Hard Start: Mars Intrigue

Fusion in a Fission World, Volume 1

S.V. Farnsworth

Published by Stone Wolfe Press, 2021.

HARD START: MARS INTRIGUE

First edition. October 10, 2021.

Copyright © 2021 S.V. Farnsworth.

ISBN: 978-1733859998

Written by S.V. Farnsworth.

Also by S.V. Farnsworth

Fusion in a Fission World
Hard Start: Mars Intrigue

Modutan Empire
Woman of the Stone
Monarch in the Flames

Standalone
A Rare Connection: Inspirational Romantic Suspense

Watch for more at https://svfarnsworthauthor.com.

Table of Contents

This adventurous science fiction novel is for the supportive family members and friends who cherish my writer's heart.

You understand why I write space opera for people who love them as much as furry, brown, Chewbacca slippers.

Chapter One

A haggard and humbled Cody Greene rubbed his newly bearded face, listening to the rasp of his bristly whiskers. He had joined Space Division when he was young. He wanted to help the Mars colonies by blasting asteroids. He never dreamed he'd be made a spy. As it turned out, his eidetic memory gave him the ability to deceive and made it possible for him to capture the vilest criminals imaginable. Unfortunately, his covert career hadn't given him the chance to find a wife.

That's why he'd been arrested on his birthday for non-compliance with the Marriage Mandate. He'd lost everything by holding out for love instead of simply finding someone willing to accept him. Now, he had eleven hours to live before he would be executed.

Here in the dark, his perfect recall of detail had provided a way to redeem his value in the eyes of his commander. Unfortunately, Cody would have to wait until the last minute to report his findings because solitary confinement didn't allow communication. His only company had been an infernal dripping faucet. The leak had driven him just crazy enough to uncover a mystery.

Footfalls echoed in the hallway outside Cody's cell. He'd waited twenty-nine days to hear those boots and that stride, but why was the commander early? Cody stood at attention.

Simon Mambwe's tone rumbled. "Open the door."

"Yes, sir." The door swung open.

The light from the corridor blinded Cody, but he didn't look away. Simon stepped into the doorway and stopped. His dark-skinned face puckered in a distasteful expression.

"You've been claimed, Mr. Greene." He clasped his hands behind his back.

Stunned, Cody stared. "Sir?"

Simon chuckled. "You'll be a married man by mid-morning tomorrow. Congratulations" He warmly clapped Cody on the shoulder, then quickly pulled his hand away with a look of disgust. "Where's your sock?"

Cody looked down at his filthy, bare foot. "The faucet drips. I used the sock to muffle the noise. I should be grateful for the leak because it unlocked a memory that for weeks had been working its way from deep inside my mind. I have a theory you need to hear."

Simon motioned for silence and moved into the corridor. "The great sock solution. I'll have to share that one. Anyway, shower and report to my rover. I've given the guards your new uniform. Oh, and do a thorough job of it. I doubt I have any nose hairs left after standing this close to you."

Cody ducked his head. "Yes, sir."

He followed the guards to the showers and scrubbed away a month of grime. He shaved his beard without mangling his face and neck. That was an accomplishment.

He dressed in fresh clothes and reported to Simon's rover. Once inside, Simon secured the transparent aluminum hatches, and Cody buckled in a passenger seat. He glanced out the observation bubble at the night sky, admiring the Milky Way. He'd missed seeing the stars.

Simon strode forward and strapped into the pilot's chair. "What's your theory, Greene?"

Cody ran a hand through his wet hair. "Someone is siphoning air from Colony THREE."

Simon eyed him in the rearview mirror as he disengaged the rover from the docking ring and accelerated away from Laser Outpost Delta. "There have been no reports of a resource theft." Simon's brows lowered. "Do you have any suspects?"

Cody met the commander's gaze. "There are only a handful of people on the planet who could pull off a heist on this scale without being caught."

The muscles in Simon's jaw clenched, and he closed his eyes briefly. "They're that powerful?"

The question surprised Cody. "They're that intelligent."

Simon squinted. "Smart enough to be listening in on our conversation now?"

Cody considered the question. "No, not here, but whoever it is could easily hack communications without leaving evidence of wrongdoing."

Simon held Cody's gaze. "This is all conjecture. Why do you think air is missing from THREE?"

Cody lifted his chin. "During my last undercover assignment there, my ears popped twice."

Simon's right eyebrow raised, but he kept his eyes on the Glass Highway. "That's how you know all of this?"

Cody smiled. "Yes, Commander."

Simon harumphed. "Fine. I'm interested in hearing more. Who do you think did it?"

Cody squared his shoulders. "There are only five or six people who have the skill set required, and three of them share the same last name."

Both of Simon's eyebrows raised. "What name?"

Cody swallowed the lump in his throat. "Shim."

Simon guffawed. "That's insanely ironic because your new wife's name is Shim."

Cody's heart thudded to a halt and then resumed beating. "Jinhee Shim?"

Simon shook his head. "No, Lisa Shim, same family, though."

Cody's chest heaved for breath. "The technology director of SEVEN wants to marry me? Why? Did Jinhee put her up to it?"

Simon shrugged. "I have no idea why a woman like that would stoop to marrying a convict on death row, but you should be grateful she has."

The blood drained from Cody's face. "I might be if she wasn't my number one suspect."

Simon's brows furrowed in the rearview mirror. "Even if she did it, she'll never see justice. We can't convict someone who doesn't leave evidence of wrongdoing behind."

Cody tensed because Simon had always trusted him in the past. "I've never failed before."

Simon relaxed in his seat. "Let it go. Lisa Shim could murder someone every week for the rest of her life and the Gold Council would look the other way. She's untouchable."

Cody scowled. "Why?"

Simon scoffed. "You know why."

Cody stared straight ahead, taking in the arid landscape and the sparkling road of glass illuminated by the rover's headlights. "She may have invented everything that makes Mars amazing, but she's not untouchable. Let me see her file. I'll find a way to force a confession. People's lives are at stake. Colony THREE has nine hundred and eleven people in it. None of them can survive without air."

Simon swallowed. "I don't need you to tell me what's at stake. I have family members in THREE. What I need to know is if you're willing to sacrifice your moral disposition to achieve your goal. If you convict Lisa Shim, then you'll be right back on death row. Trust me, no one else is going to rescue you."

Cody's heart took a hit because he had secretly hoped his mother would save him from his fate. "I understand that, sir. However, I will do whatever it takes to secure a conviction. All I ask is that you arrange a post for me on the next transport to Earth."

Simon gripped the steering wheel until his hands slipped. "You have no idea what you're saying. There is no way to grant that request. You're out of your mind."

Cody's breath caught in his throat. "Will you at least ask my mother?"

Simon scowled. "You're playing with fire."

Cody held his gaze. "Please, sir?"

Simon tossed Cody a datapad. "I'll think about it. Formulate your plan, and I'll look it over. Your marriage to Director Shim will be legally binding, but I don't mind if you investigate her while you're under her covers." He chuckled. "I'm sure she's hiding something interesting."

Cody blanched at the innuendo. He'd never crossed that line with a suspect before, and he didn't intend to start now. He cued up Lisa's profile and scanned the information.

"She's almost a recluse." Cody kept reading. "How does anyone really know what she's capable of?"

Simon sighed. "She's shy. I don't blame her. Being famous must lead to all kinds of embarrassing situations with strangers seeking a moment in the spotlight. I wouldn't mind her paygrade, though."

Cody frowned. "There's no mention of her ever having a boyfriend...or a girlfriend."

Simon relaxed in his seat. "She probably doesn't trust anyone's motives. That may explain why she redeemed you from the garbage chute. At least, you can't be a plant." He laughed. "That's doubly ironic."

Cody processed page after page of details. Lisa had written the code for the government's computer operating system and all of the programs that ran security and operations for the Mars colonies and Laser Defense Outposts. "With all due respect, Commander, I think you're wrong about why she chose me."

Simon glanced over his shoulder. "Prove it."

Cody followed his instincts and ran a compatibility comparison. The Matchmaker algorithm calculated a percentage. Stunned, he stared at the result.

He shook his head in disbelief. "I'm the only man on the planet that Lisa Shim would marry. We're a ninety-seven-point-one percent match."

Simon threw back his head and laughed. "That will do it. There's nothing like a number to make an analytical heart beat wildly."

A queasy knot of misgiving formed in Cody's stomach. Just because he could do something didn't mean he should. He said a silent prayer for the courage to go through with his plan. No answer came.

Chapter Two

Lisa Shim obeyed Martian law, exceeded expectations, met mandates, and never came in late. Unfortunately, nothing had prepared her for three funerals and a wedding within the space of an hour. All she'd ever wanted was a relationship like her parents enjoyed.

Dressed in a formal, white uniform, Lisa entered the funeral services for her fallen Technology Division workers. She had obeyed the government's order to loan them to aid in the final phase of construction in Colony TEN and now they were dead. The burden of guilt weighed heavily on her narrow shoulders.

Hesitating for a moment, she navigated the crowd of mourners to the front of the room. Stricken with regret, she knelt and bowed to the floor before the pictures of the three deceased women. Duty was no consolation at a time like this.

Resentful gazes watched her from the corners of their veiled eyes. She dropped sealed envelopes of credit tokens into the offering bowls before each picture. Perhaps, the money would help the grieving families press forward with hope.

Lisa had trained these brave women whose futures had been erased. As the tech director of Mars Colony SEVEN for the past twenty-three months, they were her only casualties. If she'd just gone with them, then she might have prevented this tragedy.

Fighting to control her emotions, Lisa dried her tears with a cloth from her pocket. She couldn't afford to mar her white uniform with makeup smudges. Oppressed by grief, she fought the urge to express her frustrations to those who blamed her. The one thing that stopped her was the knowledge that it wouldn't do any good.

The dead kept TEN's secrets. Furthermore, the Martian Colonial Government had offered no information regarding the tragic accident, making it impossible for Lisa to explain the women's deaths to anyone. Regardless, she had tried to console the families last night when she'd delivered the bad news.

A line of stricken husbands and weeping children stretched between Lisa and the exit. She bowed deeply to each of them in turn. The youngest children's tears broke her heart as she imagined their bleak futures without their mothers.

With her emotions raw, Lisa strode from the funeral. Outside the door stood a Health Division red suit with a syringe. Pulling herself together, Lisa blotted her face again.

The nurse removed the cap over the needle. "Director Shim, you need an inoculation before you transfer to NINE."

In the otherwise empty hallway, Lisa unbuttoned her uniform top to bare her shoulder. "You may proceed." The needle stabbed.

"By the way, Director, congratulations on your promotion." The nurse placed a bandage on the injection site.

"Thank you." Lisa righted her uniform and rubbed her arm as she strode along the hallway.

The intrusive nurse kept pace. "Is it true that you are to be married today?"

"Yes." Lisa paused to look out a picture window at the sweeping grandeur of the Martian landscape outside the colony. "It's an arranged match. I don't know him."

The health worker's demeanor became solemn as she bowed. "I wish you happiness, Director Shim." She walked away with slumped shoulders.

Lisa's heart sunk as she stared at the familiar, red rock horizon of her lifelong home. Bidding farewell to everyone and everything she loved was proving to be harder than she'd anticipated. Obeying orders had never been this difficult in the past, but then she had never been asked to give up this much before.

Unfortunately, she had no choice other than to accept the promotion and move to NINE because her sister's life hung in the balance. Sahra had been issued orders to report to TEN only seconds after Lisa attempted to decline the promotion. Her sister's transfer had been a warning.

Trying to make the parting from her family a happy one, Lisa had sought a reason to celebrate. The arranged marriage was to please her family. Of course, she fully intended to make the union work, but she worried that it might not be as happy as she hoped. A loveless marriage was her greatest fear.

Lisa put aside her misgivings and faced the door behind her. The sign read, "Bridal Dressing Room." Taking a deep breath, she entered to find her mother and three sisters waiting for her. Their gloomy expressions lifted as she walked into the small room.

Lisa's mother, Bethany, gathered her in a warm hug. "You made it."

Closing her eyes, Lisa enjoyed the last embrace she might receive from the woman who had nurtured her through life's challenges. Lisa's tears started afresh.

"I'm glad you're here for this." Lisa released her mother from the embrace, holding onto her hands a while longer.

"Where else would I be?" Bethany smiled through misty eyes.

The news of Lisa's transfer had prompted her to seek counsel from her mother about petitioning the government for a computer-generated match. There was no time for anything else if she wanted her family at her wedding and no point in delaying the inevitable. In less than a month the Marriage Mandate came into effect for her on her next birthday.

She opened her arms to invite her sisters in for hugs. "I'm going to miss each of you."

Jinhee and little Marha came in at the same time. Lisa's jumbled emotions made her laugh through her tears as they separated. She dabbed her face again. Normally even-tempered, she rarely cried, especially in front of others.

Sahra had held back. "It won't be the same without you. Who am I going to share my scathingly brilliant ideas with?"

Lisa hugged Sahra tight. "You'll find someone."

They were the closest in age and often confided in each other. Saying goodbye to her was the hardest. After what had happened to Lisa's techs, she prayed her sister would be all right.

Sahra kissed her cheek. "I love you, big sister." She released Lisa and walked to the farthest corner of the room.

Lisa seldom heard those words, and they touched her heart. Of course, she knew she was loved. Culturally, however, it wasn't often said.

"Call me every day." Little Marha's lip quivered.

"I will." Lisa desperately wanted to keep that promise.

Marha smiled. "I hope your husband is nice."

"He's a member of the church, and that's all that matters." Lisa wished that were completely true.

Jinhee took Lisa's hand. "I went out with him a few times. He's a bit lonely, and there's a vein of sadness in his temperament. Otherwise, he's pleasant to be around and quite handsome."

Lisa's chest tightened. "Why didn't you tell me?"

Jinhee cocked her head and raised an eyebrow. "I did. Don't you remember Mr. Possible?"

Lisa thought back. "That was months ago, and the last I heard, you said he was Mr. Impossible."

Jinhee nodded. "I dumped him for being too serious."

"What do you mean?" their mother asked.

Jinhee let out a breath. "He tried to kiss me on the third date."

Lisa didn't like the idea of her future husband kissing her sister. "What did you do?"

"I told him I was saving my kisses for marriage." Jinhee sighed. "I'm not sure why, but I always knew he was meant for you, Lisa. I told him to ask you out."

Lisa's heart sank. "He never did. You should have told me this before I agreed to the marriage."

Jinhee picked at a speck of lint on her skirt. "When would you have had the time to listen? He's a good man, and you're lucky he's still available. I haven't seen him around for months, probably because he's in Space Division. They come and go a lot."

Lisa chewed her lip. "I wonder how often I'll see him."

Sahra stepped in. "The newlywed laws ensure you'll be together for the first year. Write as often as you can, especially when you have pictures of your babies." She pumped her eyebrows.

"I plan to." Lisa's cheeks flushed just thinking about creating children with her husband.

Mother smiled. "He sounds wonderful. An associate of mine from high school says he's been working undercover assignments in the lower colonies. He's devoted his entire career to rooting out corruption. His time has run out, but she said he is worth saving."

Lisa's breath caught in her chest. "It's his birthday?"

Mother flashed a smile that soon sagged. "It happens to the best of us. But no, his birthday was a month ago. Today would have been his execution. You've done the right thing by rescuing him. Trust me, he'll thank you for it, eventually. Although, I wouldn't expect gratitude right away. He must have his reasons for failing to marry before the Marriage Mandate took effect."

Jinhee looked away with a downcast expression.

"What?" Lisa's hands trembled.

"Um, well, I may have broken his heart when I said no." Jinhee's facial features crumpled.

"No to what?" Marha asked innocently.

"When I wouldn't kiss him, he went down on one knee and..." Jinhee's eyes filled with sadness. "I've never seen anyone so crushed by the word no before." She met their mother's gaze. "It's just that he's much older than I am, and we had nothing in common."

Mother cupped Jinhee's face with both hands. "It's all right. You're barely out of high school. It was inappropriate for him to pursue you. He was probably desperate to be married since he was about to run out of time." Mother faced Lisa. "This doesn't change anything. It means he wants to be married. That's a good sign."

Lisa looked into her mother's loving eyes and remembered the peaceful reassurance that had come after accepting the arrangement. God had witnessed through the Spirit of the Lord that Cody Greene was the man for her. She allowed a sense of readiness to settle over her, calming her nerves.

However, one glance in the mirror caused dismay to set in. "I'm a mess, and he's going to think I'm ugly."

The full-length mirror made her look shorter than usual. Worse still, her makeup had washed off. She wore cosmetics, hoping to look like the Asian women she admired.

"Don't worry." Mother squeezed Lisa's hand. "He'll love you. Besides, I came prepared." Bethany opened a makeup case and in a few minutes she made everything right. "Honestly, I don't know why you cover this complexion. You're lovely without the makeup." She brushed Lisa's hair and pinned it in a Korean-style bun, then she kissed the top of Lisa's head. "Beautiful."

Bethany Carson-Shim had never been afraid to voice an opinion. In her younger years, she had defied the Marriage Mandate and refused to marry until forced. The shameful consequences had been severe and cast a burden on her children, especially Lisa.

"I wish I didn't have to leave home. Colony NINE is so far away." Lisa changed the subject, not wanting to argue with her mother today.

Bethany nodded. "I wish you didn't have to go either, but the resources you can access will help you achieve your dreams."

Lisa reflected on her future without her family nearby. "It's a great honor and a wonderful opportunity to make a difference in the world. I just wish I could stay here and didn't need to marry a stranger."

Lisa met her mother's gaze in the mirror. They shared the same striking shade of azure eyes, and both had blonde hair. Except Lisa wore dark-colored, prescription contact lenses and blackened her hair with dye.

Once again, she lamented that she didn't look Asian like her father and brothers. Even Sahra's Korean ancestry showed. It wasn't fair.

Mother's Caucasian traits were unpopular in SEVEN. Worthy men didn't admire Lisa enough to ask her out on a date. The loneliness subdued her normally buoyant spirit. Would her future husband see something in her to love?

"Stop frowning." Bethany patted Lisa's hand. "Everything will be all right. It's almost time."

Lisa faced a stark reality. "If only I could have revived the planet, then we'd be free."

Bethany squeezed Lisa's hand. "You've been dreaming of that your whole life. Ask God to help you."

Lisa took a shaky breath. "I will. He can do anything. I just wish I could be married in the Temple. You know that's why I waited so long to accept a match. If the planet were alive, then the government wouldn't have any reason to restrict our religion...or force us to love when we're not ready."

Her mother stroked her hair. "Cody is a good choice, Lisa. I promise that when this planet is green with plant life, you will have the chance to be sealed in the Temple for time and all eternity."

Lisa shook her head. "But everyone says it's impossible to restart the core. Oh, Mom, what if I fail?"

Worry lines creased Bethany's face. "I think your immediate concern should be enjoying this day. It's a once-in-a-lifetime moment. You'll regret it if you're so distracted that you can't remember the first time you met him."

Sahra nodded. "You could have told us more about him. It's crazy to have to learn things from Jinhee."

Lisa tensed with a tinge of jealousy. "I don't know anything about him."

"What?" Jinhee piped up from the chair in the corner. "You haven't read his profile?"

Lisa soberly shook her head, remembering her dead technicians. "I had other things on my mind."

Bethany rubbed Lisa's back. "I'm sorry about your techs." She had finalized the details of the marriage contract after news of the accident forced Lisa away from the negotiations.

Sahra stepped forward to meet Lisa's gaze. "Their deaths weren't your fault. They accepted the risks."

Bethany drew Lisa and Sahra into side hugs. "We all know the dangers. Now, have faith, both of you. Hard starts can sometimes lead to the happiest outcomes."

The words resonated in Lisa's heart. "Are you referring to you and Daddy?"

"Yes." Bethany smiled. "I didn't pick that grumpy man, but I love him."

Traditional Korean music started playing in the wedding hall beyond the bridal room's second door.

"It's time!" Little Marha's expression lit with enthusiasm.

Lisa's mother and sisters lined up. They departed the room and walked along the aisle, passing rows of seats filled with guests on only one side. Cody Greene must be from a distant colony because none of his family had made it to the ceremony. A nervous knot formed in Lisa's stomach.

Her father walked over with a proud expression and extended his arm. She took it with joy, loving the smell of him: green tea and ginger. It was impossible to imagine not being this close to him again. He made her insecurities evaporate without saying a word.

The two of them walked toward the front of the hall. Family and friends smiled. Upon Lisa's approach, Justice of the Peace Tehwon Kang entered from the right, and the groom came in from the left.

Lisa's breath caught at the sight of her future husband. He had brown hair, Caucasian features, and hairy knuckles. Jinhee should have told her he wasn't Asian.

Lisa scanned the insignia of his dress uniform. He was a low-ranking Health Division aide. There was something more. He was also a Bio-resource Division agricultural worker. That didn't make sense. What about Space Division?

The muscles in her face slackened, and her hands numbed. He was from THREE, a technology bereft colony settled a hundred years ago by cowboys from the Americas. This could not be happening.

Her nostrils flared, but she held her temper. Clenching her jaw, she faced Justice Kang. He was an elderly man and deserved respect.

"Welcome family and friends. We are gathered here today to solemnize the marriage of Lisa Shim and Cody Greene." The justice met Lisa's gaze and then Cody's. "Do you accept this arrangement? If so, bow your heads and say yes."

There was only one answer she could give. "Yes."

Chapter Three

Cody Greene squared his shoulders and cleared his throat at the sight of his bride. Why was he sweating? This marriage was only permanent if Lisa Shim wasn't a criminal, and he was convinced that she was.

Now, all he had to do was prove it. He knew a lot about her so why did seeing her unsettle him? Perhaps her wide-eyed look of innocence had taken him by surprise.

The two of them stood before the justice of the peace, waiting for him to pronounce them husband and wife. Lisa wasn't as Asian as she looked in her profile picture despite her being petite and slim. Her nose was Caucasian as were most of her delicate features. She had creases in her eyelids, Asians usually didn't have those.

He liked the look of her except for the caked-on makeup. The only other drawback was that she was much smaller than him, prompting him to feel protective. Of course, that was crazy because he was here to gather evidence that would secure her conviction in a court of law and lead to her execution.

Cody watched Lisa sum him up. The distaste on her face almost made him laugh. He knew he was decent-looking. So, what was her problem?

The depth of her penetrating gaze caused a queasy feeling in the pit of his stomach. She faced the justice of the peace and said yes. What was the question? Cody returned his attention to the business at hand. Oh, the commitment part.

"Yes." He had a hard time saying it even though it didn't mean anything.

"Then I pronounce you husband and wife. You may kiss one another." Justice Kang bowed.

Cody met Lisa's gaze, struck by the naïve hope in her eyes. He'd planned to graze her cheek with his lips on his way to meet her family. However, seeing the anticipation in her expression caused him to hesitate.

She lifted her chin, raised on tip-toes, and closed her eyes. His breath caught in his throat as he softly kissed her lips. A stillness settled over him, blanketing him in a comforting kind of warmth that he recognized as peace.

She broke the kiss by lowering her heels to the floor. He breathed for the first time in too long. How could he be affected like this by someone he'd never met?

Blinking rapidly, he realized he'd taken her hands in his. Small, cool, and calloused, they surprised him with their perfection. Despite the privilege of her rank, she worked for a living.

She opened her eyes, but he couldn't bring himself to meet her gaze. Instead, he hurried to speak to her parents. He could learn a lot about her character from them.

Official records had given him no indication of her motivation for stealing the air reserves from THREE. Meeting her in person had only confused him. The last thing he had expected from her was trust.

"Hi, I'm Cody Greene." He shook her father's leather-like hand.

Byeungcheol Shim had a tight grip. "Take care of my daughter."

Cody's jaw slackened. "I'll do what I can, sir."

Byeungcheol released his hand and walked toward his daughter, leaving Cody with Lisa's mother. Why had he promised the man anything? Commander Mambwe had given orders that definitely didn't include taking care of Lisa in any way a father would appreciate.

"We're happy to meet you, Cody." Bethany Carson-Shim took his hand in both of her tender ones. "Welcome to the family. I knew your father, and you look just like him. I was sorry to hear of his passing during the plague. My parents passed away because of the fever, too. It was a tragic time."

An old sadness swelled in Cody's chest. "Thank you." He'd lost his older sisters to the same illness as his father, and the pain had been unbearable.

Bethany averted her gaze, releasing his hand. "Let us know if you need anything. We'll be saving for a trip to come see you if you want us."

"Your daughter would probably like that." Cody knew it was foolish, but something about Bethany endeared her to him even though she was on his suspect list. "You're from EIGHT, right? Did you know my mother?"

His connection to Gold Council Member Addison Albright had been a well-kept secret since he'd entered the Space Academy. They had never shared a surname because Addison had retained her maiden name. Both the secrecy and the name had long been sore points with him.

Bethany's penetrating blue eyes captured his gaze. "I know better than to say yes."

He clenched his jaw. "Does anyone else know about my connection to her?"

Bethany's head shook slightly. "No, and I won't mention it. I've sacrificed my child to save your life for your father's sake, not your mother's. Please, honor my daughter, Mr. Greene."

Cody ground his teeth. "Why would you do that? I'm following a lead and nothing more."

Bethany's eyes widened. "Remember the man your father was."

Her words struck him to the core because Fortney Greene had been a better man than Cody could ever be. "I can't change the facts as I find them."

Bethany's worry lines slowly eased as she held his gaze. "That's a relief. Lisa is pure, lovely, and kind. I wish you joy together."

Cody lowered his brows to hide his doubts from Bethany. "You think this marriage is going to be successful?"

"Yes, I do." She bowed and walked away.

Cody rubbed his face and looked around. His mother was probably watching right now, listening in on the conversation. Addison had a way of spoiling every aspect of his life with her heavy-handed interference. Where was she today?

Lisa hadn't moved from the spot where he'd kissed her. If he hadn't believed she was the kind of woman who could risk the lives of people across the planet by selling resources to outlaws, then he wouldn't have married her. Why then were his instincts telling him that something was off with the investigation.

A young woman in the group around Lisa caught his eye. Jinhee waved and walked toward him, causing his heart to crash to the floor in despair. She rushed in as if trampling it all over again the way she had the last time he'd seen her.

"I told you that you should date my sister." Jinhee swept her long blonde hair out of her face. "Please, make Lisa happy."

His eyes misted. Jinhee was Lisa's younger sister. The family resemblance was unmistakable despite the differences in coloring.

Cody swallowed the lump in his throat. "I'm not sure that's possible."

A storm of emotion clouded Jinhee's expression. "Please, don't break her heart because of me."

The plea surprised him. "You shouldn't blame yourself for whatever happens."

Jinhee's eyes overflowed with tears as she grabbed his wrist and tugged him to the empty side of the room. "I told you about Lisa from the beginning. You're the same age. You have things in common that we never did. Give her a chance."

His heart swelled with sorrow. "I loved you. Do you know how rare that is?"

Jinhee wiped her eyes. "I never felt it. I'm sorry."

The words hit him like a fist to the chest. He'd thought he was over her, but surprise, he wasn't. She'd been his last hope to marry for love. Now he had nothing left except the deal he'd made with his superiors in the Space Division for a one-way trip to Earth.

"The transport vehicle is standing by. The couple will please exit to the right and the guests to the left." Justice Kang indicated the way they should go.

The announcement seemed to startle Lisa, whose ear had been tuned to the conversation. She launched into soft-spoken farewells to her seven younger siblings, her parents, and friends. How much had Jinhee told Lisa about him?

He glanced around. Not one soul in his acquaintance had come to the wedding. He had invited his mother, but she hadn't shown. It seemed that she never came to anything important to him.

Justice Kang grasped Cody's elbow and led him to the doorway on the right. Cody paused to hold it open for his new wife. Lisa embraced her large family in an enormous group hug. A stricken expression overcame her face as her family departed through the opposite door. Only after it shut did she meet his gaze, crushing him with a look of regret.

Chapter Four

Cody allowed the wedding hall door to close after Lisa walked through. The two of them followed Justice of the Peace Kang along the hallway. Ahead lay the docking hatches, and Lisa's heels clicked on the polished sandstone tiles.

Cody liked her cute walk: jaunty and feminine. He was relieved to see her bounce back after the emotional farewell with her family and friends. Catching up to her, he decided that keeping an eye on her wouldn't be a hardship in one regard: she had a great body.

Lisa glanced at him, and her nostrils flared. Her lips pressed from perfection to a perfectly thin line. He adjusted his gaze forward.

"No one forced you to marry me." He wondered what else about him she wouldn't like, and how that would affect his ability to manipulate her into confessing the truth during his investigation.

"Pardon me?" She captured his gaze.

"If I disgust you, then why did you say yes?" Cody hadn't anticipated how much he wanted to know the answer.

Lisa puffed up her chest. "I could ask you the same question."

He glanced at her lips. "You don't disgust me."

Her body language softened. "I thought you were disappointed."

He raised his eyebrows. "Why would you think that?"

She blushed, or so he imagined. It was hard to tell under the makeup.

"You walked away after the kiss." She averted her gaze.

"I only kissed you because you wanted me to. I'm sorry if it wasn't up to your standards." Why was he upset?

Lisa's lips parted as she stopped to stare at him. "It was beautiful."

He adjusted his stance. "Well, that's good, right?"

A slight smile chased away her worried expression. "Yes."

He fought the urge to take her hand. Where was this coming from? He had never reacted to a stranger like this, let alone someone suspected of a serious crime.

He ran his hand through his hair. "You didn't seem to like me when you first saw me."

A slight indication of remorse creased her brow. "I'm sorry about my initial surprise. I ranked the race of my potential spouse as a high priority. I grew up in the Korean tradition, and culture is very important to me. Jinhee didn't mention you were Caucasian."

He considered his words, carefully avoiding the topic of Jinhee. "I ranked religion as my highest priority, but I doubt they took that into consideration since I timed out."

How Lisa answered this challenge would say a lot about her. She belonged to his church, but that was a sore point since she was accused of being a lowlife thief. Might she be a coward too? He focused on a mark on the wall to avoid influencing her response.

Lisa's spine straightened. "I'm a member of the Church of Jesus Christ of Latter-day Saints, and my faith is not open to compromise. Jinhee wouldn't have dated you if you were a non-member. So, why are you playing this game?"

Cody met Lisa's gaze to be sure she wasn't afraid. In them, he saw terror. She was already questioning everything.

"Leave Jinhee out of this." He squared his shoulders. "Didn't you read my file?"

Lisa avoided his gaze. "I didn't have time. There was an acciden—"

A man in a silver uniform stepped between them to open the rover's hatch. "Let's be on our way."

Cody wanted to punch Kris Jordan for intruding at such a moment. Instead, he looked away, pretending he didn't know him. Why had an undercover agent taken this detail?

Kris wasn't a lowly driver. Perhaps that meant he had information to relay. Kris's stilted smile indicated he was enjoying the chance to harass Cody about marrying Lisa in such an underhanded way. Cody had never done anything like this before, and his less scrupulous colleagues must be laughing at him for it.

"Good luck to both of you." Justice Kang bowed in farewell.

Cody had forgotten about the elderly man.

"Thank you." Lisa returned the bow.

Kris held the hatch open. Cody guided Lisa into the rover and palmed a note from Kris behind her back. Something was happening.

Cody found a seat and buckled the five-point harness. The coded message said there would be a top priority case transfer from EIGHT to NINE. He rubbed the note between his fingers until it disintegrated.

There wasn't anything to be concerned about. Most likely, the case contained nothing more than a letter from a director to his mistress. It was disgusting, but not top-secret.

"Sedatives are available if you like. Most people take them." Kris's voice held amusement.

"No, thank you." Cody and Lisa spoke at the same time.

Kris chuckled. "Have it your way." He flipped switches and accelerated on the entry ramp to the honey-gold colored Glass Highway. "Let me know if you change your mind."

"I won't." Lisa quirked a delicate eyebrow.

Cody simmered in anger. Why was Kris risking their lives like this? It was foolish to go so fast, especially with a director onboard.

Dimples played in Lisa's cheeks as she seemed to be calculating the speed of infraction in her head. Cody's mood lifted, wishing she'd looked at him with that much enthusiasm when they first met. Of course, that was crazy since he was only here to investigate her for treason.

Lisa leaned forward in her seat, asking Kris, "Will we reach NINE in less than twelve hours? That seems incredibly fast."

Cody marveled at her naiveté. Had she never been anywhere except SEVEN? He had a hard time believing that since the famous Lisa Shim had dreamed up the Glass Highway in her childhood.

She'd later played a pivotal role on the research and development team that designed the Crawler. The gigantic machine had forged the highway. The electrical conduit inside the glass allowed the nuclear-powered laser outposts to provide supplemental electricity to the colonies.

"We'll stop at EIGHT for a new driver," Kris replied. "But you're expected to sleep on the road." He winked in the rearview mirror.

Cody caught Kris's insinuation regarding them spending their honeymoon night in the rover. Unamused, he shook his head. It wasn't funny.

"Will we have a chance to see EIGHT?" Lisa didn't seem to have noticed the innuendo. "I wish we could see it from above. The central, subterranean tube with the rectangular bio-domes fanned out around it looks like a five-petalled flower when rendered in a three-dimensional model. I've always wanted to see it."

Kris gave her an odd look in the rearview mirror. "Since you're a director, I think we can lay over for half an hour. I could show you around." Kris flashed a white-toothed grin.

Lisa frowned and looked away. "Thank you for the layover, but I don't need your help. I have all of the colonies' schematics memorized."

Irked by Kris' disrespect, Cody focused his attention outside the observation bubble at a tiny blue speck on the horizon. Earth held so much promise.

It represented freedom in his mind. Though most people considered it cursed because it had been bathed in nuclear winter for almost a century, he viewed it differently. Cody had fixated on Earth's history and culture early in life, pinning his hopes on going there someday.

He sighed and faced Lisa, but she had fallen asleep. After her conviction, he would be assigned to a cargo barge bound for Earth. It would be his salvation.

Despite this, Lisa intrigued him. Makeup concealed her complexion, adding to her mystery. Curiosity had forever been his failing, and he ached to see what she was hiding.

He hated makeup, but the prospect of seeing Lisa without it interested him. On the other hand, Lisa's sister had never worn cosmetics. Jinhee was so pretty she didn't need them.

Thoughts of the way she'd mercilessly rejected his proposal made him tense. She had told Lisa enough to jeopardize this entire mission. That's probably why Kris was here. Space Division was always listening in on people's conversations, even when they had no legal right to.

Cody let out a breath and tried to forget the strange situation he was in. At least, he wasn't facing an executioner right now. That was something to be grateful for.

He stared through the rover's observation bubble at the sky, and thoughts of long ago eased the tension from his muscles. He had loved someone before he met Jinhee, but Erica had died when they were in high school. If she had lived, then things would be dramatically different for him. For one thing, he would be married to the girl that part of him was still in love with instead of to a potential criminal mastermind like Lisa Shim.

Cody ground his teeth. Lisa wasn't a Shim anymore. She was a Greene.

Anger warmed his cheeks. He had married this woman. Sure, it was because he needed to for the investigation, but that didn't change the fact that it was a lawful marriage.

Until Lisa was executed for her crimes, he was stuck with her. He couldn't escape certain responsibilities. The weight of them settled on him like a planetoid. Why on Mars had he promised her father to keep her safe?

Chapter Five

Lisa's body lurched in the rover's seat restraints as the vehicle came to a halt. Eyes wide, she realized she'd fallen asleep. She steadied her breathing, glancing across the aisle at Cody.

"Welcome to EIGHT," announced the rover driver. "I hope you had a nice nap." He shot her a lopsided smile as he passed her on his way to the airlock at the back of the vehicle.

Lisa unfastened the five-point harness and stretched. A yawn escaped her. Outside the bubble, the fading sunlight illuminated distant ridges and unfamiliar red rock formations. On either side of the rover loomed two of EIGHT's rectangular bio-domes with their triangular latticework of transparent aluminum.

"After you." Cody motioned for her to go first.

His appraising gaze followed her. The crease between his eyebrows had deepened since the wedding. Had she been doing something embarrassing in her sleep?

"Thank you." She checked her lip for drool.

The rover driver tipped his cap from the other side of the hatch. "It was a pleasure to drive for you today, Director."

"You have my thanks." She noticed a set of double doors with a sign that read, "Commons."

"Be back in half an hour." The driver put the cap on his head.

"We will. Thanks." Cody's reply was more gravel than sunshine.

Surprised by the thrill his gruffness gave her, she stifled a light-hearted laugh. Her father was slow to warm too. She accepted the challenge of making Cody like her.

She gently took his hand. "Will you let me buy you something for a wedding present?"

Cody scowled, and she wondered if his darkened mood might be due to the driver's discourtesy toward him. It was probable that the man didn't think someone from THREE warranted direct remarks. Sobered by the thought, Lisa scrutinized her new husband's appearance.

What had happened to his career in Space Division? If he'd lost his standing because he had timed out, then even though she'd redeemed him, he'd be forced to live off of his secondary skills. That would explain his level-four stripes of red for the Health Division and level-two green stripes for the Bio-resource Division, as well as the glaring lack of medals and commendations on his chest.

"I hate shopping." Cody set his jaw.

"It's my treat." She led him through the double doors.

"Fine. Take me out to eat. I haven't had anything since this morning." He surged ahead and drew her into the mainstream of pedestrians bustling through the cityscape.

Trees reached toward the vaulted latticework above. The commons spread along a crowded promenade. Shops selling anything and everything lay on either side of the wide walkway. No space in the sun was wasted, and plants grew on the flat rooftops.

"I've never seen trees like this." She craned her neck to look at the tall, slender trunks and the plumes of strange foliage at the tops.

"Palm trees are my favorite." He ran his hand over the rough bark. "There are many varieties, and they bear a range of fruit, including coconuts. The people of EIGHT hold a festival once a year to celebrate."

The insight prompted her to give him her undivided attention. "Explain to me how you know that?" It was a perfect opportunity for him to tell her about himself.

He dropped his hand. "I like to read." His rapt expression fell into a studied reserve.

She raised her eyebrows, knowing he must have been here many times in his travels with Space Division. "What would you like to eat for your birthday dinner?"

His stomach growled. "Whatever's easy. Those are fine." He pointed to a nearby pastry stand.

They walked there together. She flashed the vendor two fingers and paid with her wrist-vid. The man wrapped a couple of pastries and handed them over.

"Where would you like to sit?" She looked around for a place.

"That will do." His gaze locked on a bench under the trees.

After they sat, she bowed her head in silent prayer glad to see him do the same. The pastry smelled delicious, but it contained spiced meat. She politely swallowed the first bite, despite finding it unpleasant to the taste. The way Cody devoured his food made her happy she'd splurged on something he appreciated even though she didn't enjoy eating it.

"I like it here." She tipped her head back and stared at the palm fronds, listening to them rustle in the air current circulating through the breezeway.

"The trees smell fresh. Rover air is stale." He finished his pastry.

She nodded. "We'd better hurry. Would you like mine?"

"Sure." Cody accepted it, finishing in two bites.

She threw away the trash. "May I buy you another gift?"

"Why?" he spoke as though he suspected her of something nefarious.

Lisa giggled. "Hurry, we're almost out of time." Common areas shut down with the last rays of the sun.

"Fine." He walked beside her to a high-end clothing store.

Inside, she surveyed the fashions with a critical eye. Honing in, she focused on khakis, a brown button-up shirt, and shiny leather shoes with a matching belt. The brown would accentuate his fine eyes.

"What are you doing?" This time he spoke all gravel and no sunshine.

"A man must have dignity." She turned around slowly to face him.

"Are you planning on buying it for me?" Cody's eyebrows lowered.

She set the items she'd intended to purchase on the table. "I don't know what's happened to your Space Division career, but dignity can't be bought. Do you still have it?" She hadn't meant to be quite so blunt.

His neck flushed red, and his nostrils flared. "I do."

"Then wear it." Her frustration with his lack of honesty about his work situation caused her to be less sensitive than she normally might have been.

"Fine." He tromped past her, selecting the proper sizes for the things she'd chosen before entering the changing room.

She watched him go and decided to dress to match. A cream-colored blouse, brown skirt, and a pair of brown leather high heels would look nice. On impulse, she selected white lingerie.

The itchy lace wasn't something she'd worn before, but maybe Cody would like the opportunity to take it off of her later. Her entire body pulsed with heat at the thought of him caressing the straps from her shoulders. Despite the challenges they faced, she hoped for a happy love life with Cody Greene.

Chapter Six

Cody undressed in the fitting room, brooding over Lisa's words regarding dignity. She didn't understand the true nature of the situation, but someone had told her he was in Space Division. That was bad news.

He'd suffered a drastic reduction in status after running smack into the Marriage Mandate. If he found evidence worthy of an investigation into Lisa, then he would be fully reinstated to his former rank and position as an undercover operative. As for now, he had been given a provisional status with a much lower rank. He would be paid in a secret account. Though, he couldn't access the money until he'd secured Lisa's conviction.

She was probably trying to help him, showing pity on him for his poverty. He resented any effort to buy his affection. Overbearing women were a total turn-off.

A garment bag flopped over the top of the stall onto his side.

"Does everything fit?" Lisa sounded hopeful.

He ground his teeth. "I don't know yet. Give me a chance, why don't you?"

Cody dressed in a hurry, stuffing his uniform into the garment bag with hers. Eager to escape, he fled from the changing room and paced the store. When Lisa still hadn't come out after a few minutes, he reluctantly returned.

"Are you all right in there?"

"Yes." Emotion thickened her voice.

"What do you have to cry about?" He clenched his fists, feeling like a brute. He hadn't intended to vent his frustrations on her, but he couldn't help it. "I'm the one who looks like his mother dressed him."

Lisa came out. "I'm not your mother, and I'm sure she taught you better manners."

Cody leaned close to Lisa's face. "She did."

His mother had taught him manners, but not gratitude. Addison always had an ulterior motive, and he resented her for it. If Lisa was the same way, then he'd make her pay.

Lisa's shoulders sagged. "I meant no offense." She looked at the floor.

He couldn't believe she'd backed down. "My mom's a touchy subject." His anger defused.

"I didn't know. I'm sorry." She kept her head down.

Regret pricked his conscience for being aggressive. "It's not your fault. The situation is complicated."

Lisa nodded with a troubled expression. "You can talk to me about her when you're ready to share."

He frowned. "Just don't bring her up until then, agreed?"

Lisa's expression lightened. "Yes. Now, may I take a picture of us for our families?"

"Sure." The photo would be a way to report his progress to Commander Mambwe.

Lisa stood beside Cody and raised her wrist-vid. "Picture in three, two, one."

The vid clicked, and a picture popped on the small screen. The image impacted him deeply. They looked far better together than he expected.

"My mother will like that." He knew Addison would see it in his file. "Send it to box number one-hundred-thirty-nine in THREE." It was the address of a safe house, not his childhood home.

He watched Lisa send the picture and forward it to her parents as well. It was sentimental, girlish behavior. Why did he like it then?

"I wonder if they miss us yet?" She took the garment bag from him and folded it over her arm.

A familiar bitterness surged inside him. "I don't have anyone except my mother."

He followed the cover story he'd put together. The closer the story came to real life, the easier it was to seem natural. He strode over to stand by the cashier, though that was a mistake because he didn't have any money.

"Will this be everything?" The clerk tallied the items.

Lisa came up beside him and paid with her wrist-vid. Cody walked out of the store to wait for her in the common area. He took a cleansing breath, aware that he might never breathe the air of his childhood home again.

Lisa caught up with him. "Maybe I made a mistake with the clothes," she spoke softly.

"What?" The tone she'd used caused him to feel penitent. "Oh, I guess I should thank you—" He tried to stop himself, but the words came out anyway. "—and tell you how nice you look in that skirt."

"Thank you." She avoided his gaze. "You're welcome for the outfit. I have to admit I used our wedding as an excuse. We'll probably be invited to dinner parties in NINE, and I want us to look our best." The brightness of her eyes dimmed. "I didn't mean to be bossy."

"I suppose you can't help it." He regretted the words as soon as he'd spoken them because she'd apologized, and he'd stuck it to her.

The hurt expression on her face made him cringe. Just then, a reminder chimed on her wrist-vid. She acknowledged the message with a tap on the screen.

"We should go." She stormed toward the docking hatches.

"I didn't mean it like that." Surprised by her sensitivity, he tried to catch up.

Seeing her temper flare sent a thrill through him he couldn't explain. Her spirited reaction excited him. With an appreciative smile, he watched her hips sway.

Her high heels were excessive. However, even when upset, she handled them with grace. Lisa Greene was a woman, not a girl like Erica had been. Yet, there was a strange commonality between the two that he couldn't quite figure out.

Chapter Seven

Cody and Lisa approached the transport hatch in EIGHT. A regular driver waited there with a sour expression. It meant the transfer case was already in place.

Cody entered the vehicle ahead of his wife. A steel briefcase nestled between the seat on the right and the bubble of the rover. He strapped in and checked the case for a telltale smudge of red paint on the corner. It was there, as expected.

Lisa settled in, closed her eyes, folded her arms, and bowed her head. Cody caught the lanky driver staring at her. He met the man's gaze, held up a hand, and twirled a finger in the air, indicating he should turn around. It was always best for a driver to focus on his job. The man returned his attention to the road ahead.

Cody gave Lisa another glance. She was still praying. While she wasn't looking, he took the opportunity to evaluate her every detail.

She smelled nice, not like perfume exactly. What was that fragrance? Coconut, maybe?

Anyway, she had the right idea. He should be praying about this whole marriage business. However, he was a little apprehensive about the answer he might receive.

He prayed anyway. Was there a possibility of her innocence? Indications of her involvement in the crime ran through his mind, crowding out an answer from the Lord.

The sound of Lisa drumming her fingers on an armrest distracted him from his concerns. Amusing. Well, if she was so impatient, then he'd make her wait even longer.

He ended his real prayer and pretended to pray for quite a while afterward. When he realized he appeared more pious than he was, he quit playing. Religion wasn't a game.

He glanced at her. She was waiting for him. Night had fallen, and her eyes absorbed the starlight. He tumbled into the deep pools of her soul.

"It's a lovely evening." Her calm voice hinted at something.

He reluctantly broke away from staring at her to face forward. "I like the way the headlights refract in the glass."

She adjusted her gaze to take in the view ahead of them. "It's more beautiful than I imagined."

He watched her. "What gave you the idea to invent it?"

She blinked. "A dream. Everything comes to me in dreams."

Surprised by her answer, he smiled. "I wish I had dreams like yours."

She laughed. "It's pretty amazing, but so much work."

He drank her in with his eyes. "I don't understand."

Her gaze returned to him. "I fall asleep each night designing solutions to everyone's problems in my head, but I wake up with more things to do than ever. It isn't very restful." She stifled a yawn with her hand.

He tried to imagine how her mind worked. "You're always trying to catch up."

She reached for his hand. "Exactly."

He accepted her touch. "Will you tell me about something you've done recently? I know you program software."

She held his hand lightly as she relaxed in her seat. "I've written most of the protocols that run the colonies. Resource conservation is my main focus. Lately, I've been perfecting sensor technology to prevent heat loss in bio-domes. That's a challenge, but efficiency will free the electricity for beneficial uses and reduce the cost burden on the colonists."

He raised an eyebrow, disbelieving her altruistic commentary. "Who wouldn't like that?"

Her eyelids became heavy. "Exactly."

He softened his tone. "Tell me more about resources."

She rested her head against the headrest. "Well, I've been working on improving the design of our atmospheric collectors. Every colony has five and each outpost has three, but they take a great deal of power to run. That's why it's so important to conserve energy."

He watched her eyelids slide closed. "Why? Don't we have enough air by now?"

Her head gave a slow nod. "Yes, each colony..."

He waited for her to finish, but she started to breathe as if she were asleep. "Lisa?"

She startled. "What?"

He squeezed her hand. "You were telling me about air loss."

Her brows pinched for a moment. "Oh, each colony sacrificed a percentage of their air and water reserves to fill the new Colony TEN. It's a fraction larger than any of the others, and even though it will eventually have seven atmospheric collectors, they take a long time to manufacture. The Crawler is our main manufacturing plant. It parked beside TEN after laying the last leg of the Glass Highway to complete the circuit around the equator of the planet."

He did some math in his head, not his strong suit. "When were the air and water transferred?"

She yawned. "Eight months ago."

That didn't explain his ears popping a few months ago in THREE. "Are the other colonies still low?"

She frowned. "No, they should have refilled their reserve tanks by now. Why do you ask?"

He released her hand, changing the subject before she became suspicious. "No reason. I like listening to you talk. It distracts me from other concerns." He'd been slated for execution today if not for her saving him.

Lisa met his gaze. "I'm sure you had your reasons for timing out. Jinhee told me you asked her to marry you."

He tensed, angry to have been discussed behind his back. "I don't want to talk about her."

Lisa's eyes widened. "You must have loved my sister very much. Do you still?"

Cody gritted his teeth. "No. I kind of dislike her." He avoided Lisa's gaze. "But mostly because I'm not over her yet."

Lisa's expression sagged in a weary, sad kind of way. "She's so young. She didn't understand what you offered her."

He narrowed his gaze. "But you do?"

She swallowed, looking upward through the observation bubble as liquid pooled in her eyes. "Yes."

The pain of Lisa's single word sunk deep in Cody's chest. "Why did you delay marriage? I know your birthday is in less than a month. What were you waiting for?"

She wiped her eyes. "I wanted to be married in the Temple."

He frowned. "That's impossible on Mars. You'd have to go to Earth for that." He knew because that was a big part of his plan.

She shook her head. "No one has gone to Earth for a century."

Anger surged in his chest. "That's not true. Transports still travel back and forth."

Lisa tilted her head. "Really? I wish someone had told me, but then, I guess it's top-secret business."

His heart pounded in his chest. Wouldn't she have worked on spacecraft design? She was a technology director and the planet's most famous scientist, why didn't she know about the space program?

"I thought you would have known." He scrutinized her expression.

Lines of concentration etched his new wife's face, creasing the thick layer of makeup. "I'm sure I'll be informed when I'm needed for a project. Most of what I do transfers over to a degree because Mars' atmosphere is so thin that it's similar to outer space."

He leaned forward in the seat, shaken by a feeling of dread. What if he'd been lied to? If there was no transport to Earth, then he'd be forced to marry someone else after Lisa was executed for her crimes.

Lisa rubbed his back. "Call your mother on the vid anytime you like and don't hesitate to ask me if you need anything else."

"I don't want your money." His mother had always used finances as a weapon. "I didn't marry you for your wealth."

Lisa withdrew her hand. "I'll grant you that because it's becoming apparent you didn't choose to marry me at all. If you had any sense, you would have chosen someone in THREE. Then you could have stayed close to your mother."

Losing control, he raised his voice. "Have you seen the women in THREE?"

Agape, she stared at him as if she'd never been yelled at before. "Why are looks so important to you? It shouldn't matter unless they have green skin and pointy ears."

He snorted to stop an inappropriate laugh. "They're not Vulcans."

Lisa raised an eyebrow. "I suppose not since few people in THREE live long or prosper."

He met her gaze, surprised that she had correctly identified the reference to an old Earth television show. "They're just not what I need."

Could he tell Lisa the truth about his struggles? No, he'd never told anyone. He slid his hands up his face and into his hair.

"Well," her voice trembled. "I don't know what you're looking for, but we're married. So, I hope you've found it." Her breathing came fast and shallow, on the verge of hyperventilation.

"We'll see." How could the marriage work out when he was investigating her for crimes punishable by death?

She huffed air like a distance runner. "We'll see what?" In her grip, the armrests squeaked in protest.

She was taking this far too seriously. He hadn't realized how invested she'd become, but then he felt like an idiot. She had everything riding on this marriage. He did too because this assignment was permanent if she wasn't corrupt. Only if she was guilty, would he have a second chance to find someone else on Earth.

He panicked. Traveling to Earth had been his plan, but now he doubted everything. Commander Mambwe had brokered the transport duty through Addison. Had she convinced him to lie? Was space travel even possible anymore?

Lisa leaned toward Cody. "Answer me, please."

He backpedaled. "A ninety-seven-point-one percent match is perfect, right?"

Her chest heaved. "It's supposed to be."

He watched her expression alter. The luster of her eyes diminished. Her lips formed a question she didn't seem to have the courage to ask.

He flinched. "We have thirty days. Let's give ourselves time to figure this out."

"You want to wait?" Her voice was small.

His jaw dropped, but he recovered from the shock at intervals. "Yes, I think we have to." He couldn't risk his heart until he knew she wasn't a criminal.

"Why?" She sounded incredulous.

How far was he willing to go to gain her trust? Thus far, he hadn't made any effort whatsoever. He hadn't even been nice.

His superiors would be displeased. He was married to her for a reason. It was a license to seduce her, but he couldn't do it.

"You can't make me sleep with you, Director." He spat Lisa's title as if it were an epithet.

He vented his animosity toward her, but he was actually mad at his mother. Had he been tricked into marrying Lisa? Why would his mother want that?

A sinking feeling settled on him. She had made this marriage happen somehow. He'd thought she'd abandoned him to his fate, but she must not have. The realization both reassured and frightened him.

Lisa's hands slowly curled into fists. "That's unfair. I would never abuse my position within our relationship."

Cody avoided her gaze, knowing he was out of line. "Are you sure? Most directors let power go straight to their heads."

A large rock lay in the road ahead with a man in an environmental suit shoving it toward the center. The rover driver jerked the wheel, but the vehicle was traveling too fast to avoid a collision. Cody grabbed Lisa's shoulder as if he could save her from the violence of the wreck. With the impact, the unsecured, silver briefcase struck him on the side of the head.

Chapter Eight

From her seat across the aisle in the rover, Lisa watched Cody's expression change from anger to alarm. He braced her shoulder before the vehicle skidded sideways and hit something. The rover flipped into the air, landing violently on its side as it bounced and continued to roll in the dirt. Slammed against her restraints, she nearly blacked out.

In the darkness, the vehicle smashed against a boulder and came to rest upside-down. The driver moaned. The rover's headlights flickered and went out. Three wheels spun wildly, but the fourth thumped against the wheel well, making the occupants rock back and forth.

Lisa disengaged her safety harness and fell onto the observation bubble. Her head bobbled. Everything was topsy-turvy.

She crawled forward to shut off the motor. They would need the power if they were to survive. She spotted the yellow emergency beacon button and pressed it with the palm of her hand. It lit up.

A hiss caught her attention. Her eyes adjusted to the dim lights from the dashboard, which provided the only illumination in the vehicle. The bubble had cracked.

She reached for the storage compartments and rummaged through whatever fell out. To her relief, she found a roll of bonding tape. Following the hiss, she located the spiderweb of cracks and pulled tape to seal and reinforce it. They couldn't afford to lose any more air to the less than one percent atmospheric pressure of Mars.

The driver gasped. "Outlaws..." A gurgling sound escaped his throat as blood flowed from his mouth.

Cody's arms and legs hung lifeless from his position in the seat. She couldn't safely release either man. Maybe she could roll the vehicle onto its wheels.

She climbed the side furthest away from the boulder. Her weight caused the rover to tip, finally slamming onto the ground right-side up. The driver plunged into his seat at an awkward angle.

Dazed by the second impact, Lisa stumbled forward to unlatch the driver's loose restraints. Why hadn't he cinched himself in better? Not sure what to do, she strained to guide the man's unconscious body to the floor.

"Is he breathing?" Cody's question startled her.

"I don't think so." She stared at the driver's chest, looking for movement.

A dark liquid trickled down Cody's face from his scalp. He unbuckled and knelt beside the driver. With two fingers, he checked the man's neck for a pulse. Shaking his head, he started chest compressions.

The driver's chest caved in on one side with a grinding sound of broken ribs. Lisa held onto the dying man's hand as she fought a wave of nausea. Cody gave two breaths to the driver. Air escaped through a compound fracture in the man's chest, spraying Lisa with his blood.

"It's no use." Cody wiped his face with his sleeve.

Lisa's hands started shaking. "Cody?" She reached out in the dark to check the wound on his head.

"What happened?" He blinked.

She could feel a swollen lump and a small cut. Something must have hit him during the crash. Properly buckled in his seat restraints, he couldn't have impacted the bubble of the rover.

"I'm not sure." She held him steady. "The driver said something about outlaws, but that doesn't make sense. This isn't the wild west."

"Why are your hands sticky?" Bewilderment dulled his tone.

"Don't you remember? The driver was hurt. You tried to resuscitate him, but it didn't work." She sat on her heels as dizziness swept over her. "We need to suit up. I think we're running out of air."

She reached for a side panel and popped it open. "Take off your clothes, and put this on." She crawled to her seat and pulled out another suit. Stripping everything, she wriggled into the pressure-tight suit and sealed the helmet and gauntlets.

Lisa switched on the external helmet lights. Cody had mostly suited up but had passed out before he finished. Panic struck, and she forced his muscular arms and shoulders into the suit. Clamping the helmet on and sealing the gauntlets, she prayed for his survival.

"Don't die on me." A shiver ran down her spine because she might be a widow before she'd fully become a wife.

Cody didn't respond.

Lisa shook him by the shoulders. His eyes fluttered open, and his pupils constricted in her helmet lights. Relief washed over her, and she crushed him in a hug.

"What happened?" He straightened his position in the seat.

"Is that your favorite question?" She laughed and held him a little longer.

He raised his arms around her. "Did you dress me in this suit?"

Heat rose in her face. "You did most of it by yourself."

"How much is most?" He reclined against the headrest.

"Don't be embarrassed. I only saw—"

He laughed in a way that hinted at vulnerability. "I remember now. I was distracted by a beautiful woman in the starlight."

She pulled away, standing in the aisle. "You nearly suffocated." She switched their lights from the exterior to the helmets' interiors. "And you hit your head. I think you're hallucinating."

His gaze met hers. "Oh, really?"

She ducked her head. "I'm not implying anything about your mental state. Please, don't be offended."

He took ahold of her hand and drew her to sit across his lap. "I was looking at you."

She shook her head. "Me?"

Half of his mouth tipped upward in a smile. "I wanted to see you before we die."

"You did?" That meant he'd called her beautiful. "But we're going to be rescued."

A tremor ran through Cody's body. "I'm sure you're right. It just doesn't feel that way. Something's wrong. We need to go. I can drive."

She stayed his rise with a hand on his shoulder. "One of the wheels is broken. I don't think this rover is operable."

He rested back in his seat. "Oh."

Despite the protection offered by the environmental suits, their body heat bled away, and the cold set in. They weren't safe yet. She left his lap, pulled a thermal blanket from a storage compartment, and handed it to him. Working her way around the dead driver to the front, she rerouted the air from the cabin to the emergency hoses. Returning to Cody, she plugged the hoses into their suits.

"This will save the canisters in the suits for later." Worry tinged her voice even though she tried not to sound frightened.

"Come here." He drew her into his arms and covered the two of them with the blanket.

Chapter Nine

Light shone through the cracked bubble of the rover.

"That didn't take long." Lisa raised herself to see the headlights of a small vehicle.

Cody didn't stir, and that worried her. Illumination flooded the area, allowing her to see the rocky landscape around them. A mangled body in an environmental suit lay prone beside the Glass Highway. No one should have been outside in the cold of night. What had caused the wreck?

A larger vehicle sped in behind the small one and fired a side-mounted laser cannon. The vehicle exploded in a flash of flame that quickly extinguished from lack of oxygen. Two figures exited the larger vehicle and walked toward her. They carried rifles.

The receiver in her helmet crackled.

"Director Shim, is that you?" a man's voice asked.

"Yes." She tried to sound unshaken by the death and destruction she'd just witnessed.

These men could be the outlaws the driver had warned her about. If so, then she hoped they were after ransom and not assassination. Unfortunately, their tactics thus far did not bode well.

"Are you hurt?" the man's voice asked over the radio in her helmet.

"No, but I think my husband has a concussion." She looked at Cody, who must be hearing this, though he didn't move a muscle.

"Mr. Shim, can you hear me?" The rifleman put a gloved hand on the outside of the wrecked rover's bubble.

"His name is Cody Greene." She took offense at the mistake.

"Oh, yes, well—" The rifleman cleared his throat. "—Mr. Greene, can you hear me?"

Cody came around enough to make a few unintelligible sounds. The rifleman opened the hatch on the back of the rover, climbed in, and pulled Cody out. He dragged him to the attack vehicle. The second rifleman never stopped patrolling the perimeter of light.

"Hey, look at this." The second rifleman's voice boomed over the receiver.

Lisa unhooked the oxygen line from her suit and climbed from the wrecked rover. The man pointed at a cracked helmet and an arm sticking out from under the vehicle. The blonde-haired woman had been pinned underneath when Lisa rolled the rover onto its wheels. A wave of nausea threatened to rise from Lisa's stomach. She had killed someone.

"I didn't know anyone was there. I righted the rover to help the others. I had no idea..." Lisa stared at the woman's frozen face unable to break away from the sight.

The second rifleman slapped Lisa on the shoulder. "Congratulations, Director. You bagged a fugitive we've been hunting for ten months. In fact, you took out two of them—although I think your driver's family deserves the reward for that one." He pointed toward the highway and the body lying beside it.

"We tried to resuscitate the driver." Her whole body shook with tremors. "My husband has medical training."

"Come with us, Director. An enemy vehicle is five minutes out. We should go." He took her by the upper arm.

Lisa shook him off. "I need to check something."

She ran to the Glass Highway and switched her lights to external. A man's mangled body lay exposed to the elements through several rips in his suit. There was nothing she could do to help the outlaw who had tried to kill her. Why had he done this?

She looked around. Rock fragments littered the roadway, and she hurried to clear them. There was no indication of fractures in the Glass Highway. Satisfied that she'd done her duty, she climbed into the assault vehicle.

Relief washed over her to have been rescued. She switched her lights to the interior of the helmet and then strapped into the seat next to Cody. His eyes were closed.

"What were you looking at, Director?" a rifleman asked as the vehicle accelerated away from the scene of the accident.

She ripped her attention away from Cody. "I needed to be sure the glass hadn't been damaged. The conduits sealed inside it carry resources around the equator of the planet. Can you imagine what would happen if they broke?"

The man cocked his head. "Resources, huh?"

She probably shouldn't have told him anything. "Air. Water. Power. Communications."

The man nodded and faced forward. "I see what you're saying. I guess it makes sense. Glad everything was fine."

She nodded. "Me too."

Lisa took Cody's gloved hand. How could the outlaws the dead driver had mentioned survive outside government-run colonies and laser defense outposts? A chill ran down her spine, the outposts were probably used for more than defending the colonies against asteroids. Her husband could probably answer her questions if he were awake. She squeezed Cody's hand.

He opened his eyes. "Is that blood on your face?" He reached toward her, bumping her helmet's visor with his gauntlet.

"It's the driver's blood. Don't you remember?" She met Cody's gaze.

He shook his head, causing it to wobble a bit. "I'm fine." He closed his eyes.

The outpost came into view. She'd never seen one this close. The solitary bio-dome lay nestled between the observatory and the laser tower.

A gate in a perimeter fence opened to admit the large vehicle. It closed behind them rapidly. The rifleman driving the assault vehicle swung it around and backed up until they docked at a hatch. Air pressurized the cabin.

"Feel free to unseal, Director." He walked past her to open the airlock.

She removed her helmet and gauntlets. "Is there a doctor here? My husband needs attention. He has a head injury." She helped Cody unseal as well.

"Of course, Director." The man nodded respectfully.

The men grabbed Cody by the arms and helped him into the facility. Lisa trailed behind them. They deposited him on a gurney where a nurse wheeled him into a room.

"Thank you for saving our lives." Lisa shook hands with the riflemen, then went with her husband.

Chapter Ten

Weak and somewhat disoriented, Cody permitted the female doctor to examine the bump on his head. The male nurse wheeled over a tray with supplies to clean the wound. The doctor did the job personally, and Cody hissed at the sting of the antiseptic.

"Thank you, Doctor. Will I live?" He hated the creepy feeling he always had in outposts.

"The wound is not severe and has stopped bleeding, Mr. Greene." She tossed the used supplies onto the tray. "You may have a mild concussion. If I had more equipment, then I'd do more tests. Unfortunately, we have limited resources here. Nurse, find a cold pack for his head, wash away the blood from his face and neck, then dress him for bed. He needs to sleep."

The doctor left the room without lingering for pleasantries, and Cody didn't offer any. The nurse gathered things from cupboards around the room. Cody didn't pay much attention to the man because Lisa's concerned expression held him transfixed.

She met his gaze from across the room. "Is there something I can do?"

He couldn't resist. "Sure." It beat the nurse doing it.

Lisa nodded to Cody and faced the nurse. "Thank you. I'll take it from here."

The older man waggled his bushy eyebrows and handed Lisa the things he'd collected from the cupboards. Once he left the room, Lisa drew the curtain in front of the door. She strode past Cody, handing him the cold pack as she went to fill the washbasin at the sink. The slope of her shoulders relaxed into one of exhaustion.

Cody sat in bed and put his legs over the side as he worked his shoulders out of the neck hole of the environmental suit. He should have taken it off completely. Except that he didn't want her to see him naked. He lifted the icepack to his aching head. At least it was a private room, and they would be alone.

Lisa brought the basin over and sat it beside him. "The water's hot."

He took the washcloth from her hand. "You need this as much as I do."

She shook her head. "I can shower. Please, let me help you so you can rest."

He sighed, seeing her logic, but unwilling to wait. "I need to know what you look like without makeup. Please, let me see you." For all he knew, she could be hiding a deformity.

She averted her gaze, taking a step backward. "I'm not pretty if that's what you're hoping for. I'm smart. That's all. Nothing more. Why did you marry me if you only care about my looks?"

His heart palpitated. "You know I had to."

She winced. "I forgot."

He frowned. "Why did you pay the fine to redeem me? I know it was a lot of money."

"My mother suggested you." She looked away. "I didn't have time to look through the potential matches."

Her mother had known his father. "Am I the only one you considered?"

Lisa nodded. "I time out in less than a month. Even so, I would have continued to hold out hope of meeting someone, if not for my surprise transfer to NINE. You were available, and when Mom and I prayed about you, we felt good about the match."

He inhaled sharply. "God told you to marry me?"

"Yes." Her breath caught with a little shudder. "I've waited my whole life for that answer."

Cody couldn't believe it. "You were surprised when you saw me at the wedding. That means you didn't even look at my profile picture, let alone read my information. That's crazy, Lisa."

She shook her head. "No, that's faith."

He raised an eyebrow. "There must have been something else to convince you to marry me sight unseen."

She looked down and to the right. "The only other thing I saw besides your name was our percentage of compatibility."

He had known from the instant he'd seen the number that she'd be swayed by it. "A computer told you to marry me, and you obeyed?"

A delicate crease formed between her eyebrows. "No, I married you because God spoke peace to my soul."

Cody gritted his teeth, knowing God loved him but rejecting the divine in this instance. Who had known about Lisa's vulnerabilities and manipulated her into agreeing to marry him? Only one person on the planet would take the trouble to save him.

Cody dared to be honest. "I didn't negotiate the details of the marriage arrangement, my mother did." That much he could say with confidence.

Lisa's eyes squeezed shut. "Your mother accepted my invitation without your consent? Why would she do that?"

He contained his anger, trying not to take it out on Lisa. "There is no consent involved with being redeemed. Either I accepted your offer or I faced execution. Regardless, my mother knows me pretty well and must have thought we'd make a good match. As for the percentage of compatibility, I don't have a lot of faith in numbers. I like you, though, so we have a chance." For the moment, guilt made him act nice when what he really wanted to do was feed his mother to a wood chipper.

Lisa clenched her jaw. "You don't think we're a ninety-seven-point-one percent match?"

He sighed, knowing the number was accurate but having no confidence about the way it was arrived at. "How would I know? If I had to guess, I'd say we're about seventy percent compatible."

Her eyes flashed with anger. "That's optimistic."

He chuckled. "Anything over fifty percent is good odds."

Lisa clamped her jaw and stalked into the bathroom. He slid off the bed to follow her, wobbly on his feet. She closed the door.

"None of this was my idea." He rested his head on the door, feeling guilty because the deception involved with an investigation was totally his fault. "Let's talk."

Lisa's sobs echoed in the tiled room. He'd heard that God counted the tears of women. Regret crushed him because his words had caused the woman he'd married to weep.

Chapter Eleven

Lisa stood in the running water of a hot shower. She had dreamed of marriage since she was a little girl. Cody wasn't what she had imagined, but there was something about him that captivated her in a way no man had before.

The nuanced attraction surprised her because his resentment didn't seem to be softening. If he never let go of his anger, then she couldn't fall in love with him. It wouldn't be safe.

She scrubbed the splattered blood from her skin. Unbidden, images of the accident played through her mind. She gripped her arms to keep from shaking.

The rover driver had died before her eyes. The man lying beside the road must have been hit during the accident. Then there was at least one person killed when the riflemen lit up the first vehicle on the scene in a fiery explosion.

All of that was horrible, but it was the blonde woman who had been crushed when Lisa righted the wrecked rover that haunted her. The flash-frozen face seemed indelibly imprinted on the insides of Lisa's eyelids. Bearing direct responsibility for her tragic end, Lisa cried until she could barely stand.

Pushing past the point of exhaustion, she shut off the water and dried her body with a towel. Hopefully, Cody had gone to bed because she couldn't face him. He didn't know what she had done, and she didn't have the strength to tell him. With a towel wrapped around her body, she left the restroom.

"Do you feel better?" Cody didn't look at her from where he sat on the edge of the recliner with his face resting in his hands.

Startled, she almost struck him. "No, and I'm not likely to anytime soon." She searched the cupboards for a hospital gown like the one he wore.

"We're married." Cody rubbed his eyebrows. "I'm not sure that can be undone unless a director has more clout than I'm aware of. You're probably thinking you deserve someone better than me. You're right, and you have my permission to submit a request for an annulment."

Stricken by his words, she stared at him. "You'd rather die than be with me?"

He rubbed his face even harder. "No, that's not it."

She concentrated on the way he avoided looking at her. "Then what?"

He shook his head. "I don't know. I just feel bad you're stuck with me. No matter what I do, I'm going to hurt you."

She blinked. "I wasn't crying about us, not really. People died tonight. It was horrible. I killed someone. It was by accident, but that doesn't matter. I can't stop seeing her face."

He sighed with his head down. "Was she the one pushing the rock onto the Glass Highway?"

Lisa paused. "No, she was the blonde I crushed when I righted the rover to help our driver. I didn't know she was there or I wouldn't have done it."

Cody rubbed his forehead. "They were outlaws. Why would you care about them?"

Lisa shook her head. "I didn't even know about outlaws until tonight. Regardless, they were people. It's sad."

He wiped his eyes. "All loss of life is a reason to mourn. Are you sure you're not just trying to change the subject? Why keep me when I'm not what you want?"

Lisa stared at the top of his head. "I'm not a quitter, Cody. We have the church in common, and I still intend to make this work.

Besides, I'm not sure I have any pull whatsoever with the government. In general, I don't think they're happy with me."

Cody lifted his head, saying, "How can that be?" His jaw dropped. "You're gorgeous."

She faced away from him as her skin flushed. "There's no need for flattery because I don't like false compliments. It does you no credit to lie to me. So, please stop before I—"

A touch on her shoulder caused her to jump. Facing Cody, she recognized a stillness that spoke of sincerity in his steady gaze. He let his hand fall to his side.

"You're beautiful. Hasn't anyone ever told you that?" His gaze traversed the features of her face.

"My mother says that, but she's biased." Lisa tried to calm her shallow breathing.

"I'm not biased, and she isn't wrong. Why do you hide your looks beneath so much makeup?" He walked over and sat on the edge of the hospital bed.

"I normally don't wear a lot, but I had to reapply after crying at a funeral." Yesterday morning seemed like such a long time ago.

He nodded. "That doesn't explain why you wear it in the first place. You certainly don't need it."

She hesitated to tell him her reasoning but took a chance that he might understand. "I was raised in the Korean tradition. That's my culture. I am Korean. However, it's tough to look Caucasian when you live in an Asian colony. The children teased me relentlessly in school. I started wearing makeup in high school because I wanted them to stop bothering me about it." The tragedy of her life lay bare.

"I hadn't thought about that." He scooted back on the bed until he rested against the wall. "How much Korean ethnicity do you have?"

"Genetically, I'm only fourteen percent Korean." She opened a high cupboard and stood on tiptoe to reach a hospital gown.

"You look more Asian than that." He folded his hands in his lap. "I have five percent black African blood, twelve percent Latin American ethnicity, and twenty-one percent Scandinavian genes. The rest is European. My ancestors came from Earth to establish ONE."

She evaluated his features with the new information. "Does that mean your ancestors came from the United States?"

He nodded. "Primarily."

She frowned. "Having been on Mars for over a hundred years—" She looked away, embarrassed by her assumption. "—um, I shouldn't have said that. I'm sorry."

He leaned his head against the wall and looked at the ceiling. "My line should have achieved more advancement as the new colonies came online? It's true."

Lisa put on the gown and tied the strings in the back, removing the towel from underneath. "What happened to your career in Space Division?"

He avoided her gaze. "I'm not allowed to talk about it."

"Oh." She hung the towel in the bathroom. "I suppose reading your profile wouldn't have done me much good then. Is there anything I can do to help?"

He grabbed the pillow and hugged it. "No. There's nothing anyone can do. But I would like to know why it doesn't matter to you who I am. Because that kind of seems like a big deal when choosing the one person you're going to live with for the rest of your life."

Lisa walked to the edge of the bed, regretting the hurt she heard in his voice. "You matter to me more than you realize. I never meant to imply that you don't. I was about to read your information when I was notified of the deaths of three of my technicians on loan to TEN. I trained them, and the authorities did not even bother to explain their deaths. Can you imagine how hard that was for me to tell their husbands and children? Their loved ones are dead, and they will never know why."

Cody held her gaze as ripples of grief played across his face. "Even with answers, it's hard to accept that kind of news. I'm sure you did your best to ease their burden, but you need to know that it's impossible to make them feel better."

Tears filled her eyes. "That explains some of the animosity I sensed. Thank you." She batted the moisture from her cheeks. "Can we rest now? I can't stay awake anymore."

He scooted off the bed. "Why don't you sleep here? I'll take the recliner."

Lisa faced him, close enough to feel his body heat. "You need to rest so you can heal. I'll take the chair."

He traced the hair that fell around her face. "All right, if you insist."

Lisa stopped breathing, unsure if she wanted him to kiss her or not. "I want you to recover."

He smiled with his eyes. "Good night, Mrs. Greene." He returned to lay in the bed and covered his lower half with a blanket.

She recovered from that smile and managed to stop staring at him. "I hope you don't mind, but I kept my name." She gathered sheets and blankets from the cupboards to make a bed in the chair.

"Of course, you did." He glared at the ceiling.

"No. It's not like that." She dimmed the lights and crossed to his side of the room.

"What's it like then?" His jaw clenched.

"In the Korean tradition, women keep their name." She touched his forearm, sorry that she'd upset him.

"Are you sure that's why?" He turned his glare on her.

She smiled at his stubbornness. "Yes, I'm absolutely sure. It's how things are done in SEVEN."

He shifted his animosity upward again. "We're not going to be living in SEVEN. Things are different in other colonies. My mother kept her name when she married my father, and it caused a lot of heartaches. I don't want to live like that."

Lisa absorbed his anguish. "Our cultures are different, but I'm willing to make certain adjustments if you are. Before we decide how to proceed, let's see how things are in NINE. I mean, a name is important. Our children will have yours. Isn't that enough?"

He looked away, moisture splashing from his eyes as he blinked. "You want to have children with me?"

His words moved her, and she grasped his warm hand. "Of course, I do. I married you because I want a family."

His Adam's apple bobbed as he swallowed. "I thought we were going to die tonight." Emotion thickened his voice.

"You nearly did." She smoothed the hair from his forehead.

His eyes drifted closed at her touch. "You're not what I expected."

"I know, and I'm sorry to disappoint you." Devastated, she tucked him in and raised the safety rail on the bed.

He covered her hand on the rail. "I meant that as a compliment. I hadn't anticipated tenderness from you. You're a powerful woman who shouldn't care about my feelings, but you do. I appreciate you for that." He looked away. "This could work, but I don't see how when so much stands between us."

Confused, she tried to sort out his concerns. "What do you need from me?"

He rubbed his face with both hands. "I'm not sure I can explain it to you."

Angered by his apparent reluctance to make the effort, her nostrils flared with a sharp inhalation. "Don't bother trying." She stomped to the chair and reclined into an acutely uncomfortable position.

"I meant no offense." He stared at her.

"None taken." Her anger burned hot, but faded quickly, replaced by a sorrow bordering on despair.

"Trust me, Lisa," he said. "I promise few things to very few people, but I always keep my word. I will try to figure this out."

She rolled on her side and pulled the blanket around her ears. "What if you can't? What if I'm unlovable?"

His eyes had a stark quality to them. "It won't be your fault. I'll take responsibility."

She cringed beneath the covers. "If our marriage fails, then everyone will know why. No one has ever wanted me. I should have known you wouldn't either."

He raised his head. "You don't understand. My reservations aren't what you think."

She understood just fine. "You're in love with my sister."

He rested his head on the pillow. "I still have feelings for Jinhee, but she was right about you. I should have asked you out. Anyway, I wasn't talking about your sister."

Lisa studied him. "Who were you talking about?"

He sighed, taking a long moment's pause before he answered. "There was someone else, long before I met Jinhee. She was my shade tree mechanic. We grew up together and fell in love in high school. She was everything to me, but she passed away. Unfortunately, love doesn't die when it should, and I'm still grieving. It's not fair to you, but I feel guilty. It's as if I'm dishonoring her memory by marrying you. I can't explain it."

The confession touched Lisa deeply. "Forgive me for being cruel." She left the chair to go to his side. "I had no idea you were suffering this way. Would you like me to hold you?"

His eyes filled with tears. "I don't know." His arm flew up to cover his face, and his broad shoulders shook with sobs.

She climbed into the bed next to him. "Loved ones are never really gone. Grieve for as long as you need to. I will never hold it against you."

Cody wrapped his arms around her and pulled her next to his side. She hadn't expected that, but she trusted him more at this moment than she ever had. She rested her head on his shoulder and held his hand until he began to breathe normally.

"What was her name?" Lisa needed to know.

"Erica." His heart rate slowed.

He had belonged to a mechanic once. Perhaps he would eventually fall in love with an engineer. Lisa desperately hoped so because she couldn't imagine being intimate with him without his love. Unfortunately, the law mandated sex within thirty days of marriage, and the penalty for noncompliance was too severe to contemplate.

Chapter Twelve

Cody awoke to the sound of Lisa arguing with a woman. He rubbed his eyes and rolled onto his side to see who was there. Cody's mother's assistant, Tammy, was on the vid.

"I will not accept a reward for what happened last night." Lisa's voice was low but emphatic.

The conversation captured Cody's full attention. Did his mother intend to pay Lisa to seduce him? He narrowed his eyes at Lisa. Fortunately, she had her back to him and wouldn't realize he'd overheard her confession.

"Director Shim, you are being honored for saving your husband's life." Tammy's color piqued.

Lisa shifted her weight. "Anyone would have done that."

"I'm not sure that's true, Director." Tammy's gaze shifted to meet Cody's. "Things weren't going well between you two. It would have been easy to allow him to expire. Then you could have chosen a new husband."

"I'm not a murderer." Lisa's voice raised.

"Agreed, Director, and your government thanks you for that." Tammy let out a slow breath with puffed cheeks. "There is another matter to discuss. Your belongings could not be retrieved. A salvage team searched for the wrecked rover this morning without success. It appears the outlaws have stolen it along with everything except the environmental suits you were wearing."

Cody groaned inside. The silver briefcase had fallen into the hands of the enemy. That could mean serious consequences for the colonies, depending on what information was in it. For him, it would trigger a reprimand in his Space Division record and possibly worse.

Lisa's body sagged. "No. Please. Are you sure?"

Cody lowered the rail on the side of the bed and sat with the covers over his lap.

Tammy gave Lisa a long-suffering look. "Yes, Director, it's been confirmed. Ah, Mr. Greene, I'm glad to see you survived the night. I'm sorry to inform you that your belongings have been lost. It is unfortunate, but everything was cataloged, including your recent acquisitions. Both of you will receive replacement items or reimbursement when you arrive at NINE. You must not speak of this incident with anyone except to say it was an accident. Do you understand?"

Cody clenched his jaw. "Yes."

Lisa cast a stricken expression at him before turning her attention back to Tammy. "I agree to your terms, but can't you look for our things again?"

Tammy frowned. "I will submit your request, Director."

Lisa's body became rigid. "Thank you."

"You're welcome, Director." Tammy cut the connection.

Lisa let out a grumble of discontent and rubbed her temples as she paced the hospital room. Cody enjoyed seeing her temper burn hot. Anger heightened the color in her cheeks, making her stunning.

Her small hands clenched into fists. He found that adorable. At least, he would have if she weren't being paid to sleep with him.

She glanced his way. "No amount of 'reimbursement' can replace my Korean ancestors' table. It's three hundred years old." She paced the other way. "I knew I shouldn't have let my father give it to me." She sat on the arm of the recliner and buried her face in her hands.

Cody studied her, fighting the urge to comfort her. He'd almost believed her to be compassionate. Last night, she'd held him tenderly. It had been innocent, or so he'd thought.

Her tears in the shower had disarmed him. All her talk about lives lost had fooled him. Obviously, she'd been crying over a lost table. She didn't care anything about their relationship.

He decided to up the theatrics. "That's bad enough, but I was transporting a packet of seeds for a super-plant that could have fed countless people and reseeded the planet someday. It took twelve years to create and a year to collect the seeds. Try explaining that to my boss when I'm not allowed to say anything. I'll be lucky if they don't hang me from the trusses in a bio-dome." He had transported top-secret seeds a while back.

"What? Are you sure? I thought my father sent those months ago." She met Cody's gaze.

"That's what they told me." He'd been caught in a lie. "Is your father a botanist?"

She nodded. "The best on the planet."

"Oh." He avoided her gaze.

How could he have forgotten that detail? He never forgot anything. He left the bed to pace the room, causing his gown to flap open in the back. That seemed to distract her. He let a little more show.

She turned pink and looked away. "Forgive me. I should have listened to your troubles."

He faced her from the farthest point in the room. "I feel like I'm cursed. Do you think I'm cursed?"

"What is 'cursed?' Is that Martian? What language are you tossing in here and there? You're confusing me." She frowned with that adorable crinkle between her eyebrows.

"Huh? Cursed. You know, when everything you do seems doomed to failure." He stood dumbfounded.

"That's not a Martian word." Her gaze drifted to the V-neck of his gown and the sparse showing of chest hair there.

"Really?" He straightened his spine. "I thought it was." Where had he picked up that word? Probably from one of the cowboy songs he liked to listen to. "Everyone uses it in THREE." Another lie.

Lisa's critical gaze deepened. "I wonder if people in NINE speak differently than either of us. We'll have to keep that in mind. I suggest we train for the adjustment. We don't want to stick out in society and have problems at work...or at home." She walked to the sink and brushed her teeth.

Cody stared; her pragmatism was impermeable. "Where's the doctor? I want out of here."

She kept brushing.

He stalked over to join her. "You know," he spoke around a mouth full of foam, "I'm not entirely sure they want to let us out." He spat in the sink.

Let her chew on that idea because it was the truth. Both of them had seen too much. By now his superiors in Space Division knew he was here and everything that had happened.

Lisa rinsed, padded barefoot to the door behind the curtain, and then returned. "We're under guard. How did you know?"

"Oh, probably because I'm cursed." He tossed the toothbrush in the sink and strode to look out the door. "You weren't kidding." He realized she was probably never kidding.

She shook her head. "If by kidding you mean lying, then no."

"What's up with that?" He meant her lack of sarcasm. Was it cultural?

She sighed. "I'm sure the guards are here to make us feel safe." She tidied the sink.

He couldn't keep his eyebrows in check, and they raised halfway up his forehead. Gullible was too mild a description for her. She wanted to believe everything was fine, so she did. That was called willful ignorance.

A knock sounded on the door. The same doctor and nurse from last night walked into the room. The hairs on the back of Cody's neck raised because at least the nurse should have gone off shift by now.

"Good morning, Director Shim. Mr. Greene, you're looking well. Place your thumbprint here, and you're free to go." The doctor handed Cody a datapad.

They were being watched.

Cody pressed his thumb on the screen. It was a good thing nothing had happened with Lisa last night. He wouldn't want a copy of it out there for people to see.

Anger quickened his pulse. What right did anyone have to make a recording of him and Lisa in bed together? He cringed. His mother had no scruples whatsoever.

The nurse placed a stack of gray utility clothing complete with hospital socks on the counter by the sink.

"Thank you, Doctor." Lisa included the nurse in a nod as well.

Cody was glad to see them leave. He sorted through the pile of clothes. What he found affronted his dignity.

"They call this underwear?" What good would this flimsy mesh do to keep things under wraps?

Lisa gathered identical gray clothes in a smaller size from the counter. She slipped on the socks first. With a demure glance in his direction, she walked into the bathroom with her clothes and shut the door.

"Why are they gray? Only kids wear gray." He put on the underwear, sweatpants, and shirt.

The socks were nasty with treads glued on the bottom that made his feet sweat. His mother must be trying to humiliate him. Why was she doing this?

Lisa came out of the bathroom with a glum look on her face, pinning her hair in a bun at the back of her neck. She wasn't paying attention to him. He lowered his gaze to admire her pert nipples through her shirt.

"I wish they'd recovered our things." She sighed. "We can shop when we reach NINE. Let's go home."

He followed her jaunty stride out of the hospital room. Shopping was not what he wanted to do with her. The impulse to sleep with her took him by surprise because he seldom had those types of thoughts about anyone. Maybe it was a good sign.

Chapter Thirteen

The rover driver for the last leg of the journey to Colony NINE was Cody's commanding officer, Simon Mambwe. The man had a scowl on his face the entire trip. Cody had messed up by losing the briefcase, but honestly, it wasn't his fault.

He laid back in his chair and pretended to sleep. What had been inside that case? He had tried to snoop, but it had been locked tight.

When they docked at NINE, there was a greeting party for Lisa. All the directors of the colony had sent underlings with fruit baskets full of goodies and gifts. Lisa greeted the group with a shy smile.

"Please, convey my thanks. I feel very welcome in NINE." She collected the cards from each offering. "I would be grateful if you would deliver these baskets to the orphanage. Thank you." She sidestepped through the middle of them.

Commander Mambwe's strong hand clamped on the back of Cody's neck. "You need to placate that idiot savant. Thanks to last night, she knows more than she should. The council wants you to keep her out of trouble."

Cody tensed. "Lisa didn't even know outlaws existed. She couldn't be selling resources to them. Has anything turned up with the other suspects?"

Simon nodded. "We found some dirt on the programmer in SIX."

Cody dropped his chin. "Is Lisa cleared?"

Simon's brows lowered. "Not yet. Keep asking her questions. Make nice with her and she'll probably tell you everything."

Cody stiffened. "Do we still have a deal? I want on the next transport."

Simon's grip on Cody's neck tightened. "That's out of my hands. The council wants to find the thief, but they also need Lisa to be productive in her new position as tech director. This colony depends on her doing her job well. Your investigative assignment has changed to more of a support role. Do it right, and you'll be rewarded." Simon gave him a shove.

"Yes, sir." Cody hurried to catch up with Lisa.

The bald inference that she was a genius in one area and suffered from mental retardation everywhere else shocked Cody. She wasn't handicapped, just socially awkward, introverted, and completely naïve. He had found hope in those qualities until this moment.

Had he been mistaken about Lisa's good nature? The Gold Council seemed overly invested in Lisa's job performance. Had she arranged to receive this massive promotion to NINE in exchange for something? He glared at her back. Had he become a bargaining chip in the negotiations?

Department directors in NINE worked at the pleasure of his mother. It was clear that Addison had a hand in the marriage. Had she traded him for Lisa's compliance?

Cody joined Lisa in the elevator. They descended five floors to the residence. A drab hallway led to their apartment, unlucky number thirteen.

Why had Lisa chosen to live among the common people? The elite had luxury accommodations on the lower ninth level. His mother lived there.

Lisa had already thrown her money at him. That led him to believe she wasn't cheap. Therefore, why pretend to be normal when she was just as much of a monster as the rest of the ruling class?

Lisa punched in the key code, but the lock beeped in protest and flashed red lights. "Looks like someone forgot to change the code after the last occupants moved out. Don't worry. I can fix it."

She knelt and drew a hair pin from the bun at the back of her neck. Bending the pin, she pried the lock away from the door a crack and stuck the pin into the gap on the center-right of the lock. The lights started flashing. She keyed in numerals one through five in ascending order. The door opened.

"That's not reassuring." He'd set up this test to see if she was good at bypassing security measures. "We might as well not have a lock."

She stood and met his gaze. "There's very little crime in NINE." She strode into the apartment with a smile. "We're home."

He stood dumbstruck in the doorway. "What is this?" The place was empty.

"Korean-style housing. I asked for your approval and received it, but..." She invited a conversation with her eyebrows.

"No one bothered to ask me." His mother must have accepted Lisa's terms without any attempt at negotiation.

This was a catastrophe. He stepped into the entry area. Confused, he took a half-step up onto the spongy, beige linoleum flooring. A narrow rectangular room with a kitchen on the right wall and storage cabinets on the left wall comprised the living area.

Straight ahead lay three doors. He looked inside. The first was a bedroom. The middle was the strangest bathroom he'd ever seen. It had tile everywhere, a squat toilet, and a showerhead on the wall with a clothes washer and dryer at the back of the room. The third was another bedroom. Neither bedroom had anything except floor-to-ceiling cabinets on one wall.

"Where are the beds?" It didn't make any sense.

"Koreans sleep on the floor." Her expression fell from apologetic to dejected. "There are blankets in the cupboards."

His anger increased. The second bedroom was cold enough to catch a chill. He tried to flip on the light, but it didn't work.

"Why isn't there any power in here? It's freezing." He came out, leaving the door open.

She ducked her head. "I thought we would save on the electric bill until our children are old enough to need the room."

He ground his teeth at the mention of children. It wasn't right. In twenty-eight more days, he would be forced to sleep with Lisa or be executed, and at the moment, he didn't want to.

He looked around the apartment with a scowl. There wasn't even a place to sit and put his feet up. Homes were for relaxation and food.

He hadn't eaten since the shopping trip in EIGHT. Strange. He usually had a healthy appetite.

"I'll turn the electricity on, but the floor heating will take a while to warm the room." She walked past him into the bedroom.

He watched her open a panel, engage the controls, and activate the power. Her no-nonsense attitude chilled him emotionally. Seeking comfort, he searched the kitchen cabinets for food.

Unsuccessful, he couldn't even find the ingredients to make something good to eat. There was nothing except shelf-stable packages of food substitutes. Each cabinet held a separate color: yellow, green, pink, and orange.

"There's nothing to eat, other than dietary chews." He confronted her. "I mean, look, you have a rice cooker, but no rice. Where are the groceries?" The culinary arts were one of his passions.

Her shoulders slumped further. He didn't care. He'd had more than he could stand, and he was throwing a fit.

Her eyes reddened as they welled with tears. "I will cook when we have something to celebrate. Koreans are all about food, but we don't like to eat alone. I'm going to be at work all the time." She shook her head. "I'm sorry. Dietary chews are convenient."

Anger narrowed his vision. "You know these are made of fish scales and vegetable peels, right?" About now, he would practically kill for one of those fruit baskets she'd given away.

She rolled her teary eyes. "That's a rumor."

"Nope." He couldn't take any more of this. "They're also laced with hormones, and I'm not going to eat them." He shook his head because she had no idea how sexually confused the chews made him feel.

She wiped her eyes and strode forward. "There's a bin of rice under the kitchen sink and kimchee in the refrigeration unit." She knelt beside him to pull a heavy container from under the counter.

He watched her struggle to remove the stubborn lid. "Here, let me help."

Their hands touched as he took over prying the impossible lid from the bin. He expected her to retreat, but she didn't. Together they finally broke the seal and accessed the rice. She stood, and he hefted the container onto the counter.

"Do you like kimchee?" She seemed to be holding her breath for the answer.

He watched her for a moment, debating whether to admit it or not. "I like cabbage kimchee, but radish is my favorite, and nothing beats cucumber kimchee in the summertime when it's fresh. Does that surprise you?"

She nodded, swallowing as if she fought an emotional response. "Kimchee is at the heart of Korean culture. I was worried that you would find the smell distasteful and ban it from the apartment."

He raised an eyebrow. "You'd let me order you around like that?" He took the pot from inside the rice cooker and scooped rice from the bin into it.

She rubbed her temples. "I wouldn't like it, but I would understand. Most people who visit SEVEN say it smells of garlic and avoid returning. We have a reputation."

Cody chuckled as he rinsed the rice grains with water. "I like garlic."

She leaned against his arm, tilting her head to touch his shoulder. "That's really good news."

He liked the feel of her next to him, and that made it worse. "Will you eat with me? I'm making plenty."

She glanced at him. "Yes, thank you. I just wish we had our table. I don't know how I'm going to explain losing it to my family."

He couldn't understand her stupid obsession with the table. "I guess we'll have to stand at the counter or sit on the floor until the replacement is delivered." He placed the pot into the cooker.

She pressed the button to start it. "I expect it will be ready in less than an hour."

He reached around her to open the refrigeration unit, and his hand glided along her trim buttock. The sensation sent a thrill through his entire body. An involuntary smirk pulled at one corner of his mouth.

"Excuse me." He hadn't meant to send mixed signals because that was against his rules of dating.

Was this a date? He scowled as he grabbed the kimchee out of the unit and set it in the sink. A bulge formed in his sweatpants, and he headed toward the bedroom before Lisa noticed.

She followed him. "I want to negotiate a compromise concerning the thirty days."

He grabbed a stack of blankets from the cupboard, concealing his display. "I think it's best if we talk about that tomorrow. You can have this bedroom, and I'll sleep in the living area. Maybe by tomorrow, the other bedroom will be warm enough to use."

She averted her gaze, looking disappointed, but resigned. "I thought you would at least want to share a room."

He ground his teeth. Why was she acting like this? Directors weren't demure, and this act didn't fool him.

He shoved the blankets at her. "I'll take the room, and you can sleep in the living area."

She grabbed them before they fell, then gasped and backed away. "What's that?" She stared at his groin.

He glanced down. "That's none of your business." Mortified, he slammed the bedroom door.

Chapter Fourteen

Cody stayed in his room as much as possible. He was the worst spy that ever lived. He should have used sex as a tool to coerce her confession. He'd been ordered to go to bed with her. Regardless, he couldn't face her after his embarrassing display last night.

At lunchtime, his naïve wife came to his bedroom door, knocked, and asked to talk to him. He didn't dare say a word. Every time she crossed his mind, his hormones took over again. Something was seriously wrong with his self-control.

After she'd gone, he opened the door to find his replacement items stacked neatly on the floor. Surprisingly, she'd included a wrist-vid with a card that read, "Happy belated birthday." Why was she being so generous?

The sound of what he assumed was traditional Korean music came from her bedroom. He quietly walked over to figure out what she was doing. Through a crack in the door trim, he watched her dance with a pair of ribbons.

She twirled them in the most intricate patterns. Her grace and poise impressed him, as did her refinement and physical appeal. Even in gray sweats, he had trouble resisting the temptation to go to her.

To his dismay, she never stopped frowning. He had caused that. With a sigh, he rested his shoulder against the wall to observe her further.

He would give a lot to see her smile again, but not his virtue. He needed to be sure she wasn't a criminal before he committed the rest of his life to her. Thus far today, he'd combatted the attraction with sit-ups, pushups, crunches, and squats.

Nothing had helped, and watching her dance was acute torture. If only he could resist seeing her, thinking about her, and dreaming of all the things he'd like to do with her in bed. He sighed heavily.

Lisa stopped dancing. Had she heard him? Cody fled to the bathroom.

He tossed his sweaty clothes in the washing machine then started the shower running. Stepping into the water, he lathered his hair with Lisa's coconut shampoo. A noise made him open his eyes. She walked behind him to the far end of the room. Startled, he covered his body with his hands. Had she seen anything?

"Forgive my intrusion." She stripped in front of the washing machine.

He stared at her backside and immediately regretted it. "I'm almost finished." He faced away, rinsed his hair, and reached for a towel, wrapping it around his middle.

"You spend more time in here than I thought you would." She showered in front of him.

He leaned against the wall, trying to appear calm, but staring at her breasts. "I like to exercise."

"I do too." She shaved her legs.

"I can see." He watched the razor glide across her toned calf. "Why do women do that?" Even after seeing a demonstration, he still had no real clue.

"What?" She tracked his gaze to the razor in her hand. "Regulations."

He noticed her hand tremble and nick her skin with the blade. It was the first sign that she was nervous. Now, he felt guilty because he'd been taking in the sights like an eager tourist.

He shook his head. "I almost believed you had no shame."

She shut off the water and faced him with her gaze on the tiled floor. "I have feelings for you."

"Why?" His confusion overruled his good sense. "We don't even know each other."

She crumpled like a wet paper sack. Once again, he'd said exactly the wrong thing. Shaking as if in shock, she walked to where she'd set a pile of clean clothes on the dryer.

"We're married, right?" Her posture remained defeated.

"Yes." What did she mean by that?

"Why did you ask for thirty days?" Her voice quavered.

He grabbed a second towel and closed the distance between them, wrapping it around her shoulders. "I won't settle for less than true love." He dropped his hands.

"What if..." She closed her eyes. "What if you can't love me?"

He took note of her pained expression. "If I can't love a woman like you, then I'm a fool." He touched her cheek with the back of his index finger. The smooth, blemish-free skin turned him on.

She shook her head. "I'm not what you expected. That's what you said. What did you want in a wife? I can't be someone I'm not."

He considered her question. "You surprise me in a lot of good ways. I expected you to be horrible. I guess I still do. I'm looking for your flaws. It's unnerving that you don't seem to have any."

She frowned. "I don't hide my shortcomings. You've seen my temper."

He smiled. "Your personality quirks are charming." He slid his hand down her slender neck as if she were a live statue from ancient times.

Heat radiated from her skin. "I'm not sure how this is done."

He caressed a little lower, enjoying the way she flushed in response to his touch. She closed her eyes and came in hot. He employed evasive maneuvers.

"Hold on, now." Avoiding her hands, he held her at arms' length.

Confusion overwhelmed her expression, and she swallowed a sob. "I need you."

He took a deep breath and relaxed his defensive stance. "Be patient." Forcefully drawn to her, he almost couldn't resist her offer.

She stilled. "I've never felt this way before. What do I do?"

He retrieved her towel from where it had fallen to the floor. "This is new for me too. I just want to be sure about you. Besides, a director deserves better than me, and I have no idea why you want me."

She met his gaze with an intensity he'd never seen before. "I married you for the only reason that matters."

"God?" What could he say to that?

He'd never met anyone this sincere. Her dedication to their marriage was one-hundred-percent. She held nothing back. That made him feel even worse because he was lying to her about almost everything.

Lisa accepted the towel and faced the washing machine. "The honeymoon is over." She dried her hair and dressed in baby blue pajamas. "We have work in the morning, and there's an award ceremony in the afternoon." She passed him on the way out of the bathroom. "Don't miss the ceremony because they expect you there. I won't be home for dinner. My schedule won't permit it."

He couldn't breathe. Their opportunity to know each other was coming to an end. Furthermore, he'd wasted his best chance to investigate her involvement in the resource thefts.

Panic set in. "Wait. You're not even a director here until the current director leaves for TEN. Why are you working so much?"

She stopped without looking at him. "Director Xyler has ordered me to conduct individual interviews with everyone in the division. It'll be sixteen-hour days until I've completed an extensive orientation process."

Dismay hit Cody like a pulse rifle. "The proximity regulations limit the time we can spend apart. We're newlyweds. We need to bond." He resisted the urge to take her hand.

She shook her head. "I need to work."

"Then I'll help you." His heart pounded in his chest.

"Do you have any tech skills?" She faced him. "I don't need a distraction."

He delighted in her candor. "I have skills that might be useful, but I can't guarantee I won't, um, be distracting."

Her pupils dilated. "Perhaps, you might be helpful."

He swallowed a lump in his throat. "Kiss me."

Her expression collapsed. "I don't want to embarrass myself again."

His heart skipped a beat. "I'm the one trying not to..." He drew close. "I'm having self-control issues."

"I am too." She looked away. "All I want to do is make love to you."

He marveled at the level of tension in her body. He adjusted the angle of her face and laid a chaste kiss on her lips. Her eyes drifted closed. Did she have any idea how much he needed to kiss all over her body?

She took a half-step back. "Thank you."

"Anytime." He couldn't help smiling at the confused look in her eyes.

"Is now too soon?" Her pupils became wide pools of black.

"Take it slow." He relaxed his stance and let his hands fall to his sides.

She stood on tip-toe to lay a feather-breathed expression of love on his lips, chin, and Adam's apple. Warmth filled his chest. He wanted her. All she had to do was ask.

"I'll wake you at half-past three in the morning." She smiled on the way to her room and closed the door.

Chapter Fifteen

Cody set an alarm on his wrist-vid for three twenty so Lisa didn't walk in on him while he was sleeping. Morning came far too soon. Yawning, he dressed in a green jumpsuit because he would be going to his bio-resource job at eight o'clock.

He stumbled to the kitchen and ate leftover rice and kimchee. Even cold, it was better than a dietary chew. Lisa came out of her room in a crisp, blue uniform. When had she found the time to press it?

"Good morning." She smiled at him as she walked over, stood on tip-toes, and kissed him on the cheek.

"Good morning to you too." He offered her a bowl of rice.

"Thank you, but I've already eaten. Are you ready to go?" She slipped her feet into a pair of sensible shoes in the entry area.

He put the food in the refrigeration unit. "Um, just a minute." He hadn't even used the restroom or brushed his teeth yet.

"I'll wait." She picked up her toolkit from beside the door.

He hurried; already sure this day was going to be miserable.

Following Lisa to the interview room, he dreaded the hours of meetings that lay ahead. Of course, he would have a break in the middle to do four hours of agricultural work and another four of Health Division services before he rejoined his wife to finish the rest of her schedule.

Lisa pushed open the door to a small conference room and took a seat on the far side of a table. She had a good view of the door. He sat as far from her as possible, trying to be inconspicuous.

She tossed him a palm-sized ball. "Would you like one of these? They reduce stress."

He squeezed it and leaned back in his chair. "I guess so, thanks."

Beside Lisa lay several cartons holding more items. During each interview, she gave away one of the items to a tech worker. Cody liked the two-colored meditation timers. When you turned them over, the liquids inside traded places in a swirling process that was supposed to help you relax.

Cody's favorite things Lisa gave away were small, flat rocks. At first, he hadn't realized what they did, but she demonstrated that the thin, smooth stone could be used for hand massages. Now he wanted one of those instead of the stress ball.

Each break between interviews, Lisa stood and stretched with deep, slow, bends. He tossed her the ball after watching her the fifth or sixth time. He'd already lost count.

"Can I have a rock instead?" He grinned as she missed catching the ball and chased it to the far end of the room.

She stooped to pick it up, making him wish he could misbehave. A uniform had never looked so good on anyone as Lisa's did on her. He planned on taking it off of her as soon as he was sure she wasn't a traitor.

"I have plenty." She dropped the ball into a container and crouched to rummage through the stones. "What color would you like?"

He righted his tipped chair and planted his feet on the floor. "I'd like a dark shade of sandstone red. Do you have any like that?"

She brought a stone over and sat in the open chair beside him. "May I show you how it works?"

He nodded, eager to see her try. She took his hand, though she hadn't done that with anyone else. Slow strokes of the stone's blunted edge across his palm relaxed him until he nearly fell asleep. Then she caressed his fingers with it, and that's when he had an unexpected reaction.

He hoped she wouldn't notice what she'd done. "You're better at this than I thought."

She met his gaze with a peaceful look in her eyes. "I find it easier to make it through a day when I employ relaxation techniques at regular intervals."

He leaned toward her. "I've heard that the best way to relax is to—"

A knock sounded on the door. "Come in." Lisa placed the rock in his palm and strode to her seat.

He slid his legs under the table to hide his reaction to her touch, pocketing the rock. He wouldn't be using that again today. Fiery asteroids, she made him hot.

Chapter Sixteen

Lisa endured a second day of tedious employee interviews and orientation meetings with patience. Normally she would be more excited about her work, but this was no fun. Cody entered the small conference room after his shifts ended.

"Long day?" he asked.

She gave him an exhausted smile. "Tomorrow will be better because I finish the interviews tonight."

He sat at the far end of the room, yawning into his palm. "Does that mean we'll be sleeping more?"

She sympathized with the level of fatigue in his posture. "I'm sorry you have to go through this with me. It isn't fair to you."

He held her gaze. "What's on the agenda for tomorrow?"

She pulled up her schedule on a datapad. "Well, I'll be watching orientation videos from four in the morning until six. After that, I'll have separate meetings with the innovation teams for each division, culminating with a luncheon for all of us. From that point forward, I'll be following various inspectors as they complete checklists on the equipment in the colony."

Cody pursed his lips. "I thought engineers conducted experiments in a lab and invented exciting things. Can't you show me something amazing?"

Lisa's heart warmed that he had a high opinion of her work. "Saturday, I'll be setting up my prototype laser array for testing. If it works, then we may be able to coordinate the firepower of the laser outposts to eliminate larger asteroids. It will reduce the risk of a direct hit to any of the colonies."

Cody stood and trotted over to kiss her cheek. "Now that sounds more like it."

She shied away from the public display of affection. "I was hoping you would say that because I plan to let you flip the switch."

He lifted an eyebrow before he slowly returned to his chair. "I thought you liked kisses."

She met his gaze out of the corner of her eye, unable to look at him directly. "I like them at home."

He leaned back in his chair. "Oh, I see, you don't like them."

She chuckled. "Tease me all you like, it won't help. There's just too much to do. I expected this colony to be functioning at peak capacity, but it's seriously underperforming."

Cody leaned forward in his chair. "Really? What's going on?"

Lisa sighed. "I shouldn't say anything until I'm sure where the fault rests."

A frown creased Cody's brow. "What's your biggest concern?"

She studied him, deciding whether or not to tell him the truth. "I've been reviewing reports and there have been unexplained fluctuations in air pressure over the past several weeks. It seems to have stabilized now, but without an explanation, I'm worried it may happen again."

He held her gaze with an unusual intensity. "We just arrived, and already you have life and death scale dilemmas to face. What will you do?"

She couldn't figure out what he was driving at. "I'll make sure there are no leaks as I go around with the inspectors. Furthermore, I plan to conduct a complete check of every system related to the atmospheric collectors as soon as possible."

He avoided her gaze. "Are you saying we don't have enough air?"

Her wrist-vid chimed with a message from her next interviewee telling her he would be late. "No. We must have plenty of air because the readings reported by the computer indicate the reserve tanks are full." She didn't want to worry him over a hunch.

Cody looked at her sideways, folding his hands on the table. "They're reported as full, or actually are full?"

Exasperated by the line of questioning, Lisa tossed him a meditation timer. "Relax. We're fine."

He shook his head and placed the timer on the table. "If you say so." He watched the liquids trade places until his eyes closed, and he fell asleep on the table.

Lisa envied him. Just then, someone knocked on the door. An unassuming, elderly man peeked inside the room.

She put on a smile for the tardy technician. "Please, come in and take a seat, Mr. Albright. I look forward to hearing about your work with the matchmaking software."

He shuffled inside, eyeing Cody. "I've made improvements to the compatibility algorithms."

Lisa raised her eyebrows. "I recently benefited from your expertise. This is my husband, Cody Greene. My apologies for him being asleep, but I've been keeping him busy with all of the preparations for my promotion."

Mr. Albright nodded. "A ninety-seven-point-one percent match. I remember you. That's the highest percentage of compatibility on record."

Lisa didn't miss the twinkle in his eyes. "Is your work accurate?"

He met her gaze and held it. "I guarantee it."

She relaxed. "That's good to hear because I had begun to wonder."

The old man chuckled softly. "This young man is worth waiting for, Director Shim. Everything will be all right."

Lisa warmed to Mr. Albright's confidence. "I'm sure you are correct. Now, tell me about the improvements you've made."

He nodded. "It has everything to do with data points. People lie, even to themselves. I have found a way to interpret genes that provides greater insight into complimentary pairings."

Lisa frowned, discomforted by the age-old and often abused concept. "How can genetics dictate love?"

Mr. Albright grinned. "Haven't you heard the adage that opposites attract?"

She shook her head. "No. What does it mean?"

He faltered. "It means that people are like puzzles. Some pieces fit together, genetically speaking, and some don't."

Something about this didn't feel right. "Are you talking about nature versus nurture? Because people are free to choose, and having excellent parents makes a huge difference in a child's life. Genes are a factor, don't mistake my meaning, but they are less important than free will."

Mr. Albright tsked. "If you say so, Director. I learned long ago never to argue with my superiors."

He unsettled her, though she couldn't explain why. "Please, submit a full report on every aspect of your responsibilities and all recent matches. I want to be certain your work is benefiting the couples you've paired. Perhaps, you are right, but we can't afford to trust a theory when it comes to the happiness of real people."

Mr. Albright's brows lowered until she could only see the glint of his eyes. "Yes, Director. As you wish." He stood and shuffled from the room.

Lisa glanced at Cody. "What about our DNA makes him think we're meant to be?" She shook her head and let out a breath. "I seriously hope he's not delusional."

Cody's breathing remained steady and deep. It melted her heart to watch him sleep. Yawning, she wished she could join him—at home, that is.

She groaned. "This day is never going to end."

Chapter Seventeen

Friday, Lisa completed a strenuous day of in-depth inspections. There were no air leaks in NINE. That only deepened the mystery. Where was the air going?

She'd looked at the lungs with her eyes, instead of relying on gages, reports, or censor logs. They regulated pressure in the colony and were inflated to half-capacity. That was normal and reassured her that there was sufficient air in all of the bio-domes and the central tube.

As soon as she had time, she planned to check the five atmospheric collectors and their supporting equipment. Four of the collectors worked, but the fifth was offline with serious problems. She had the authority to order it repaired, and completed a work order form.

For now, she needed something that didn't require any brain power. Exhausted, she checked the task board. An oxygen sensor in a storage room indicated a malfunction. Perfect. She accepted the job and requisitioned a replacement sensor at the parts bay.

"Thank you, Mr. Dean."

"You're welcome, Director." The bald man nodded without really even looking at her.

She strode to the elevator. It concerned her that she didn't have the authority yet to command the allocation of energy to put an atmospheric collector into operation. Fortunately, all of them were running at the moment, except for the broken one. She chewed her lip as the elevator descended to sublevel eight.

She strode the dim corridor. Color-coded pipes lined the ceiling. She calculated exactly where she might reduce power usage in the colony in an emergency.

If her ears popped due to a change in pressure, then she'd know the readings on the reserve tanks were faulty. They were supposed to automatically open to compensate for air loss. The lungs expanded if there was an air gain. Everything was supposed to work smoothly.

Someone's heavy footfalls behind her preceded his gruff voice, "Why are you down here by yourself?"

Startled, Lisa dropped her toolkit, grasping her chest with both hands. Cody scowled at her. She'd been lost in thought and hadn't realized the lateness of the hour. Stooping to pick up her scattered equipment, she noticed him looking at her backside.

She waved the sensor's shockproof container to distract him. "I'm checking the status of an oxygen sensor. I'm perfectly safe. Sensor checks in storage rooms are like scrubbing toilets, no one is going to offer to take the job from you."

His dour expression altered to include a twist of humor. "Do you wield a toilet brush often, Director?"

His half-smile lightened her mood. "Every day in our apartment, or hadn't you noticed, Mr. Greene?"

He raised his shoulders and opened his palms with a playful look in his eyes. "Don't ask me to take the job away from you."

She laughed, tempted to do all kinds of things with him that had nothing to do with household chores. "By the way, what does this gesture mean?" She repeated what he'd just done.

He quirked an eyebrow. "Don't Asians shrug?"

She shook her head "Shrug? No. I've been seeing people do it here, and I don't know what it indicates."

He chuckled. "It indicates the person doesn't know something, isn't sure, or is shirking responsibility."

She considered his explanation as they walked along the corridor. "So, I take it you don't want to scrub the toilet in our apartment."

He smiled. "I'm glad to share the work at home. I was teasing you."

She stopped at the correct storage room door, noticing the disengaged locking mechanism. "That's strange."

He leaned against the wall to meet her gaze. "Oh, really? Don't the husbands in SEVEN pitch in with housework?"

The question confused her. "Of course, they do. Why do you ask?"

He laughed. "You have a one-track mind."

More confusion assailed her. "What's that mean?"

He came closer to kiss the arch of her ear. "You focus on only one thing at a time. I like that about you, especially when you're focused on me."

An intelligent reply escaped her at the moment. "Oh."

Why did Cody have the power to turn her into an adolescent girl having her first infatuation? She had experience with how to deal with unwanted attraction, but it did her no good when it came to him. She wanted to go home, strip naked, and engage in what married people were supposed to do after a day of work.

He pulled away. "What's wrong?"

She swallowed a lump of emotional frustration, changing the subject. "The door shouldn't be unlocked."

Cody put a hand on her shoulder, moving her away from the door. "This is why you shouldn't be in a remote area of the colony without someone to back you up if something goes wrong." He opened the door, flipped on the light, and searched the storage room. "All clear."

She strode into the room. "The sensor is sending an error signal to the main computer. I brought a replacement." She held up her toolkit. "Hopefully, I didn't damage it when I dropped everything."

He frowned. "I wasn't trying to sneak up on you earlier."

She opened the panel to access the sensor. "I wasn't paying attention to my surroundings. I have a lot on my mind."

Lisa replaced the oxygen sensor chip. The unlocked door to the storage area was an infraction of protocol she'd have to report. If it had been the only instance of negligence she'd stumbled upon today, then she wouldn't be concerned, but it was one of many.

Cody held the door open, squinting at a stack of containers in the opposite corner. "Are you about done?"

She hit reset on the wall-mounted sensor. "Green lights." She stowed the old chip in the case and deposited it in her tool kit on her way out of the room. "I'm sorry if my work bores you."

His frown deepened as he followed her. "What are you really doing down here?"

She was too tired to argue. "I have a duty to the colonists to fix things when they break."

He grabbed her by the shoulders and pressed her against the wall in the hallway. "Don't pretend with me. Who were you meeting?"

Her jaw fell open as she processed his accusation. "No one."

The anger behind his words sent a flash of fear through her mind that shut it down almost completely. Confrontational situations had always intimidated her. That's why she spent most of her childhood in a laboratory. She shied away from him, avoiding eye contact.

He took a half-step backward. "You're trembling."

Lisa forced herself not to cry about whatever it was that had just happened. "I have work to do. Go home if you want. I don't need you bothering me." She engaged the locking mechanisms on the storage room door and scurried to the stairwell.

He pursued her. "You know I have to stay with you."

Completely rattled, she couldn't quite calm her nerves. The man she had believed to be gentle, except for his grumpy nature, had proven himself to be far more intense than she'd anticipated. She wasn't used to volatility.

Calm. Predictable. Orderly days were her norm.

"I won't tell anyone if you go." She made an effort to sound calm, stopping on the landing in the stairwell.

Cody was changing everything in her life, or maybe it was her transfer to NINE that had removed her too far from her comfort zone that was the problem. Either way, she sought balance. Fixing things usually helped center her because it leveled her focus and gave her something to concentrate on until everything else fell into place.

"Wrong answer." He scowled at her.

Heat flushed her cheeks. "I can't do anything right with you, can I?"

He squared his stance. "Capitulation is a sign of weakness. Promising not to tell is the fastest way to be victimized. You should always report someone who is intimidating you, Lisa."

She met his gaze because his tone had softened. "But you are my husband."

He nodded. "And if I ever were to hurt you, then you must report me just the same as anyone else. No one has the right to scare you into submission."

She took a deep breath, easing the tension from her shoulders. "I was bullied in school. Avoidance is my coping mechanism."

His arms fell to his sides. "Why would anyone mistreat 'the most promising mind of this century?'"

Lisa winced, remembering the words on a poster of her distributed around the planet when she was in junior high. She curled inward. Her classmates had mocked her over it without ceasing.

Cody came close, touching the sleeve on her forearm. "What did the children say to you about it?"

She shook her head. "It doesn't matter."

He lifted her chin. "Please tell me."

She met his gaze and relented because of the tenderness of his touch. "They said the government singled me out because I'm a blonde Caucasian. They said an Asian wouldn't be celebrated."

He leaned closer. "That's why you altered your appearance?"

She inhaled his citrusy scent. "Not until high school. I was confused by what they had said for a long time and didn't make the connection."

He laid a soft kiss on her lips. "And hurt by it, I can see."

She relaxed as he rested his hands on her hips. "It made no sense because I lived a traditional Korean lifestyle when most of them didn't even speak an Asian language."

He pulled her close and rubbed her back. "You are Korean. I haven't fully respected that about you, and I'm sorry."

She wrapped her arms around his middle and hugged him. "I miss my home."

He sighed. "Is that why you're working such long hours?"

She stepped back, shaking her head. "No. Well, maybe a little, but there are dozens of projects that need to be done, and most of the technicians don't seem to know how to do them."

Cody frowned. "That doesn't make sense, but I've sat through enough of your interviews with them to know it's true. Anyway, where are we headed now?"

She took a deep breath to clear her head. "Sublevel nine to inspect the safeties on the Administrative Division's private elevator. A report came in voicing a concern about a half-second delay when it lifts and a slight thud when it descends. I think it's slipping."

Cody's expression became severe. "Super important stuff like this should always be attended to by the director herself and not some first-year flunky."

Lisa descended the flight of stairs. "Are you being, um, what's that word?" She couldn't think of what to call it.

Koreans were always sincere. They joked sometimes, but in a distinctive way. If they told lies, they always did so in an exaggerated manner that let the other person know it was a falsehood meant to amuse and not to deceive.

"Sarcasm." He descended the stairs with her.

"Yes. That's it. Koreans don't have sarcasm." She exited the stairwell and opened the access panel to the elevator shaft in the bright, shiny hallway, dropping into a greasy-smelling crawl space.

He leaned into the opening. "Why?"

She considered the question as she shone her light around the mechanisms that raised and lowered the elevator for the elite class. "It confuses us. Perhaps, we're too literal. I think of it as sincerity."

He reached for her shoulder, coming up short. She caught his hand and met his gaze. He squeezed her fingers.

"I'll try to speak plainly." He didn't release her.

"Why?" What was he attempting to say?

"Because I'd rather we understand each other from now on." He drew her to him.

Stooped, she came toward him awkwardly. "That's probably best, since I never know where I stand with you, and I'd like to."

He nodded. "We need to be on an equal footing." His voice had deepened a great deal.

She closed the distance between them, tilting her head as if to kiss him, but stopping a millimeter from his lips. "Koreans don't engage in public displays of affection."

He smiled and pulled away. "Ah, that's too bad."

Deeply disappointed with herself, she watched him withdraw just out of reach. "We can go home after this inspection. Though, I have reports to file and schedules to set for tomorrow. And I could still be called out for an emergency." She rubbed her hand across her forehead. "I haven't eaten all day, I'm filthy, and the laundry needs folded."

He chuckled. "A million things more important than what I have to offer."

Her lips parted as her heart sank. "I didn't say that. Forgive me for...offending you? You don't look offended."

He smiled. "I'm not. I'm amused by your order of priorities. Have you considered the probability that our relationship should rank higher on the list?"

Her heart pounded in her chest. She desperately wanted to put him at the top...on top, or whatever way worked best for them. She'd done a little homework, but the rudimentary sketches in the sex education digital pamphlet had left her more confused than ever.

She searched his open expression. "You are my top priority, Cody. I just don't know what to do to please you. Everything I've done so far has upset you, and I don't know why."

His features sobered. "We've been experiencing some miscommunications."

She batted two large tears from her eyes with her lashes. "Is that all that's gone wrong between us?"

He slid his feet into the opening, and she backed further inside. Crouching low, she retreated as he slid into the tight space. Maneuvering his arm behind him, he closed the access panel until only a sliver of light shone on her face.

Sitting on the dirty floor, he motioned for her to come to him. "We're not in public anymore."

Even so, her anxiety level remained high. "What are you planning to do?"

He patted his thigh. "Let's talk."

She raised an eyebrow. "Here?"

He drew her into a sitting position across his lap. "How about here?" His lips captured hers.

Her eyelids fluttered and closed as her last ounce of reluctance evaporated. Floating on the sensation of softness combined with the scratch of stubble on his face, she raised her hand to caress his jawline. For the first time, she dared to breathe while kissing him. He smelled wonderful, warm, and masculine, everything she wanted.

Cody broke the kiss, leaning his head against the wall with a satisfied-sounding sigh. "Now tell me why you don't have time to do more of that?"

Lisa smiled. "I'll make time."

In the dimly lit space, his expression remained somber. "Is that a promise?"

She flushed, embarrassed and not sure why. "Yes, if I say something, then I will do it. Koreans are honest and generally don't make casual commitments."

He hugged her, pressing her shoulder to his chest. "We have that in common."

She sought him with her lips but only managed to reach his chin. Kissing the stubbly skin, she remained patient until he met her halfway. This time, he didn't pull away.

Sliding his fingers through the gaps between the buttons of her uniform, he caressed her midriff. She moaned from her core, incriminating herself completely. Mortified, she crawled away, silently berating herself for indulging in a moment of weakness when she should be doing her job.

Cody raised his knees and rested his arms on them, watching her. When he didn't say anything, she felt even worse about what she'd done. He must think she had no self-control whatsoever.

Frustrated, she suppressed the urge to cry and focused on her work instead. Shining a light on the elevator engine and the pully mechanisms, she realized the luster of the cables didn't look bright enough. Moving closer, she inspected the metal cables to find one of the strands frayed. If any more splitting took place, then it might fail. She photographed the cable with a datapad from her toolkit and filed a work order for tomorrow.

She crawled in Cody's direction. "We can go home now."

"Oh." He climbed out through the access panel.

She followed him and secured the panel behind them. "I'm shutting down the elevator until the cable can be replaced." She pushed the button on the elevator and inserted a key in the red slot, twisting it until the lights in the elevator turned off and the doors stayed open.

He watched her intently. "Did I do something wrong?"

She removed the out-of-order sign from the box inside the elevator and magnetically secured it above the button on the outside. "No. Why would you say that?"

He captured her fingers. "Because you pulled away from me."

The desire to hide from her shame made her shy away from his touch, lest he cause her to do something inappropriate again. "I shouldn't have—" She shook her head and started walking toward the service elevator.

He caught up with her and pressed his lips firmly together. "How often do elevator cables fail?"

"Not often with regular maintenance." She pushed the up button.

Cody's brows lowered. "Are you worried?"

Lisa massaged her shoulder to ease the tension enough to restore blood flow to her brain. Her head pounded with the lack of oxygen. The entire day had been stressful in the extreme.

She glanced at him. "Not overly. The biggest problem I've discovered is that reports are unreliable, and the technicians here in NINE aren't trained as well as I would like." The service elevator opened, and they stepped inside. "There's no reason for you to be concerned. I'll have this colony in excellent shape before anything terrible can happen."

He scowled, punching the button for sublevel-five. "So much for NINE being the shining example of advancement. No wonder the elites are leaving for TEN before long."

She softened her stance toward him. "A place is only as good as its people."

He stared at the control panel. "Why did you pull away from me earlier?"

She composed her thoughts but had no idea how to explain what he'd done to her. It had never happened before. She'd wet herself over his touch. However, that was far too embarrassing to admit.

"Is it possible to have an, um, oh, I can't even say it." She faced away from him and darted between the elevator doors as soon as they opened.

Practically running down the hallway to their apartment door, she keyed in the access code and entered with him close on her heels. They slipped off their shoes, and she fled to the bathroom sink to wash her hands and face.

He came in beside her and washed his hands too. "What can I do to make this right?"

Surprised that he didn't condemn her, she met his gaze. "You're not appalled?"

His brow creased in the middle. "By what?"

She took a step backward, lowering her chin. "I had an orgasm. At least, I think I did. It's never happened before."

He grinned in a conspiratorial way, shutting the bathroom door with both of them inside. "What did it feel like?"

Her body pulsed with heat as she stood her ground. "It was wonderful. I didn't know something like that could happen without coupling." She shook her head and faced away from him, ashamed. "I shouldn't have let it happen in public. Please, forgive my indiscretion."

He came to stand behind her with his hands on her shoulders. "Please don't be embarrassed. I'm the one who lured you into being intimate in a place that made you feel uncomfortable. I want you to know that the way you respond to me makes me feel ten feet tall and bulletproof."

She shut her eyelids, trying to block the thought of how close he stood. "I have no idea what that means, but I've never felt this way before. I don't know how to act or what to say. I have no idea what's happening to my body, and no framework by which to weigh your reactions. All I know is that I want to be with you in every way possible."

He stepped toward her, pressing his body against her back. "I feel the same way." He raised her hand to kiss it over her shoulder. "I have an embarrassing confession, too. I had a wet dream about you last night."

She found it difficult to hear when he kissed her so it took a moment to process his words. "Wet?" She swallowed. "That's what happened to me." Heat flushed her cheeks.

His voice held a smile. "We're even."

She frowned. "It was involuntary."

He nodded and kissed her hand again. "Yes, same for me. I'll let you shower while I make dinner." He left the bathroom and closed the door behind him.

Chapter Eighteen

Saturday, Lisa worked overtime on a project that had taken on renewed importance after learning of the atmospheric fluctuations in NINE. Her dream of restarting the core and restoring life to Mars was the only way to ensure the survival of everyone she loved. The colonies were just too fragile.

Cody strode into her laboratory as the eight-hour maximum they were allowed to be separated lapsed. A thrill ran through her at the sight of him, causing her concentration to unravel. Instead of focusing on the prototype model of a laser array that she needed to test-fire, her gaze flitted around the well-lit area to find a private place to ask him for a kiss.

He followed her gaze with a knowing smile. "Are we alone?"

She set down the laser control pad. "Yes."

Drawn to him, she strode in his direction. Smugness tipped the corners of his lips. Aching for his touch, she ignored the implication that she was making this easy for him.

"I've missed you today." He caressed her face with the fingertips of one hand then drew her by the neck into a kiss.

The softness of his lips caused her to want to explore their fullness. She wrapped her arms around his neck, running her hands through his hair. This kiss was different than the others because she gave herself over to it completely.

Inexplicably, the desire to taste him overwhelmed her inhibitions, and she extended the tip of her tongue. His lips parted, allowing her access to his mouth, and he met her in an ever-deepening expression of sensuality. She had waited forever for this moment.

Cody lifted her off her feet. Dizzy, she didn't realize he had carried her across the room until he laid her on the sofa. The weight of him on top of her did delightful things to her body.

His lips traveled her jawline, and the sensation of his breath on her ear made her gasp. His mouth captured her earlobe, causing her to cry out in a most undignified way. What if someone walked in?

"Take me home," she whispered.

He stilled, releasing her ear. "What am I doing?"

Disoriented, she watched him push off of her with his arms. The bulge in his pants dispelled the haze from her brain and triggered a panic attack. Heart pounding, she fell off the sofa.

"What is that?" She couldn't take her eyes off of it as she scrambled backward across the floor.

He glanced down then grabbed a throw pillow from the sofa to cover his midsection. "What did you think would happen with that much kissing?"

Her chest heaved for breath, but the tightness made stars float before her eyes. She collapsed as darkness crowded the edges of her vision. He came to her side, making it worse.

"Lisa, calm down. You're going to be fine." He held her hand in both of his. "Slow your breathing. Take a deep breath. Hold it. Now, let it out."

He placed the pillow underneath her knees. She could hardly hear what he was saying, but she did her best to obey his coaching. It took a while for her breathing to begin to stabilize.

She covered her eyes with a hand, fighting a blinding headache. "I'm all right."

He lay beside her on his side, propping his head with his hand. "What were we thinking?"

She watched his cheeks flush with color. Rolling onto his back, he stared at the ceiling. His body still strained the fabric of his pants.

"Health class didn't prepare me for this." She counted the ceiling tiles.

His chest heaved with a sigh. "Me neither. I sure didn't expect this level of desire. I'm out of my mind over you."

Was that a declaration of love? "I thought I was imagining things the other night."

He met her gaze. "Imagining the attraction between us?"

She shook her head, focusing on her breathing. "No. I'm relieved you're returning my affection. It's just that I wasn't prepared for that." She pointed toward his zipper unable to look.

His eyebrows raised. "You mean my, um, difficulty staying calm around you? Is that what triggered your anxiety?"

She nodded as she climbed to her feet. "It's too big."

He stood beside her. "It? What do you mean? I'm not that big."

Moisture flooded her eyes at the hopelessness of the situation. "The tolerances are too tight. It's never going to fit."

He pulled his shirt lower. "I think you misunderstand what's happening here. I have no intention of finding out how well we do or don't fit together tonight."

She made her way to the sofa and sat at one end, wiping an unending stream of tears. "Tonight, or next week, it doesn't matter when. It just isn't going to work out between us."

He sat at the opposite end of the sofa. "I thought you wanted to sleep with me."

Her lower lip quivered. "I did, but now I'm not sure."

He frowned. "What can I say to make this right?"

Her pulse pounded in her temples. "I'd feel better if I knew what I was in for."

His face twisted in confusion. "I'm not sure what you're saying? Are you being coerced into sleeping with me?"

Surprised, she met his gaze, blinking away enough moisture to see properly. "We'll be punished if we don't comply."

His expression became grim. "What do you know about the birds and the bees?"

She wiped her runny nose with a cloth from her back pocket and tried to think past the headache. "I'm familiar with the phrase because of my mixed heritage. Other than that, all I know is that I take you in, but I'm telling you it's not going to work. You're too large for me to accept without excessive damage."

He scowled at his hands. "It works for everyone else. It will work for us."

She shook her head. "No. It won't."

He sat back on the sofa, sliding his knee into the center as he faced her. "Just so you know. This bee has no intention of stinging that bird anytime soon. Despite what happened a minute ago, I plan to wait until I'm sure about you."

Conflicted by the answer, she organized her thoughts. "You keep saying that, but it doesn't make me feel any better. We almost made love. Why would you do that if you don't have feelings for me?"

His jaw clenched. "I want to be with you so much it hurts. I'm literally about to explode, and my brain has been completely hijacked. I just don't understand why?"

Anger threatened to rise in her chest, falling into her churning stomach instead. "I know how you feel."

He met her gaze, placing his hand on his knee. "You do?"

She covered his hand with hers. "Fear is the only thing that has kept me from letting you 'sting' me, Mr. Bee."

A pained expression raised the center of his brow. "Well, Mrs. Bird, what can I do to ease your concerns?"

"Are you sure you want to?" She held her breath for the answer.

He met her gaze. "Yes. I definitely do." He scooted beside her.

She leaned against his shoulder and rested her head, absorbing the comfort of his proximity. "I'm afraid."

He held her hand. "Me too, but I think you're forgetting something."

"What?" Her eyes drifted closed as she inhaled his warm scent.

He cleared his throat. "Well, babies are born from there, and they're much bigger than I am."

The logic didn't reassure her. "I've never heard of childbirth being pleasant."

He chuckled and laid his head against the back of the sofa. "No, I guess you're right. Though, most people say sex is wonderful."

She nestled beside him, and he put an arm around her. "I always thought it would be too. My parents are private about it, but they have eight children and are very happy. I guess I should have asked my mother more questions. It was foolish to assume that our relationship would be easy."

Cody hugged her. "Your parents have been married a long time. You and I just need to figure things out."

She considered that. "Anatomically?"

He kissed her head. "Emotionally."

Her chest tightened. "I'm an engineer, and I think spatially." Curiosity built in her mind.

He faced her. "Well, I'm just a man, and I think...I usually think with my heart." He lifted her chin and leaned in for a chaste kiss.

She accepted his lips, melting into the tenderness. He didn't stop, though the intensity remained steady. His eyes closed.

At some point in the process, he took her hand and began to slide it downward. She pulled away, gasping for breath. What was he trying to do?

He met her gaze. "I thought you needed to know."

She raised her eyebrows. "I thought you were too modest."

He swallowed. "If you don't want to—"

"—I do." She definitely did. "I've just never seen—"

"—No looking. Just feel me with my clothes on. That's all I'm letting you do." He tensed.

She shook her head. "It feels like an intrusion. I have no desire to molest you simply to assuage my fears."

He chuckled and reclined his head fully with his arms along the top of the sofa's back. "How innocent are you?"

She searched his expression for a clue to his meaning. "I had never kissed a man before you, and I thought you were inexperienced too. Though, I know you tried to kiss Jinhee. It's clear that our cultures are different. Does that mean you've kissed other women? Please tell me you haven't been intimate with anyone in other ways."

Cody met Lisa's gaze from his reclined position. "I haven't slept with anyone. As far as kissing Erica, well, that's none of your business."

Lisa adjusted her expectations to accept his answer. "Fine. Now, are you going to assist me with the test-fire or would you like to continue this conversation?"

His right eyebrow arched. "Let's take a look at your laser array."

Chapter Nineteen

Sunday morning, Lisa dressed for church and started on her makeup in the bathroom. She wanted to look her best when she met the congregation. She worked six days a week, but always observed the Sabbath and attended her meetings on the Lord's Day. It was the first Sunday of the month, a fast and testimony meeting.

She wore the outfit she bought in EIGHT. Well, at least it was a close approximation of that outfit. Everything she and Cody had now was a replacement.

A knock came at the bathroom door.

"Almost ready." She hurried to finish.

Opening the door, she strode into the living area and slipped into her high heels. An alert popped on the datapad on the floor where she'd left it last night. She accessed a report, reading the information.

Cody came up behind her and swept the hair away from her neck. The brush of his hands on her skin thrilled her senses. However, the news on the datapad stunned her.

"What are you reading?" He leaned over her shoulder to look at the screen.

His proximity fuzzed her brain in a warm and very welcome way. "I'm not sure."

His eyes tracked the data as a frown darkened his expression. "This shows unusually high hormone levels and some kind of drugs. Are your techs in trouble?"

She faced him, allowing him to hold the datapad. "Not my people." She ducked her head. "Those are our numbers. It's the urinalysis report from our time here in the apartment, but it makes no sense."

He took the datapad and scrolled through the information. "Are we on drugs?"

She nodded, unable to speak past the lump in her throat. The ramifications could be catastrophic for her career. They would both be jailed if anyone found out.

He scowled at the report's conclusion. "We were dosed with hormones and a slow-release drug combination to lower our inhibitions. Our numbers have risen all week, and today is the first day they've begun to come down. How did you obtain this information?"

Lisa's heart raced. "I was ordered to send three techs to replace the women who died in TEN. Since they had a layover in NINE, I asked them to install a prototype toilet I've been working on with Health Division's research and development team."

Cody's eyes narrowed. "Why would you do that?"

Her cheeks warmed. "I wanted to be notified as soon as I became pregnant. I knew I wouldn't have time to visit the doctor, and I thought this would be the best way."

Cody captured her gaze. "Lisa, we haven't—"

She faced away from him. "I know we haven't, but I thought we would by now. I've been thinking about it, and I'm willing to try. I want to be with you, Cody."

He grabbed her shoulders. "No. I really don't think you do. Drugs are influencing your decision. Did you receive an injection before our wedding?"

"Yes." She searched his pallid expression. "It was an inoculation."

He frowned. "I was given one too. The nurse said I was due for a booster shot, but that's not true. That's when they dosed us." He shook his head and took a step away from her. "I can't believe this is happening. I actually thought I had feelings for you."

Lisa fought for air, suddenly unable to breathe. "You do, and I love you, too." She'd never said those words out loud before.

He shoved the datapad into her hands. "It's not real. All of this between us is a lie. Our feelings are nothing more than something the government cooked up in a chemistry lab."

A chill settled over Lisa and traveled down her spine in a way that made her feel faint. "I'm in love with you."

He backed away from her. "No. You're not. We don't even like each other. Remember when we met? All we did was argue."

She lifted her gaze to look into his brown eyes. "I love you."

He scoffed. "Not even close. You hated the sight of me."

She took his hand, rubbing her thumb over his fingers. "I hated your hairy knuckles. You being Caucasian frightened me because deep down I knew it meant the compatibility percentage was off somehow. I reacted badly, and I'm sorry. It doesn't matter anyway because those things are trivial compared to your attributes. I'm happy with you. I even like your grumpy ways."

Cody scowled. "And I like your Asian temper, but that doesn't change the fact that we've been drugged. I'm never this sexually frustrated. I've been fighting an unreasonable urge to sleep with you all week. I should have known it wasn't real." He gripped her hand fiercely. "And if I find out you were involved in this, then I'll never forgive you."

The accusation struck fear into her. "I would never—"

He jerked his hand away. "You're a director."

Anger drove away reason. "What does that mean? Are you saying I'm lying to you?"

He turned on her. "Power corrupts."

Agape, she realized his masculine strength for the first time. "I'm not like them."

He rushed in like a wave of heat. Fortunately, his anger gave way to passion as his mouth captured hers. She reciprocated, and his hands crushed her clothing in his grip as he pulled her against his body. Fear fled in the face of her desperate need. She dropped the datapad and wrapped her arms around his neck.

He lifted her off the ground squeezing her thighs with his large hands. His mouth hungrily explored her neck. Pain opened her eyes to her peril. He had sucked her throat brutally. She reached for the place to be sure he hadn't broken the skin, but there was no blood, only tenderness.

She met his gaze, witnessing the frenzy of his passion dispelled by the realization that he had hurt her. The tight skirt she wore had stopped her from wrapping her legs around him, and because of that, she recognized his readiness to make love to her. She wanted him, yet feared him. Her apprehension caused her to hesitate.

He dropped her, taking a step backward. She landed on her feet, though her knees buckled. Recovering, she gasped for air. An expression of acute regret and shame overwhelmed Cody's features.

Catching her breath, she changed the subject before he could run away. "What is that you're wearing?" She couldn't help the disapproval in her tone.

He had dressed in brown slacks, a white collared shirt, and something else. She'd never seen anything like it before. He cinched the thing around his neck, withdrawing from her in a way she'd observed him do often.

"It's a bolo tie. My ancestor was an Eagle Scout. He made this from an arrowhead when he was a kid and brought it with him to Mars." Cody shuffled his stocking feet. "My mother sent it to me after she found it behind my dresser." He cocked his head. "What? Don't you like it?"

She took a deep breath and let it out slowly. "It's fine."

He looked like a yokel. She moved to open the front door, and Cody caught her by the shoulder. He released her as soon as she stopped.

"You can't go like that." He avoided her gaze.

Had he left a mark? She strode to the bathroom, examining the place on her neck in the mirror. A bruise stood out on her skin. Above the collar of her blouse, it would be noticed by everyone.

Cody slipped into his shoes, standing by the apartment door. She opened the medicine cabinet and found a concealer. Liberal application of the cosmetic covered the bruise. A sliver of doubt entered her heart. Did she really love him?

Chapter Twenty

Lisa knew the way to the common use, nondenominational chapel. She had memorized Colony NINE's schematics when she redesigned them for TEN's modular construction. The chapel wasn't far from their apartment and technically belonged to the residence, as did a preschool and a grocery store. Cody surged ahead with brisk strides to hold the door open for her.

"Thank you." She accepted his kindness without the warmth she might have felt if the nature of their relationship wasn't in question.

An older couple came forward.

"Hello, I'm Jane Rosales." The woman extended a hand.

Lisa and Cody each shook it in turn.

"And I'm Branch President Jorge Rosales. Welcome. We're happy to have you in the congregation." President Rosales shook their hands.

"It's nice to meet you, President and Sister Rosales." Lisa liked the friendly couple right away.

"Sister Shim, would you offer the opening prayer for us today?" President asked.

"Yes, I'd be happy to." Lisa enjoyed being included in the program.

"Brother Greene, would you be willing to bless and pass the Sacrament with me?" President Rosales smiled.

"Of course." Cody's posture eased. "Thank you, President."

Cody's sudden smile turned Lisa's insides into a quivering mess. She tried not to stare, but she couldn't pry her attention away. Talk about a hormone rush. Dosing her had been completely unnecessary because she had plenty of passion, she simply kept it in check. That must be why they drugged her. They needed to reduce her ironclad self-control. Embarrassingly, the plan had worked.

"How many members are there in this branch?" Cody glanced around.

"Including the pair of you, there are five adult members and three young children. You see why we're glad to have you. We haven't had the Sacrament since Kelly Kramer's husband, Luke, transferred to TEN. He went as part of the finishing crew, so it's been almost three months." President Rosales' brow creased.

Cody nodded. "I'm glad to be part of the branch. Let me know how I can help. Well, let us know how we can help."

Lisa refrained from rolling her eyes. "Yes, President, please let us know what we can do."

She took Cody by the arm and drew him over to sit in a pew. Sister Rosales sat in the same row on the opposite side of the aisle from Cody and Lisa. President Rosales walked to the front of the chapel.

He stood at a lectern. "I'd like to welcome everyone to church today. Sister Rosales will lead us in the opening hymn while I play the keyboard. Lisa Shim will then offer the prayer. Afterward, the Sacrament will be blessed and passed to the congregation."

When the Sacrament portion of the meeting ended, President Rosales offered the first testimony. Lisa fell asleep. She couldn't help it, and there was no disrespect intended.

The sound of a baby crying woke her, and she lifted her head from Cody's shoulder. When had she let herself lean on him? Sister Rosales stood bearing her testimony and hadn't yet finished her lengthy list of things she was grateful for, including the ways the Gospel had changed her life.

The testimony was worth listening to, but the baby turned Lisa's head. It was a little girl. She was so tiny.

Sister Rosales wrapped up her remarks in a hurry, leaving the lectern vacant. Lisa hoped the mother of the children would sit by her and let her hold the baby, but as she led her children along the aisle to find a seat, she sat in Sister Rosales' pew. Sister Rosales gathered the infant into her elderly arms with an expression of joy that made Lisa jealous.

With a disappointed sigh, Lisa sat back in her seat. She'd been straining to see around Cody's broad shoulders as the woman walked in. Then she had leaned forward to see around his chest when Sister Rosales took the baby. Now, sitting properly, Lisa noticed his critical expression for the first time.

"I never figured you for baby crazy, Director." Cody whispered, but everyone heard him due to the acoustics in the room.

It boggled her mind how he always managed to say the most annoying thing possible at exactly the wrong time. With a scowl, she stared straight ahead at the empty lectern. She wasn't overly eager to have a baby, was she?

Seven younger siblings had required a great deal of child care from her. That could have put her off of having kids, but it hadn't. She enjoyed them.

In this instance, however, her ticking biological clock provided a compelling drive. Many women complied reluctantly with the four-child requirement dictated by law after the pandemic decimated the population, but she would not be one of them. Her children would never feel like she didn't want them because she absolutely did.

The way she saw it, she had two choices. She could come kicking and screaming into marriage as Cody had, or she could utilize her time before marriage and children wisely. She had chosen the latter, and now felt completely prepared to raise a family.

Cody's thigh pressed warmth against her leg. Her abdomen clenched, and her need for him deepened. She swallowed, closing her eyes against the urge to lay hands on the man. At this point, she couldn't be sure she wouldn't rip off his clothes.

Slow, steady breaths cleared her thoughts. Cody pushed away from the bench and strode to the lectern to bear his testimony. She met his intense gaze.

"I'm thankful for many things today," he said. "The Gospel of our Savior strengthens me in all my trials. I've been recently married, and my wife is an amazing woman. I'm grateful for her patience with me. I know the Lord will bless us as we keep his commandments and try to be like him. I say these things in the name of Jesus Christ. Amen." He spoke with a sad chord in his tone.

The Holy Ghost's influence entered her heart, prompting her to understand that rough times lay ahead. Fortunately, another impression also came to her. If she didn't abandon her feelings for this special man, then the two of them would find a way to love each other in time.

The word that had come to mind wasn't the Martian word for special. It was the Korean word. The meaning was roughly the same, except with a deeper connotation of priceless worth.

When Cody returned to sit beside her, she took his hand and squeezed it. What she had to say was for his ears alone so she maintained her seat hoping the meeting would close. After a few minutes, it did. However, that brought the bustle of Relief Society, Priesthood Quorum, and Primary meetings.

Sister Rosales took the little children to Primary, even the baby. President Rosales led Cody away for Priesthood. That left Lisa and the children's mother, Kelly, for their Relief Society meeting.

Kelly asked Lisa to give the lesson. A few minutes into it the young mother fell asleep. The poor woman looked like the baby was keeping her up at night.

Lisa pressed on as if she hadn't noticed. The Old Testament lesson about David, King Saul, and his son Jonathan warmed her heart with the Holy Ghost, despite the lack of commentary from Kelly. Lisa offered a closing prayer, and when she opened her eyes, the young mother had awakened.

Kelly stifled a yawn. "I'm sorry. I didn't mean to fall asleep."

Lisa had to laugh. "I was the one dozing earlier." She came to sit beside her new acquaintance. "Your children are beautiful."

Kelly smiled. "Oh, thank you. I love them dearly, but it's not easy without their father. He's always been a big help, especially with the boys." Her bottom lip protruded, and the corners of her mouth turned downward. "I need him to come home."

Lisa worried for her. "Hasn't he contacted you lately?"

"No. I've sent messages nearly every day, but he hasn't replied. It's been months."

Lisa frowned because this was not the standard procedure. "I'll inquire after him. Perhaps I can set up a vid conference for you and the children to speak to him." She put her hand on the woman's shoulder. "I'm sure he's fine." She hoped she was right.

Chapter Twenty-One

Cody and President Rosales left Lisa and Kelly in the chapel and walked to Jorge's office for their Priesthood meeting. It was a tiny space, but necessary to conduct the business of the church. Things were different on Mars than they had been on Earth centuries ago.

First and foremost, there were no temples on Mars. The ordinances that made eternal families possible were not available here. The Martian Colonial Government wouldn't allow that much religious freedom, providing another reason for Cody to go to Earth.

"You look troubled." Jorge leaned forward in a seat behind a compact desk.

Cody let out a sigh. "Since when have I ever had any trouble?"

Jorge chuckled. "Since forever I guess." The older man leaned back and continued to smile.

Cody had known Jorge since he was the youth leader at church growing up. The older man had taken Cody under his wing after the deaths of Cody's father and three, older sisters during the plague in EIGHT. Jorge had also consoled him when Erica had been killed in a freak accident in the mechanic's shop. Cody had missed Jorge when the man had been promoted to NINE, but it was a joy to find him here now.

"I guess you know the predicament I'm in." Cody rubbed his face with both hands.

Jorge's eyebrows raised. "No. Am I missing something? I noticed you were married when the membership records came in a few days ago. When did you meet Lisa?"

Cody tipped the folding chair backward and crossed his arms over his chest. "Take a look for yourself. You have my permission."

Jorge pulled a tablet from the bottom drawer of the desk. As an analyst in Space Division, he had clearance to see almost everything. Jorge's expression of acute concentration deteriorated, and a frown overtook his features. He shut down the tablet and locked it away.

Letting out a slow breath through pursed lips, he finally looked Cody in the eye. "I'm guessing it's not going well. I'm sorry."

Hearing those words of sympathy released a flood of pent-up emotion. A sob shook Cody's shoulders, and he wept like he hadn't since Erica's death. His mother had set him up. He had begun to suspect her interference, but he hadn't anticipated this level of betrayal.

"Why would my mother drug me?" Anger surged in Cody's chest. "If Lisa isn't guilty of a crime, then I might have actually grown to care for her. I like her. I just can't trust anyone right now."

With Jorge, he could be completely honest. Jorge knew things that weren't in those files. He understood why Cody had struggled to fall in love again after Erica's death. They'd never actually put Cody's infrequent and confusing bi-sexual attraction into words, but Jorge had been helpful with good advice over the years.

Jorge's brows lowered. "The reasoning for the chemical intervention is not recorded in the files, but I'm fairly certain your mother has guessed your secret. She's the only one who would care enough to go to these lengths to ensure your union is successful."

Resentment hardened Cody's heart. "The only thing she wants is to avoid a scandal. She doesn't care about me. I've disgraced her by timing out. I thought she wouldn't care because she doesn't acknowledge that I'm her son, but it's clear that I made a serious error in judgment. She should have let me die."

Jorge's brows piqued in the middle. "Don't say that. Lisa redeemed you, and you have a chance at happiness with her. Your mother loves you. She'd do anything to help you. Maybe she pulled a few strings, but she didn't force anyone into this marriage. Well, other than you, but timing out was your choice."

Cody shook his head. "If my mother loves me, then why lie to me? Why drug me? Why manipulate Lisa into marrying me?"

Jorge shrugged. "I can speculate, but there's nothing in the files that give me anything concrete. Your mother is afraid of you. Your eidetic memory has allowed you to see through her duplicity since you were a child. She's hiding from you."

Cody winced. "You think she'd be a part of my life if she wasn't concealing corruption?"

Jorge shrugged. "I can't be sure, but I know she's not as bad as you think. She does what's expedient in her line of work. She lies. She cheats. She bribes. It's her job as a politician, and she can't do those things around you because you always piece together the truth."

Cody rubbed his face. "Not lately. I can't read Lisa, and it's making me paranoid that she's better at hiding things than I am at rooting them out. I'm second-guessing my second guesses."

Jorge's kind eyes met Cody's gaze. "Lisa has nothing to hide. Forget about your mother's motivations for putting you and Lisa together, and open your heart to your wife. Lisa obviously loves you. Anyone can see that. Have the courage to trust her, and I think you'll be happy with the results."

That wasn't the answer Cody had been anticipating. He'd hoped for sympathy, but expected chastisement.

"How can I fall in love with Lisa when she works for my mother?" Anger surged inside his chest.

Jorge chuckled. "She doesn't work for your mother any more than you or I do. Besides, they dosed Lisa as well as you. That tells me, she wouldn't have been easily deceived by your cover story. She's intuitive and would have sensed that something was wrong. Anyway, she's nothing like your mother. I've met both women and have read their profiles. There's little in the way of similarity."

"Lisa's pushy." Cody grimaced, regretting his petty complaint.

"She's assertive."

"I'm not a chauvinist, President."

"I know that. You're just an old bachelor paired with an old maid. Sparks are likely, and clashes are inevitable. It's a big adjustment for both of you."

"We're not that old." Cody groused.

"Mature enough to be set in your ways. Besides, this is a complicated situation that Lisa doesn't even partially comprehend." Jorge folded his hands on his desk and looked at them. "Have you been intimate?"

"Not completely." Cody was still chewing on the realization that Jorge obviously didn't think Lisa was guilty of treason.

Jorge looked up. "How can that be?"

Cody scoffed. "We've been too busy fighting with each other to feel comfortable giving in to the hormones."

"By 'we' you must mean you. Am I right?"

Cody paused, thinking about Lisa's concerns. "You're not wrong."

"That gives you absolute power over her," Jorge said.

Cody met his critical gaze. "I didn't ask for this."

Jorge nodded slowly. "Unfortunately, there are many things in life that are unfair and against the will of the Lord. We are still responsible to keep the commandments. We're obligated to do the right thing by others."

"And what is that?" Bitterness overwhelmed Cody's mood.

"Love her," Jorge said.

"I thought I was in love with her. In fact, I was almost ready to forget about the whole investigation and be with her for the rest of my life." Cody's heart ached from an old wound enlarged by recent events. "Do you know what loving Lisa could have meant for me? I was happy until I found out we were being drugged. Our feelings for each other are nothing more than the result of hormone injections."

Jorge leaned forward in his chair. "I think the chemistry between you two is real."

"Real?" Cody leaned back in his chair. "I can't be attracted to Lisa because she's nothing like Erica."

Jorge cocked his head. "I disagree. Lisa is everything Erica wished to be."

The words hit Cody hard. The girl he'd known had spent every waking hour dreaming of the things she was going to invent. Tragically, all of her ideas were ridiculous. Of course, he'd never told her he thought so because it would have crushed her.

Erica simply didn't have the talent required to be anything like Lisa. A memory came unbidden, floating in the middle of the room as if he was looking at it right now. There had been a picture pasted inside the lid of Erica's toolbox. It was of Erica's idol, an adolescent Lisa with blond hair, a shy smile, and the bluest eyes behind dark-rimmed glasses.

Cody clenched his jaw. "You're right." Why hadn't he put this piece of the puzzle in place before?

"It's why you like Lisa." Jorge's expression lightened into a pleasant one.

Cody stood and paced the small room. "What if I'm not genuinely attracted to Lisa? What if, after the drugs wear off, there's no spark between us?"

Jorge sighed. "She is the right woman for you."

"But how do you know?" Torment gripped Cody's soul in agony.

"You're married." Jorge extended his hands face up in an open gesture.

Hurt mingled with other dark emotions in Cody's heart. "So, that's it? I'm stuck? I have no choice?"

Jorge's expression saddened. "You had a choice, and you made it. Now the consequences are out of your control. If you change your mind, then Lisa pays the price."

Cody pounced on the opening. "I'm investigating her for resource theft. Are you forgetting that?"

Jorge let out a breath. "The investigation appears to be going nowhere. There's no definitive proof that resources have gone missing from THREE. All I know is that Lisa was commissioned by the Gold Council to write the source code for a protocol that transferred a fraction of each colony's reserve resources to TEN. However, that was eight months ago, and everything went smoothly. Maybe, your mother let you investigate Lisa as a ploy to convince you to marry her. Addison must have realized that you needed the hope of a way out of the marriage if you were going to commit."

Stunned by the extent of the depraved scheme, Cody's hands fell to his sides. "And now I'm trapped."

"No. You're married. Be happy." Jorge smiled warmly.

Cody stood in silence for a very long time. It would be so easy to succumb to the hormones. All he had to do was say he loved Lisa, and she would give him everything she had to offer.

He couldn't do it, not when he wasn't sure. "What if she becomes pregnant?"

Jorge folded his hands on the desk. "I imagine she will. Why does that worry you? You've always wanted children."

Cody met his gaze, tormented. "I can't bring a child into the world until I feel like it's safe."

Jorge's eyes became peaceful. "The Savior is our only safe harbor. You have patiently trusted in him your whole life. So, what's bothering you now?"

Cody searched within himself for the answer, but clarity eluded him. "I don't know. The evil in our culture and the unfair way our society is structured scares me."

Jorge nodded. "Is there more to it than that?"

Cody sighed. "I guess, there is. I've been thinking about the way the government let so many people die in quarantine during the plague.

Losing my father and sisters ruined my mother. She's become a monster."

Jorge let out a slow breath beneath heavy brows. "And you think it will happen to Lisa if you lose a child?"

Cody's breath seized in his chest. "No. I'm afraid it will happen to me."

Jorge's eyebrows lifted. "It won't. You have something your mother never accepted, the Atonement of Jesus Christ."

Cody's eyes filled with tears. "What if I don't have enough faith?"

Jorge met his gaze. "Whether you think you do, or you think you don't, you're right."

Cody took a shaky breath then relaxed. "I choose. Is that what you're saying?"

Jorge nodded. "I remember your mother before grief changed her. She loved your father and adored each of her children. She didn't join the church, and I've always wondered why. Regardless, she was open to religious freedom. She realized Fortney's religion made him the man she wanted to father her children. Don't make the mistake of forgetting about that when you look at her today."

Cody had blamed his mother for being distant. However, he had been just as callous toward Lisa at times. There was no excuse for it, and he needed to change his attitude.

Cody ducked his head. "I should apologize to you, President. I've been sitting here trying to justify the need to reject Lisa when I have nothing to back it up with other than my insecurities. It's exactly what my mother does to me."

Jorge's expression saddened. "You should spend considerable time in prayer. Ask the Lord for a way to heal. Tell Lisa you need some time. She'll understand."

Warmth gradually filled Cody's chest. "I will, President."

Jorge stood and walked around the desk to put a hand on Cody's shoulder. "Repentance brings healing through the Atonement of Jesus Christ. You can become the man you want to be."

Cody nodded, unable to speak past the lump in his throat.

Jorge opened the door to his office. "Be faithful, Cody. God will provide a way for you to find the joy you seek. What he fixes stays fixed."

Chapter Twenty-Two

Lisa and Cody returned to their apartment after church. Cody headed for his room, but she caught him by the elbow. He faced her without meeting her gaze.

"Please listen to me." Lisa searched his expression. "The government is manipulating us, but I trust in the Lord. I'll be patient with you, I promise."

Cody paced the living area, trying not to show her how upset he was. "Why don't we have any furniture?" He went to the bathroom and pulled some tissue from the roll, blowing his nose.

Lisa looked around the apartment, knowing he had changed the subject to avoid talking about their relationship. "Koreans sit on the floor."

He came into the living area and leaned against the wall. He looked so emotionally devastated that she pitied him. What had he and President Rosales talked about?

"I can order something." She avoided his gaze, sensitive to the gulf of economic disparity that lay between them.

"No, it's fine. I'm sure you realize how nice this place is. I mean, we never run out of hot water." He slid down the wall to sit on the floor with his knees upright in front of him.

She knelt facing him and sat on her heels. "Who runs out of hot water?"

He chuckled and swiped at his eyes. "Everyone."

She frowned. "Why is that funny?"

He waved a hand. "It's not. I miss my old life. None of this feels right. I don't fit in here."

She bowed her head, regretting his discomfort. "What can I do?"

He dropped his knees and crossed his ankles. "I don't mean our place, exactly. I kind of like our Korean-style apartment. It's nice. Comfortable, except for the lack of a couch." He shook his head. "I hate the squat toilet, but I'm already used to it." He blushed and looked away.

"It makes potty training easier." She had thought ahead when she designed the apartment.

His brows crashed downward. "Don't even joke about kids."

She tilted her head in confusion. "When the thirty days are up, don't worry about hurting me. I overreacted. It's going to be all right."

He shook his head. "It's good that you're willing to wait because I can't control myself right now. You'd better stay clear of me until the drugs are out of my system."

She nodded in agreement. "I'll monitor the reports and let you know when it's safe to try."

He clenched his fists and squeezed his eyes closed. "I hope we work this out between us soon."

She wished he would look at her. "Me too, Cody. Waiting doesn't feel right."

He leaned his head against the wall. "There's a chance that I'm not actually attracted to you. If that's true, then we have a serious problem."

The depth of his concern made her smile. "God did not put us together to fail."

He swallowed. "What makes you think you want me? You didn't like the look of me when we first met."

She pondered the question. "It started with your confidence at the wedding, your secret smile when you thought I didn't see you looking at me. But the first time I knew it would work was when we kissed, and you took my hands. Something happened, and I could tell that you felt it too because your eyes were unguarded and surprised. I was stunned when you walked away."

He took her hand. "I'm...sorry."

His apology confused her. "For what?"

He stroked the back of her hand with his thumb, staring at the opposite wall. "For not being honest with you about who I am. In my line of work, I'm simply not permitted to share my true thoughts and feelings with the people I spend most of my time with. I haven't even told you how much I like cowboy poetry or black and white westerns. You don't know me at all."

She moved to sit beside him, transferring his hand into her other one. "I like old movies, too. Color versions are better, but there was just something magical about the characters in them. The wide-open sky above them and the stretching vistas of vegetation are restful to the soul."

Cody looked at her. "There's something peaceful about it. That's why I like working in the bio-domes. I could earn more money doing other things, but I crave nature."

She smiled. "I usually look at it through the observation deck glass."

A crease formed in his brow. "Why? The smell of the ocean is powerful. I like it almost as much as the aroma of fertile soil." He chuckled. "You probably think that's crazy."

She shook her head. "No. It's wonderful. I just don't go inside the domes often because I have allergies to some of the flowering plants and trees."

Cody squeezed her hand. "Take an antihistamine, and I'll show you the most beautiful spots in the colony."

She blinked at the warmth in his eyes. "I'd love that."

His gaze lingered on her face, sweeping across her features until it focused on her lips before it darted away. "I specialize in dive harvesting in the ocean habitat. You haven't lived until you've tasted my seafood."

She leaned against his arm, imagining him in swimming trunks. "I'm looking forward to spending time with you. I'll try whatever you cook. Will you taste my traditional Korean cooking? I desperately hope you like it, but I want you to be honest if you don't."

He turned her hand over and traced his fingertips across her palm. "You cook?" His voice thickened.

She glanced at his misty eyes. "I'm the oldest of eight children. Of course, I cook." She smiled. "I guess that doesn't mean that I enjoy it, but I do. I just don't care for washing dishes."

He placed his palm on hers and laced his fingers between hers. "I promise to do all the dishes."

Her breath caught in her throat. "Forever?"

He met her gaze. "Always."

She blushed at the warmth that surged between them. "What do you want in exchange?"

He quirked a short-lived smile. "I'll let you know when the drugs wear off."

She averted her gaze. "Oh, that. Well, I'm yours whenever you ask unless I'm so tired I can't manage it. I'm trying to reduce my workload. It will be nice to have more time with you in private."

He raised his knees, pressing the hand he held in his lap with his thigh. She wondered how close her hand was to things she'd better not ask about right now. He didn't seem to notice her train of thought.

His brows pinched in the middle as he gazed at the wall. "You seem comfortable with the idea of making love to me. I wish I felt less anxiety over it. I'm not ready to be a father."

She read the depth of his concern. "Is it because the government will use our children against us?"

He met her gaze and nodded. "Yes, but not only that. I'm afraid of caring too much about anyone. That's why I don't have any close friends."

Lisa understood his loneliness. "Where do you put all of your tender feelings?"

He tapped the center of his chest with his other hand. "Right here, in a tight knot."

She reached across her body to place her hand on his chest. "I'm sorry that you've been alone for so long. I know it must hurt."

He covered her hand with his and closed his eyes. "You have no idea. Your family loves each other. You have people who would do anything for you. You're very blessed. I hope you know that."

She gripped his shirt in her hand and pulled, causing him to look at her. "You have me, and we have them. You're not alone anymore."

He teared up and swallowed. "You don't even know me."

She lifted her chin. "God does, and he recommended you. That's good enough for me until we become better acquainted." She released his shirt, and he released her hand.

He still held her other one and gave it a reflexive squeeze. "I've been praying, but I haven't received an answer about you. Am I asking the wrong question? What did you ask when you prayed about me?"

She thought back to that day when she'd gone to her mother for advice. "Mom and I knelt and prayed that if you were the one for me that I would have perfect peace."

Cody stared at her. "And did you?"

She nodded. "Yes. I've never felt anything like it."

"Peace." His gaze became contemplative. "Every time I touch you, I feel peace."

She raised her eyebrows. "I was sure you'd say something else."

He met her gaze and chuckled. "You set me at ease. That's the only reason I can feel those other feelings for you. It's never happened to me with anyone else. Even with Erica and Jinhee, I was worried that I wouldn't be able to perform."

His confession baffled her. "What do you mean?"

The animation left his features. "I don't often feel romantic about anyone."

Still confused, she prompted him, "Romantic in what way?"

He blushed. "Physically. You're the only woman I've ever been this turned on by. It's probably just the drugs and hormones. What if I'm not excited by your body after they wear off?"

Lisa looked at their hands, meshed together in his lap. "Have you touched other women? Have you kissed them? I'm fine before you come up to me and caress my skin, but after that, I can't even think. What we have is stronger than I expected, but I have no fear that it will go away, not if we don't want it to."

He leaned against her and squeezed her hand. "I don't want it to go away."

She breathed a sigh of relief. "Neither do I. If you have trouble with it in the future, then you should just say so. I've been reading some pamphlets on married life. There are a few suggestions that I'd like to try."

The corners of his mouth quirked upward. "Oh, really?"

Warmth flooded her core. "Really, really."

He chuckled. "I may just let you do that sometime soon."

She sighed. "Not soon enough for me. I've been holding back all my life. You may not have enough in the way of unbidden urges, but I always have."

He smiled a broad expression of amusement. "Tell me one thing you'd like to do with me?"

She avoided his gaze, singling out only one thing was hard. "Um, well, I want to touch you."

He narrowed his gaze, though his smile persisted. "What part of me?"

She extended her index finger from his grip on her hand in his lap. "Here."

He shifted her hand over until she touched the bump in his pants. "Satisfied?"

She stroked the fabric, extending all her fingers to investigate the shape of his body. "I can't feel much beneath your clothes."

He allowed her to explore him without letting go of his grip on her hand. "You may not, but I do."

She curled her fingers around his hand and eased back to where he'd held her hand before. "Is my touch unwelcome?"

He sighed. "No. That's the problem, or the solution, I'm not sure. I want you all the time. I see you even when you're not there. I hear your voice, and replay our conversations until every nuance of your expression and inflection of your tone is indelibly imprinted on my mind's eye, ear, and all across my body. I want you, Lisa. I just have to know it's real. I have to know you're not like everyone else."

Hearing his concern hurt her. "I would prove it to you, but because of the drugs, you wouldn't trust my love. You would receive my gift and still not believe in it."

He searched her expression. "It?"

She held his gaze. "My virtue. My first time."

He stared. "It would be my first time too, but I don't think we'd be giving up our virtue. There would be nothing wrong with us making love. It's virtuous for married people to be happy together like that."

She couldn't look away. "You're right. I used the wrong word. Our virginity is what I meant."

He reached across his body with his free hand to caress her face. "I saved myself for love...for you. Can you be patient for just a little while longer?"

She nodded, captivated by the feel of his fingertips on her skin. "Please, don't make me wait too long."

He pulled away. "You may have to wait forever because my answer isn't guaranteed, and I won't pretend to be in love with you."

The ache in her chest intensified to the point of agony. "What have I done to cause you to doubt your feelings for me?"

He clenched his teeth. "You were a director in SEVEN. You earned that position somehow. Now, you've jumped two colonies to land at the top of the heap in NINE. No one has ever been promoted the way you just were. Something is wrong."

The anger in his voice surprised her. "I didn't ask for this job. I tried to turn it down."

He glared at her, though he still gripped her hand. "Explain."

Her heart rate skyrocketed. "I didn't want to leave my family. The Gold Council made me come here."

He held her gaze. "How did they force you to do what they wanted?"

She wasn't sure she should voice her fears, but she took a chance. "They are taking my sister to TEN. I have the impression that Sahra won't be coming back if I don't do what they ask. I have lines that I won't cross, but sacrificing closeness with my family is a small price to pay for Sahra's safety. I had to agree to the transfer."

He ground his teeth. "And me. Do you have to do me too?"

She couldn't help smiling at his pouty response. "No. You have nothing to do with that. I asked for a match so I could have my family at my wedding. God gave you to me so I wouldn't be alone. You are my consolation in the lone wilderness of this crumbling colony of strangers. You are my only joy, Cody, and I thank God for you every day."

The tension in his body relaxed a fraction and then some more. "Oh."

She harumphed. "'Oh?' Is that all you can say?"

His face eased into a knowing smile. "The communication you crave has nothing to do with talking, and since I'm not ready to convey the messages you long to receive, I will just say, 'Oh.'"

She looked away. "Fine. We can change the subject."

He laughed, adjusting her hand in his lap. "What's on your mind?"

She gathered her courage. "How many children do you want?" She hoped he'd say a large number.

He skewered her with his gaze. "It's your body."

Her jaw dropped. "What does that mean?"

His brows drew together. "I don't have the right to dictate to you how many times you risk your life to bring my children into the world, especially since I'm not even ready to have kids yet."

She stared at him. "Don't you want children?"

He narrowed his gaze, avoiding hers. "My feelings don't matter because we don't have a choice."

The torment in his statement stabbed her heart. "I care about your feelings. It matters to me that you're able to love our children. I want as many as I can have without jeopardizing my health. My parents have eight children, and I'd like a big family. Even so, if you don't want them, then we'll just have the required four." Her lip quivered until she clamped it in a pout. "I will love them enough for both of us if I have to."

His brows lifted in a pitiable way. "That's not what I'm saying. I will love our children, but I need to tell you something about my—"

A digital bird song sounded throughout the apartment, cutting him off. The interruption came at the worst possible moment. Relieved to know their children wouldn't grow up without a father's love, but still concerned about why Cody was struggling with the idea of having them, Lisa climbed to her feet to answer the door.

"What is that noise?" Cody wiped the moisture from his eyes. "I've been hearing it all week."

Lisa crossed the room. "It's the door."

"That's the doorbell?" He looked confused.

"Bell?" She glanced at him sideways as she opened the front door.

"Director Shim, your table is finished. Where would you like it?" A delivery man stood in the hallway.

"Right here, please." She ushered him toward the dining area and overlooked the fact that he didn't remove his shoes.

He set the short wooden table on the floor. It was not like the one she had inherited. The dimensions were the same, but nothing else.

"Thank you." Still mourning the loss of her family heirloom, she stared at the table in despair.

"You're welcome." The man tipped his cap and departed.

She closed the door. The new table had none of the ornate carvings along the sides or any of the aged patina she had loved about the original. With a sigh of resignation, she faced Cody.

"You wanted furniture." She knelt beside the table. "This is our furniture." She slid her hands across the smooth wood. At least it had been stained cherry and had a durable clear coat finish.

"You always make do, don't you?" Cody's expression held disbelief mingled with irritation.

"I can't change reality." She sat on her heels and folded her hands in her lap.

"So, you alter your expectations?" He shook his head. "I can't do that. It doesn't work that way for me."

"What exactly are you saying?" Fear lanced through her chest inciting her to anger.

"You wouldn't understand." He retreated to his room and closed the door.

Her heart ached. Why wouldn't he ever listen to her? She had something important to tell him.

Chapter Twenty-Three

Early the next morning, Lisa went in for an appointment at the hospital. Her surprise transfer to NINE had come at a bad time. She wished she could put off the surgery, but her request for a postponement had been denied.

Her best friend, Andrea Tran, should be the one performing the procedure. However, Andrea wasn't due to transfer in from SEVEN for a couple of weeks. Andrea would be the new health director of NINE, and she was an incredible doctor.

Lisa and Andrea had worked on the implant Lisa would receive for the past twenty months. All of the trials for the experimental procedure had gone flawlessly. So, why did Lisa feel uneasy?

"Are you ready, Director Shim?" The surgeon entered the pre-op room.

"Yes, Doctor Harper." Lisa's neck and shoulders locked with tension.

Sleep hadn't come easily after speaking with Cody last night. He'd had something to tell her but had given up. She sighed because she'd wanted to fill him in on her surgery.

"We'll be injecting a local anesthetic. The incision will be small and heal quickly. We expect no side-effects." Doctor Harper's gaze rested on the screen of a datapad in his hand.

"Thank you, Doctor. I'm eager to return to my duties." Lisa wished the man would look at her when he spoke.

Doctor Harper nodded distractedly. "In and out. Nothing to worry about." He left the room.

Orderlies wheeled Lisa's bed to the operating room. She moved to the operating table to lie on her stomach. The room was icy cold.

A nurse shaved and sterilized a small patch of skin behind her ear. The local anesthetic injection pinched and burned. She wished she'd told Cody about this.

Doctor Harper came alongside her. "You're going to feel some pressure."

She tried not to tremble as he injected a neural mesh receiver. The device would integrate with her hearing and her brain to convey information from the main computer as well as messages for her ears only. It was one of the reasons she had been promoted to the position of tech director of NINE. The implant was among dozens of medical devices she had designed concepts for in the past few years working with Andrea.

"That's it, Director Shim. You did great." The doctor touched her shoulder. "They're going to take you to a recovery room. I'll be in to test the receiver in about an hour."

The operating room staff helped Lisa move to a gurney, then wheeled her to a recovery room. She shivered as she made her way into the hospital bed. The female nurses fluffed her pillows and piled warm blankets onto her.

Doctor Harper entered the room sometime later. "How are you feeling, Director?" Unlike before the operation, his intense gaze focused on Lisa.

"I feel fine, Doctor." She hadn't noticed the color of his black eyes before.

"We're going to send a test message to the receiver." He pressed his index finger on the datapad in his hand.

A flash of pain lanced through her head along with the word "alert." The room seemed to spin a revolution or two before it twisted. She nearly passed out, overwhelmed by the agony that assailed her.

"Director Shim, look at me." Doctor Harper brought his face close to hers. "What are you experiencing?"

"A sudden headache and vertigo." She blinked until everything felt right again. "I'm fine now."

Doctor Harper typed on the datapad. "That wasn't supposed to occur."

Lisa's stomach acid climbed her throat. "I know, Doctor. It never happened in the trials. Do you think the device was damaged somehow?"

Doctor Harper met her gaze. "No, but I'm sure you would have felt better if you had inspected it before the surgery."

Lisa controlled her tone so as not to express her frustration. "I've always done so in the past." Her request had been denied without explanation.

The doctor patted her shoulder. "You're in good hands, Director. Let's try this again." He tapped the screen.

The words "emergency alert" sounded in Lisa's ear.

Her head fell onto the pillows. Helpless, she watched the room spin. Swallowing madly, she tried not to vomit.

"Tell me exactly what happened, Director." The doctor's gaze probed her intently.

After a moment, her head and stomach quit trying to embarrass her. "I experienced no pain this time, but vertigo and nausea were severe." Something was wrong with her invention.

He reviewed whatever information was on his datapad. "It must be your size. The power drain required for the receiver is something you're just going to have to become accustomed to. I wish you'd factored that in before you elected to have the procedure, Director. This is most unfortunate."

Lisa wilted under the censure. "I'm sorry, Doctor." She redid the relevant calculations in her head but couldn't find an explanation.

"I'm lowering the settings on the implant to the minimum energy requirements. You may be a bit dehydrated. Drink plenty of electrolytes, and rest a full eight hours tonight. I know you don't normally sleep much. Thus, I'm ordering a full body massage to relax you." Doctor Harper typed on the datapad. "Vertigo should be temporary, but let me know if you have further complications."

The burden of her shameful failure wilted her confidence. "Yes, Doctor."

Chapter Twenty-Four

"Your three o'clock is here, Mr. Greene. Doctor Harper sent this one over especially for you. It's a deep tissue massage." The female appointment aide handed Cody a chart.

"Thank you." He read the name and quirked an eyebrow.

"It's a post-op patient. Apparently, elective surgery was too stressful on her." The aide smirked.

He looked over the information on the chart. There wasn't much of a medical history other than a vague notation about the aforementioned elective surgery. What had Lisa done to herself? His mouth went dry.

The mere sight of Lisa's name had caused his heart rate to increase. Sweat broke out on his brow. What secret was Lisa keeping from him?

He gathered his courage as he walked along the hallway. Upon entering the room, he couldn't help being surprised to see his wife lying face down on the massage table. She wore pink panties and a matching bra.

"I know the receptionist said to undress completely, but I've never done this before. I hope this will be enough." Lisa spoke through the opening for her face on the table.

"Mm hum." A mischievous thrill ran along his spine.

He walked over and placed his hands on her shoulders, moving her hair away from her neck. A small incision behind her right ear was visible through a clear, sterile patch. Had she had a facelift?

He unfastened her bra. To his surprise, she held her breath. That thrilled him in a way he hadn't expected.

He cued up faint ocean sounds on the player. She liked coconut-scented shampoo and conditioner so he selected a tropical fragrance in massage oil. Why was he being nice when she had kept something as serious as surgery from him?

He laid into her shoulders too forcefully, causing her to wince. Remorseful, he worked on each part of her petite frame with finesse. She resisted his efforts to relax her until, at last, he won her over with a foot massage.

Touching her body turned him on more than he'd anticipated. He admired every curve and reveled in the softness of her skin. He resisted the urge to invade her panty line. A massage therapist would never do that. Though, a husband might.

Too bad he probably wasn't actually in love with Lisa. He stood there contemplating the difference between attraction and affection until he heard her crying. Tears fell through the table onto the floor as her shoulders shook.

"I'm sorry." She lifted her head without looking at him. "I feel like an idiot. Please, may I have a tissue?"

He hastily pulled one from a box and placed it in her outstretched hand. The tears kept coming. He longed to hold her. Regrettably, his doubts held him paralyzed.

Lisa blew her nose. "I've had a rough couple of weeks, and today was a complete humiliation. I'm sure you don't want to hear about it. Do many of your clients respond this way?" She looked at him and gasped.

"Not often." Why did she look surprised to see him?

"Cody?" She blinked the moisture from her eyes.

"Of course, it's me. Who did you think it was?" How could she not have known?

He raised the lighting and noticed her eyes were a brilliant blue. That made sense because she wouldn't have been permitted to wear her colored contacts or her makeup in the operating room. Her entire body flushed pink, and she avoided his gaze. Much to his shame, the hickey he'd left on her neck before church yesterday was plain for anyone to see.

"I only agreed to have this massage if the therapist was a woman." Lisa reached for her bra in a clumsy attempt to fasten it.

"Let me help you." He leaned in to do it for her.

When their hands met, she pulled away. He fastened it, wishing he were taking it off rather than putting it on. As soon as he finished, Lisa fled from the table.

"You could have told me who you were when you came in." She pulled on her blue uniform. "I would have felt differently about the experience if I'd known it was you."

His brows crashed together. "Why?"

The muscles in her jaw bunched. "Because I thought a stranger was touching me like that, and I was uncomfortable. It felt like a betrayal of you to be..."

He couldn't speak. Touching her had involved a lot more than he'd expected, and he was confused by the experience. He'd been aroused, and that had never happened before during a massage. He only worked on women and had been waiting for this to happen with one of them for years. Now he questioned if it was merely a lingering effect of the hormone injection or something genuine.

"I turned you on?" he asked.

She nodded, avoiding his gaze.

"And that bothered you because you thought I was a woman? Are you attracted to women?" He held his breath.

Wide-eyed, she met his gaze. "Very rarely, but yes. I've seen a counselor about it. She says it's my loneliness manifesting in what I perceive to be attraction simply because I have no one to invest my romantic feelings in. She did all the evaluations on me. I'm not homosexual. So, don't worry."

He absorbed the emotional hit. Lisa was just like him. He'd experienced the same feelings but had never dared talk about it. His fears had isolated him and intensified his suffering.

"You could have told me." He wondered why it wasn't in her file.

"It's personal. Besides, I was sure it would go away after I married." Her face pinched as a sob escaped her. "Instead, I feel like I'm being torn apart with wanting intimacy I'll never have."

He sighed, frustrated because he wished he could trust her with his heart but couldn't. "And I suppose that's my fault?"

She turned away. "I said I would be patient. I didn't say it would be easy for me."

He bristled. "You may be waiting forever. And as for my job, you know what I do for a living." He noticed the hurt in her eyes.

She pulled her hair back and tied it with a band. A shiver of fear traveled along his spine. Was he to blame for this? His fingers had strayed a fraction out of the safe zone, but not by enough to warrant a reprimand from the health board.

Lisa's face blanched. "Your file says you're a level-four medical staffer."

The rushing of blood in his ears deafened him. "I can't help what my file says. Just like you probably can't help what yours doesn't."

Lisa slipped her socks on and stepped into her shoes. "Is this what you do all day? With other women?" She grabbed her glasses from the countertop.

He stood in front of the door. "Why didn't you mention you were having surgery today?"

She gingerly put on her black-framed glasses. "I planned to tell you last night, but you didn't give me a chance."

He strode forward to move her hair away from the incision, scrutinizing the wound. "It doesn't look like cosmetic surgery."

Her eyes widened and then narrowed. "What makes you think I would do that?"

He let her hair fall into place. "You alter your appearance to look more Asian than you are."

She frowned. "I'm Korean."

Anger surged to overwhelm his sense of caution. "Why do you hate Caucasians? You are one, you know."

She gritted her teeth. "My mother is Caucasian, and I don't hate her."

He leaned closer to Lisa's face. "Who said anything about your mother?"

She shook her head. Huffing air, she strode to the other side of the room. She grabbed her toolkit and thwacked it on the massage table.

"I don't hate you, Cody." Lisa stared at the wall. "Are you saying I hate myself? I don't think that's the case, but I've had to live with my mother's disgrace all my life. Perhaps, it's manifested in an aversion to certain physical traits. I don't know."

His children might one day feel the same about him. "What is it about your mother that you don't like?"

Her jaw clenched, and she winced. "My mother allowed her time to run out just like you did. Except, she did it as a means of protesting the Marriage Mandate. My father compromised his marital preferences to spare her life. My mother was penalized and sent from EIGHT to SEVEN. She lost her career as an intelligence analyst in Space Division and was given a job in the nursery to keep her away from anything sensitive. Her dishonor is a shameful reminder of what not to do in life."

Cody hadn't realized how much her mother's disgrace had shaped Lisa's choices in life. "Yet, you saved me the same way your father saved her. Are you secretly angry with me, too?"

Lisa avoided his gaze. "I don't keep secrets. When I'm angry, you'll know it. Anyway, you timed out because Jinhee refused to marry you. She broke your heart. Your excuse is better than my mother's."

He fumed. "Being broken-hearted isn't an excuse. It's a reason. Answer my question, why did you save me?"

She stared at him agape for a long time. "You needed a wife as much as I needed a husband. I hoped for love, but I'm willing to settle for stable home life and children. I'm in love with you, and I'm still hoping you find a way to feel the same, but it may not happen. Somehow, we have to move forward. This is killing me, but I'm not too proud to beg you to trust me with your happiness."

He scoffed, facing partly away from her. "You mean sex."

She paled. "I mean a physical relationship based on respect."

He turned his back on her. "You don't respect me or you wouldn't be pushing me into this. You conform to the wishes of others. You meet their expectations and surrender your own. I don't. I can't."

The sound of Lisa's ragged breathing filled the otherwise silent room. "What do you mean, I have no respect for you? I've been nothing but respectful. I respect you, Cody."

He balled his fists. "No, you don't, not deep down inside you where you fear failure."

She moved into his peripheral line of sight. "I couldn't be in love with you without the utmost respect for who you are."

Something about her tone triggered a suspicion. "Your mother's principles shame you, don't they? I'm guessing that means you have none of your own."

Her fingers curled into her palms. "What?"

Cody finally understood his wife for the first time. "That's why you accept every betrayal the government throws at you without question." He could never trust her now.

She stood agape. "I have ethics."

He shook his head. "Not really. You accept whatever is expedient. There's a huge difference between pragmatism and morals."

The flush in her cheeks deepened. "Now you doubt my virtue?"

Without gobs of makeup on her face, he could read her easily. Her passionate response did things to him that he liked, distracting things.

"Not that kind of virtue. I'm talking about religious principles as opposed to political correctness." He took a step closer.

She massaged her temple on the right side. Creases indicating pain deepened in her expression. Her breathing rate had increased to the point of being dangerously close to hyperventilation.

"You think my faith is only skin deep?" She clenched her jaw.

"I think you do what you're told." He had the sudden urge to take her right here, but he ignored the uncharacteristic impulse.

"You thought I had cosmetic surgery?" She backed away from him. "Why? To please you?"

His attention drifted to her perfect, little breasts. "I thought for a minute or two that you'd done something like that."

She shook her head. "A facelift? I don't have wrinkles."

He tried not to stare. "Um, no, that wasn't my first thought."

"Then what?" She followed his gaze. "My breasts?"

Embarrassed, a short laugh escaped his throat, and a lopsided smile spread across his face. "Maybe, but when I saw you lying face down on the table, I knew better."

She balled her fists. The silence between them chilled him. A baffling compulsion caused him to meet her gaze. Her angry expression immobilized him.

"I'm never going to mutilate my body to please you." Her voice quavered with intensity.

His jaw dropped. "I don't want you to. I was worried that you were trying too hard. It wasn't a turn-on, trust me."

She breathed in and out through her nose, but he could see the tears welling in her eyes. "The surgery had nothing to do with you. It was for my job."

His sense of relief was soon crushed by a feeling of dread. "What did you have done?"

She took a shaky breath. "Doctor Harper implanted a neural mesh receiver. Now I can hear sensitive information while I'm working. Not every emergency needs to be broadcast to the whole colony. Peace of mind is a fragile thing for the populace."

Bitter disappointment knocked the wind out of Cody. "You won't mutilate yourself for me, and that's good, don't misunderstand me, but you'll do it for the government?"

She jabbed him in the chest with a finger. "You're an irritating man. Do you know that? I invented the implant." Her posture deflated. "It's supposed to be harmless."

He caught the implication. "What's wrong with it?"

She walked to the far corner of the room. "It gives me vertigo. The doctor says it's temporary. He said my size is a factor. He postulated that the power draw overwhelms me for a split second, but that shouldn't be happening."

Cody's tendency toward paranoia kicked in, making him suspicious of governmental tampering with the implant. "What did Doctor Harper recommend? Aside from a full body massage?"

Lisa glanced at Cody. "Fluids. Sleep. Nothing useful."

He walked over and took her hand: a jolt of sensuality coursed through him. "Take the day off. I'll be home in a few hours to make dinner."

She stared at their hands, breathing quick, shallow breaths. "You would do that for me, even when you're upset with me?"

He stroked his thumb across the back of her hand. "I make excellent stir-fry."

Her eyelids drifted closed. "That sounds nice."

He watched her relax. "You must be exhausted."

She nodded. "I don't like arguing with you."

He began to realize just how persuasive touch could be. "I'm sorry."

She swallowed. "You can't love until you've fought." Her tone expressed warm emotions.

He didn't know how to take that. "What's that mean?"

She shook her head. "It's a Korean adage. I never understood it until I married you."

He scrutinized her expression. "Explain it to me."

She met his gaze. "It has something to do with honesty. I guess, when you're angry you tell the absolute truth. It's cathartic."

He smiled in amusement. "Is that Martian you're speaking? You keep throwing big words into our conversation. I'm just a dumb farmer from THREE if you remember."

She chuckled, ducking her head. "You're anything but stupid. I'm sorry if I made you feel that way."

He took her by the shoulders and met her gaze. "I'm sorry for a lot of things, but I hope we can work this out. Maybe, we should fight more often."

She blushed. "Only if we can make up like they do in those classic films where the couple kisses and the bedroom door swings closed behind them."

He touched her face. "I'd like to date you first."

Her lips parted. "I've never been on a date."

Disbelieving, he had to ask, "How can that be true?"

She shied away. "I've never been asked by a man I wanted to date."

Her lack of confidence about her looks probably stemmed from her inexperience with the opposite sex. "I'm guessing you think that's because the right men don't admire you, but you're wrong. I think it's because your accomplishments eclipse everyone on this planet. It can be intimidating. Either that or you just never noticed they were flirting with you because you had your eyes pressed to a microscope or something."

The slight crease between her delicate eyebrows made an appearance. "Why did you ask my sister out on your first date?"

Surprised by the question, Cody gave an honest answer. "Well, I saw Jinhee in the commons area with her friends. They were laughing and speaking Korean. The other two were Asian, but Jinhee is a blonde. The mystery of it caught my attention, so I introduced myself and asked her out."

"She's tall and beautiful." Lisa glanced at him out of the corner of her eye. "She noticed you do a doubletake. You were in full shock gear when it happened, disappeared, then came back in civilian clothes to ask her out."

Cody's eyes crinkled in the corners with amusement. "She's attractive. You're beautiful. Besides, she's not that tall. Anyway, how did she know it was me? Shock gear is designed to conceal the wearer's identity."

Lisa avoided his gaze. "Jinhee said, you had helmet impressions on your head."

Cody let out a breath. "So much for my covert skills."

Lisa faced him with an intense look in her eyes. "I need you to answer my question honestly and without holding back. What drew you to Jinhee?"

He could see how much it mattered to Lisa. "It was the smudge of grease on her cheek and the dust on her knees that convinced me to ask her out. The first date was a bust. I let her choose where to go, and she chose frozen yogurt." He rolled his eyes.

Lisa's gaze drifted away. "You're quite a bit older than her. She said you had nothing in common."

He analyzed that comment. "I've told myself the same thing a thousand times, but I don't fall in love often. In fact, Erica is the only other girl I've ever loved."

Lisa looked crestfallen. "I guess it's only fair after what Jinhee did to you that I love you, and you don't love me. It just doesn't feel fair because it hurts so much."

The pain of Jinhee's rejection hit him in the chest, but it had faded considerably. "That's why you and I need to date."

Her brows came together. "I don't know how dating works."

He inhaled, then let out the air. "It goes like this. I cook dinner for you tonight, and we talk about the little things. We find common interests. That'll be our first date. After a few more, then we'll see where things lead."

Lisa's cheeks flushed, and she veiled her eyes with her eyelashes. "Buy whatever you like for dinner. I'll grant you full authorization to use my funds from now on. You can order that sofa you've been wanting, too, if you like."

Her guileless offer surprised him. "I'll wake you when dinner's ready."

She raised on tiptoes to kiss his cheek. "Thank you."

He wrapped his arms around her, surprising himself. "I hope you like my cooking."

Her lips parted as if to speak, but he didn't let her. Instead, he kissed her. Tasting her lipstick-free mouth, he inhaled the scent of her clean skin. She breathlessly met his passion with earnestness.

"Mr. Greene, you're overdue for your next appointment. She's in room four." The aide held a chart in her hand, extending it to him from the open doorway.

Surprised by the intrusion, he lowered Lisa's feet to the floor. "You can count on me."

Lisa's already heightened color turned bright red. "Excuse me."

He watched her walk away with his mind taking much the same course as hers must have, straight to the bedroom. The aide cleared her throat. He nodded and held out his hand to receive the chart without taking his eyes off of his wife.

Chapter Twenty-Five

The aromas of home cooking roused Lisa from a profound sleep. Rubbing her eyes, she opened her bedroom door to see the kitchen. Cody poured a rich brown sauce over two plates of omurice.

The sight evoked a pang of homesickness, and a vision of her mother floated before her eyes. "How did you know how much I've been missing my family?"

He startled and nearly dropped the saucepan, but he smiled when he looked at her. "Because you have a family." He set down the pan and picked up both plates, bringing them to the low table. "I hope I made this right. I found the recipe in your archive under cookbook."

Lisa's eyes misted as she knelt beside the table. "You made barley tea."

He knelt and said a prayer of thanksgiving for the meal. Gratitude filled her heart for this thoughtful man. The first bite tasted heavenly.

"It's perfect." She nodded her satisfaction. "Mom often makes omurice for breakfast. My friends and I love to go out to lunch. I usually order this because it's my favorite." She continued to enjoy the meal.

"I didn't know it wasn't a dinner thing. I'll do better next time." Cody relaxed into a cross-legged position and dropped rice all over his khaki pants as he tried to eat. "I thought I could handle this flat spoon, but it's not working out."

Lisa's good mood bubbled over into polite laughter. "It's not the spoon's fault. It's the table. You have to sit on your heels like me."

He cleaned up the mess. "I hope the sauce doesn't stain."

She smiled at his guilty look. "It does, but I can take it out."

He knelt the way she did and scooted closer to the table. "This isn't very comfortable, but at least I'm closer to my plate."

She watched his positive reaction to his first successful bite with an abiding joy in their connection. "You may sit more comfortably if the host asks you to. Just rest your hip on the floor. It takes some pressure off of your lower legs." She didn't move.

He gave her a quizzical look. "Am I the host?"

She had to think about that. She'd assumed as much, but what was the protocol in her tradition? "You are the presiding host. Though, technically we share the position."

His eyebrows raised. "Because I'm male?"

She giggled. "It's a sign of respect. Everyone knows the woman conducts the household. Except in this instance where you prepared the meal."

His expression sobered, and he rested his spoon on the edge of his plate. "I don't deserve your respect as the head of this household until I've earned it. I was angry this afternoon because I feel guilty about keeping my covert career in Space Division from you. I can't respect myself for lying to you. I should have had the courage to tell you that I'm investig—"

'Emergency Alert' sounded in Lisa's implant. Her head dove to the right. Pain sliced through her scalp as her skull scraped along the table's corner. Cody reacted fast enough to break her plummet to the floor.

"What happened?" He cradled her head with one hand and steadied her fluttering hands with the other.

Lisa moaned and rolled onto her back, closing her eyes against the spinning world. Just like that, it was over. She hadn't even comprehended the message that must surely have come across with the alert.

"I'm fine." She struggled to sit up, feeling hot blood ooze from the throbbing point of impact. "This is my fault. The implant sounded in my ear, and I nearly passed out. I'm a failure." The shame of her blunder with the invention had her questioning her abilities and regretting her ineptitude. "Twenty months and an abundance of resources have been wasted because of me."

He scooted close, pulling her shoulder to his chest. "All I care about is you." He kissed her forehead, wrapping her in an embrace.

She lived in that moment for as long as it lasted. "Thank you. That means so much to me right now."

He chuckled. "You're always polite. My mother must have recognized that you and I would have that in common."

Lisa melted into his embrace and rested her head on his shoulder. "I'd like to meet her."

He stiffened. "You can't." He released Lisa and stood, walking to the kitchen cabinet. "My mother has taken a turn for the worse and is in the hospital under sedation."

Lisa's heart went out to him because he was lying again and she was beginning to understand what it cost him. "I'm really sorry to hear that. Will she be all right?"

He shook his head. "No, and it doesn't matter because I knew this day was coming."

"Still, it must be devastating for you." She realized that someday her parents would grow old and die. "I can only imagine how you're feeling right now."

"I feel nothing." He gripped the edge of the countertop with both hands until his knuckles turned white.

No longer wobbly, Lisa went to his side. "Is there anything I can do to help?"

He faced her with an intensity that sent a shiver of fear along her spine. "Are you offering to comfort me in bed?"

She wasn't opposed to consoling him, though she hadn't considered where it might lead. "Not if you say it like that."

She opened the drawers, looking for the medical kit. They had one because she'd made sure the apartment was fully stocked with necessities. Once she found it, she tore open a disposable antiseptic wipe and cleaned the scrape on her scalp.

"Let me." Cody took over.

She permitted it because he had medical training. "You're pretty good at this."

He scoffed. "That would be the only thing."

She couldn't help but smile. "We'll see about that."

"What's that supposed to mean?" He parted her hair with his fingers and peered at the scratch.

She carefully considered her answer. "We're both passionate people. It stands to reason that we'll be good in bed as soon as we allow ourselves to love each other."

He threw away the wipe and the packaging. "Allow?"

She captured his gaze. "Yes. You don't seem to think you deserve happiness in marriage. Why is that?"

He hunched his shoulders and stared into the sink. "I keep too many secrets."

Conjecture swirled in her mind, but a peaceful solution formed in the center of her chest. "Then show me your heart, and don't worry about the things you're not allowed to tell me."

All at once, he engulfed her in a childlike embrace, clinging to her as his tears came in raucous sobs. Stunned, she belatedly held the tall, muscular man close. Her brothers had sometimes needed this kind of compassion, and she gave it to Cody freely.

Chapter Twenty-Six

Cody knelt in the fertile soil of a bio-dome, enjoying the earthy smell. The agricultural crews would be planting fruit tree seedlings around the edges of the ocean habitat today. The arduous work would wear him out during a four-hour shift. Then he'd shower and go to his other job in the physical therapy clinic.

He smiled despite himself, thinking of Lisa on the massage table yesterday. His pulse picked up. What would it have been like if she'd known it was him?

One of these days, he'd like to take off her pink, cotton undergarments. A picture of her rushing him like a runaway rover squashed his fantasy. He shook his head, frustrated by his lack of nerve. Nothing on the planet had ever scared him like his misgivings about being able to please his wife in the bedroom. Was it first-time jitters or something more?

"Pass me that flat of plants, will you?" a coworker asked.

Cody located the flat and crawled over to hand it to the man. Wiping the sweat from his forehead, Cody glanced upward. Lisa stood on the catwalk high above his head, inspecting the emergency lighting. A pang of longing assaulted him. She faced him and smiled. He waved.

Without warning, Lisa folded like a collapsible box. Landing on the catwalk grating with a clang, she almost tumbled from the fifteen-meter height. She lost her grip on her toolkit as she grabbed for the railing.

He jumped to his feet as her tools dropped onto the rocks at the edge of the ocean habitat. There was nothing he could do to save her if she followed them. Adrenaline battled with a queasy feeling of helplessness in his stomach. Fortunately, Lisa pulled herself upright.

She took two breaths before running along the catwalk to exit the bio-dome. An alert on her faulty implant must have caused the collapse. Was there an emergency?

"What's the holdup?" Cody's supervisor asked.

"Nothing, sir." He wished he had listened to Lisa when she had tried to tell him about the surgery because he would have talked her out of it. "I noticed the tech director dropped her toolkit in the water."

Cody suspected that the device had been tampered with. What if the government had added a tracker? In the planning phases of this assignment, he had expressed a wish for an unhackable way to know where she was at all times. Her suffering could be his fault.

Cody's supervisor gave him a funny look. "Isn't Tech Director Shim your wife?"

Cody nodded. "Yes, sir."

He sniffed. "Well, I'd say it's your responsibility to retrieve her tools. Hit the lockers and put on a swimsuit, I seem to remember you have dive training."

Cody shook off his worries and grinned. "Yes, sir."

Cody's father had taught his children to swim, loving every minute he spent with them. As a marine biologist, he'd had free access to the ocean habitat. He had made sure his children were confident in the water.

Cody found a pair of swimming shorts in the locker room. The only ones that fit were a bit tight. However, accommodating his modesty wasn't a possibility since there weren't a lot of options available.

He grabbed a dive mask and jogged out to the ocean habitat. Lisa's tools had scattered all over the rocks. He gathered them from the crevices and crags where they'd settled.

The kit that had held them was smashed. However, most of the contents looked undamaged. He donned the mask and jumped into the bracing water, diving to retrieve a wrench and a pair of pliers. Swimming out further, he grabbed a bobbing can of sealant.

He lobbed it to the shore and took a moment to enjoy the water. The waves rose and fell in a soothing rhythm. He closed his eyes, floating on his back.

Experiences like this reminded him of better times. When the rest of his family had been alive, his mother's negative attributes had been tempered by love. He'd been happy then.

The deaths of his father and sisters had incited Addison to become overbearing to the point of cruelty. It was how she'd dealt with the grief. He, on the other hand, had shut down emotionally, especially after Erica's passing. It was no way to live.

An acrid smell distracted him from his sorrow. A faint grinding sound came from the direction of the spout that fed salinized water to the ocean habitat. It belched smoke, and the flow stopped. A thin, black film spread around the opening.

Cody swam closer to investigate. He stopped short when the substance floating on the water tangled in his hand. Long, black strands clung to his fingers. Hair.

Jolted by the realization, Cody swam to the rocky shore and climbed out of the water. Whose hair was that? A cold sense of foreboding worked through him. Could it be Lisa's?

Chapter Twenty-Seven

Lisa responded to a fire alarm in the water treatment plant. She entered the elevator and descended to the trouble zone. Taking a deep breath, she slid through the doors as they opened to a smoke-filled chamber.

Equipment screamed like the bearings in one of the pumps had seized. She racked her brains to remember the layout of the room and the location of the emergency cutoff switch. It was twenty paces along a narrow walkway over the water to the correct controls near the far entrance to the plant. She followed her ears to be sure she found the proper pump.

Along the way, she tripped over a body and slid beneath the railing into the swiftly moving water. Her uniform sleeve snagged on a tether hook, ripping the cuff. A lucky save, it prevented her from going completely under.

Against the current and her rising panic, she strained to grab the grating of the walkway. The cuff tore off just as she obtained a good grip, but she managed to climb to safety. Coughing because of the smoke, she realized she'd almost drowned and wished she'd learned to swim when her mother had tried to teach her.

Lisa hacked with every breath as the acrid smoke burned her lungs and stung her eyes. She crawled toward the wall, groping for the emergency cut-off switch. There it was. She slammed it down.

The screeching came to a halt, but the smoke didn't clear. Why wasn't the ventilation system working? Desperate for clean air, she made her way toward the enormous body she'd tripped over and dragged him to the elevator.

When her rear-end hit the doors, she slapped the button. It took an eternity for them to open, but she hefted the unconscious, blue-clad tech worker inside. Losing consciousness, she hit the button for the hospital level as she fell to the floor.

Chapter Twenty-Eight

Cody ran for the elevator in the bio-dome. His heart pounded as he descended to the water treatment facility. The doors opened on a hazy scene of chaos.

"Are you the diver? The pumps are shut down. Jump in there and retrieve the body." Police Director Godfrey waved Cody toward pump number four.

Lisa's black hair floated on the water with her head submerged below the surface. Trembling, Cody's heart wrenched in agony, and tears pricked his eyes. He had failed to keep his word to her father.

Steeling himself for the shock of seeing the body, he followed the director to the railing. Barefoot, Cody opened the gate and backed down the ladder into the tepid water. Near the pump, Lisa's arms were only slightly submerged. Her leg had been sucked into the intake.

Cody reached under her arms and pulled her body free. She surfaced, and he held her as he fought against the onset of shock. Weakening, he kicked to the side before his symptoms progressed and he lost consciousness. At least he had been able to give his wife dignity in death by being the one to recover her body.

At the railing, red-suited med-techs reached for Lisa, lifting her onto the walkway. Half-naked with her panties below her bruised backside and her pants missing, Cody stared in horror. They laid her on a gurney.

"Was she sexually assaulted?" Director Godfrey asked.

"It will be in the medical examiner's report, Director. I'm not qualified to make that determination." The med-tech unfolded a white sheet.

The other medic swept Lisa's hair away from her face. Unfamiliar eyes stared into nothingness. It wasn't her. A spasm of relief gripped Cody's chest.

"Let me give you a hand." The black-uniformed director reached down.

Cody took the man's hand and climbed the ladder. "I thought it was my wife." Cody couldn't keep his eyes off of the dead woman as the medical technicians covered her with the sheet and carried her body away.

"She's someone's wife," Director Godfrey said.

Chapter Twenty-Nine

"Director... Director Shim..."

Many hands lifted Lisa onto a gurney. People wheeled her somewhere, snapping an oxygen mask over her mouth and nose along the way. The band pinched her ear. A light flashed in each of her eyes, and she focused on the face of the medical technician.

"Here she is. Welcome back, Director." Relief filled the man's voice.

Lisa tried to speak, but her throat croaked. A deep cough racked her chest, causing intense pain. She blinked her swollen eyes to clear the soot from them, but the stinging irritation only heightened.

"Don't talk, Director. You're going to be fine. Let's change you into a hospital gown." The med-tech motioned to a nurse.

The woman swooped in to help. The technician pulled a curtain to divide the room with him on the other side. It provided a modicum of privacy. Shaky, Lisa undressed and slipped into a hospital gown.

"Excellent work rescuing that intern," the technician said. "He thought he'd be a hero, but that turned out to be you." The tech chuckled. "He should have looked at the medals on your chest before he thought to best you. Isn't that right, Mr. Praetorius?"

A hoarse laugh came from across the room. "I won't try it again." The deep voice was raspy.

"He almost made it." Lisa managed to croak in a semi-intelligible way as she entered the bed.

The men laughed.

She didn't find any of this funny. Why would two systems fail at once unless they had been neglected? Her initial inspections had revealed nothing wrong with them.

She didn't know where the problem lay, but she would have this colony in tip-top condition or die trying. The dark humor lifted her abysmal mood. She felt responsible somehow and not at all like a hero.

This would be yet another award she didn't deserve. She thought back to her recent commendation, the one she couldn't talk about. At least this time she hadn't killed anyone.

"No one died, did they?" She couldn't face it if they had.

"Not to my knowledge. It looks like the only ones injured were the two of you. We were fortunate." The medical technician's voice traveled toward the door. "A doctor will check on you as soon as the labs from your blood work are in. Both of you should rest."

The nurse inserted an intravenous line into Lisa's arm, drew blood, then connected a bag of fluids. The woman withdrew the curtain for Lisa and did the same for the intern. When both patients were comfortably situated, she dimmed the lights.

"Director Shim, would you like your husband to be notified?" The nurse stood in the doorway.

"No, thank you. I'll tell him after his shift ends." She'd been raised not to bother people at work.

"As you like." The woman left the room with the blood samples.

Lisa ached all over. She wanted to stay awake, but it hurt to keep her eyes open. Her lungs burned painfully. Unable to do anything to improve the situation, she concentrated on not coughing and allowed sleep to overtake her.

Chapter Thirty

Cody needed to find Lisa, but his skin crawled after handling a dead woman. He returned to the locker room for a quick shower. Toweling his hair dry, he dressed in civilian clothes.

If she was hurt, then the hospital would notify him as her spouse. Even so, he checked the admittance log. Her name wasn't on it.

Using his wrist-vid, he sent her a message. No reply came. He tried to call her, but she didn't respond.

He then accessed the surveillance network. Most of the colony could be seen by any citizen. He'd have to request special clearance to view the rest, but he started with what was readily available.

When that turned up nothing, he requested and received full access to the live feed from the police cameras. He cued up facial recognition and searched for Lisa. However, his wife wasn't anywhere to be found.

He checked to see if Lisa had been implanted with a tracker. That would make this easier. However, he could not access any information regarding the device.

He tensed, suspecting that he was right about the government tampering with it. There was no reason to wipe evidence of Lisa having the surgery, but it hadn't been on her itinerary yesterday and wasn't in her file now. He suspected a coverup.

He'd worry about that later. For now, he still needed to find her. That left the secret infrared scanners that the Administrative Division had installed.

Lisa had invented them to find heat leaks in the dome. Of course, the Gold Council wasn't using them for their intended purpose. Would Lisa approve of citizens being monitored with them? He hoped not.

Regardless, he couldn't locate her. He slipped out of the locker room and looked for her in the usual places. On any given day, she performed a myriad of tasks on the move instead of sitting in an office like she was supposed to.

Cody wasn't making any progress. How on Mars was he going to find her? He checked the police report on the drowned Technology Division worker. The preliminary findings indicated it was a murder, but the finger-shaped bruising on the woman's neck had told him that much already.

The other tech workers reported that the ventilation system had been sabotaged. There was no report from Lisa, and that troubled him. She should have had time to file one by now.

Cody skulked around the less reputable places in the colony's underbelly. Following a hunch, he listened in on a conversation between two bootleggers. One of them bragged about forging documentation granting illegal entrance to the colony for a man yesterday in exchange for ongoing illicit sexual favors. Could the infiltrator be the killer?

Cody checked into it with a confidential informant. The man reported that a Technology Division intern kept showing up in the oddest places. Mr. Praetorius, as he was called, frequently appeared near Lisa on surveillance footage from this morning.

The intern's credentials appeared to be legitimate, but Cody recognized him from somewhere. He searched his memory, dredging up images from his last investigation in THREE. Mr. Praetorius might be a grownup version of an unidentified child victim in a pornographic recording of unknown origin.

Could Mr. Praetorius have become an assassin? Cody reported his findings to Commander Mambwe, recommending that the man be apprehended. It stood to reason that Mr. Praetorius might have murdered the water treatment tech due to a case of mistaken identity. If Lisa was his intended target, then she was in danger.

Chapter Thirty-One

Hours of investigation didn't help Cody find Lisa. He was being an idiot, but he dreaded the alternative. Clenching his jaw, he did the one thing he'd vowed never to do under any circumstance. He called his mother from the nearest safe house. She would have access to Lisa's tracker if there was one.

Addison's face popped on Cody's wrist-vid. "What's wrong, Son?"

"I can't find Lisa." Cody refused to bite the nail that called to him.

Addison's blonde eyebrows raised. "Let me see what I can do."

He could tell she was in bed. Was it already that late? He checked. It was after midnight. She accessed a tablet and scanned the screen. Her delicate eyebrows crashed together.

"What? Is Lisa safe?" He stood and paced the room, looking at the vid on his wrist with a frown so deep it hurt his head.

His mother's face blanched. "Your wife is in intensive care. The doctors aren't sure she'll survive."

Cody bit the first knuckle on his right hand as the pit of his stomach dropped. Sobs broke free to shake his shoulders. He'd failed to save her after all.

"Stay where you are. I'm coming to you." Addison ended the vid-call.

Cody wiped his eyes. Shaking, he sat before he fell. Why would anyone want to hurt Lisa?

He could think of one reason. If Lisa was corrupt, then she would have made enemies in her rise to power. Perhaps, she was exactly like his mother after all. He just didn't want to believe it.

Addison rushed into the room. Cody stood and dried his eyes on his shirt sleeve. Without hesitation, she gathered him in a firm embrace.

Stunned, he eventually clung to her.

When had his mother become small? At that moment, he realized he hadn't hugged her since he was much younger. How could that be? What was wrong with him?

"The latest update indicates that Lisa has a fifty-fifty chance of survival." Addison rubbed his back. "That's an improvement from a few minutes ago. They're working on her now. It will be a while before you can see her."

Cody took deep breaths. "What happened?"

His mother held his hand. "It was an assassination attempt by an outlaw who recently infiltrated the colony. I'm sorry, Son. We had no idea he was after Lisa. Law enforcement is on high alert, and she's under heavy guard."

Cody forced his way clear of the trauma-induced brain fog. "Why wasn't I notified when she was taken to the hospital?"

Addison looked away, dropping her hands to her sides. "She was admitted for smoke-inhalation, nothing more."

He shook his head. "How is that possible? I thought she was in intensive care."

Addison's jaw clenched. "Lisa rescued the murderer from the water treatment facility. No one suspected he was responsible until they found her strangled when the nurse returned to the room."

Cody's hands went numb. "Did he sexually assault her?"

Addison shook her head, still not meeting Cody's gaze. "No, he didn't, but he raped the water treatment worker. I have little doubt that he would have done the same to Lisa if he'd had more time."

He sat down with a thud. "Why would the nurse leave the room?"

Addison's brow creased. "Lisa asked that you not be informed of her hospitalization. The nurse went to stop the notification from being sent and dropped off blood samples for testing. By the time she returned to the room, the intern was gone, and Lisa wasn't breathing."

Cody's heart twisted with pain. "How long was her brain without oxygen?" Why hadn't Lisa wanted him with her?

"I don't know, Son." Addison's expression hardened. "I should never have manipulated Lisa into redeeming you. She's far too independent to be a good wife."

Cody's resentment toward his mother's meddling ways solidified. "You issued Lisa's promotion, didn't you? And then, when she wouldn't accept it, you transferred her sister to TEN as a threat. Worse than all that, you sabotaged our marriage by drugging us." His anger turned to rage, and he balled his fists.

"I had to do it, and I think you know why." Addison held his gaze.

Cody stood in outrage. "Whatever my shortcomings are, there's no excuse for what you've done. I suppose this means that you want me to believe that Lisa had nothing to do with the air thefts in THREE? I can't accept that. There's only one method by which air can be seamlessly removed, and Lisa wrote the protocol."

Addison squared her narrow shoulders. "Let me worry about Lisa's involvement in the theft. It's over and done with and no one has died. I'm sure I can smooth it over with the Gold Council. What is important is that I love you, Son, and I couldn't let you die simply because you were unable to find a wife. You were too proud to ask for a match, and Lisa was hiding in a lab. You needed me to intervene."

Cody couldn't believe what he was hearing. "Why did you dose her with drugs and hormones? Was it to throw off my suspicion?"

Addison shook her head. "Drugging Lisa was Commander Mambwe's idea. He said she was too intelligent to be deceived by my ruse for long if we didn't. Unfortunately, it wasn't enough to force the two of you to overcome your inhibitions. Why haven't you made love to her? She wants you."

Cody swallowed the lump in his throat. "She wants me to love her, and I'm not convinced that I do. I still have drugs in my system and so does she. Regardless, the relationship never had a chance because I haven't been honest with her about why I married her."

Addison reached for him but withdrew her hand before she touched him. "I know how hard you've struggled with falling in love again after Erica's death. I wish I could have saved the girl from her fate, but I couldn't. Grief over your father and sisters' deaths blinded me to your pain, and I'm sorry I wasn't there for you. Even so, you should have come to me when you met people you liked. I could have made things happen for you."

He clenched his jaw, angered that she knew about his struggles with bi-sexual attraction. "You mean, you would gladly have forced whoever I was attracted to into a marriage?"

She lifted her eyebrows. "Well, I would have exerted my influence, at least. Regardless, the law makes allowances for differences in preferences. You shouldn't be ashamed of your inclinations. I have never seen anything wrong with same-sex marriage."

Cody's heart wrenched in his chest. "I want to be heterosexual for religious reasons. Sex is voluntary, I have a choice in who I commit to love, honor, and cherish. You shouldn't have tried to force Lisa and me to have sex. Bypassing our consent is rape. I would have been a rapist because I lied to her about who I am and why I'm with her."

Addison took his hand. "You should tell Lisa everything about your personal struggles. You know she shares them. Anyway, she already knows you're an undercover operative in Space Division. It won't be long before she figures out that you've been investigating her, and it would be best if the news came from you. Of course, you can't tell her about me, but I'll just have to live with that."

He met his mother's gaze. She was to blame for so many of the reasons why his marriage to Lisa had failed. However, liberated from the burden of his deepest secret, he dared to change the outcome. Now all he needed was for Lisa to survive.

Chapter Thirty-Two

Cody had never prayed for anyone the way he did for Lisa, yet she languished in a coma for over two weeks. He sat beside her bed, worn to the bone with worry. Her limp fingers offered little comfort to his troubled soul.

"Why didn't you want me to know you were in the hospital?" He couldn't understand why she had told the nurse not to tell him.

When he had first arrived in Lisa's room after the assassination attempt, he'd found a male nurse removing her hospital gown. Cody had grabbed the man's shoulder and nearly punched him before the nurse could explain he was simply there to bathe her. Cody had asked him to leave and requested permission to be Lisa's caregiver. On the condition that Cody completed his education in the physical therapy program, he had been granted the opportunity to take over the duties of caring for his wife.

"I'm sure you'll be upset that I've invaded your privacy, but what else was I supposed to do?" He talked to Lisa through the long days and longer nights.

Two guards stood outside the hospital room door around the clock. The entire colony was on high alert, searching for Mr. Praetorius to no avail. Where was that slippery murderer hiding?

The doorknob turned, and in walked Cody's trainer. "Good morning, Mr. Greene. Are you ready to finish your last module?"

Cody pulled his hand away from his wife's. "Yes, Nurse Strickland, I'm looking forward to having a new stripe on my uniform."

The elderly mentor smiled. "You're almost there. After today, all you'll need to do is pass the exam."

Cody groaned. "I forgot about that, but I'll study hard and make you proud."

She beamed. "You already have. You're my brightest pupil."

Cody warmed to the praise and worked twice as hard because of it. Twelve hours of intensive training later, he had achieved his goal. Nurse Strickland departed on her way home to her multi-generational household of eleven. He admired her fortitude and missed her cheerful company.

Alone in the room with Lisa, the silence overwhelmed him. He should study, but exhaustion held him immobile. As soon as he passed the exam, he would be a level-five Health Division staffer with physical therapy credentials.

The pay raise would be nice. Furthermore, Lisa would approve of his increase in status. Plus, it meant he only needed to do agricultural work when he wanted to pick up extra hours or smell the fresh air.

Cody crossed the hospital room to stare at his comatose wife. She was the reason for his success. Caring for her provided ample opportunity for education without ever leaving her side. That was sure to trigger an angry response when she woke up, but he'd give anything to see it.

He collapsed in the recliner by Lisa's bed. "I hope you appreciate what I'm doing for you. That last stretching routine was hard for me to do without embarrassing myself in front of my trainer."

He chuckled. "Does it bother you when I talk like this? Just how mad are you going to be with me when you learn that I've been bathing you?" He sighed. "Your body is so beautiful."

He took Lisa's hand, rehabbing the fingers to prevent the loss of dexterity. "I never thought I could feel this way about another person. The drugs are gone from my system, and I still have feelings for you. In fact, I want you more than ever."

He watched her for any sign that she'd heard him. "I know you're nervous about it, and I want you to know that I understand what you were saying to me in the lab. I'm sorry to tell you that I think you were right, it's going to be a tight fit. I wish I had a painless solution to our dilemma. I mean, it's not going to be a problem for me. Mr. Bee is looking forward to stinging you, Mrs. Bird. I'm just sorry for you because you're definitely going to tear, and I don't want to hurt you."

He leaned forward, lifting her palm to his cheek. "Lisa, I'm lost without your half of the conversation. Please come back to me."

A knock sounded on the door, and the new Health Director, Andrea Tran, walked into the room. She had transferred from SEVEN to NINE a couple of days ago. He vaguely remembered seeing her at his and Lisa's wedding. Andrea said she was Lisa's best friend, and she'd been visiting often.

"Hello, Mr. Greene." Andrea closed the door behind her. "How's Lisa tonight? I meant to make it in to see her earlier in the day, but I was caught in a meeting all afternoon."

Cody stood to face Andrea. "There's no change, Director."

Her eyebrows lifted in the middle. "I was hoping you would have seen something promising." She crossed the room to the other side of Lisa's bed. "Lisa's been my best friend since high school. She didn't deserve to go out like this."

Cody bristled. "My wife's not dead."

Andrea nodded, taking in and letting out a shaky breath. "I know, but there's only a slight chance she'll come out of the coma."

He scowled at the cruel reality that he understood far better than this so-called friend of Lisa's ever could. However, denial was the only option. Accepting this was unthinkable.

He met Andrea's gaze. "Lisa will live, Director. She has every reason to pull through."

Andrea wiped tears from her eyes. "I'm sorry for your loss." She shook her head. "I'm even sorrier for what I've been ordered by the Gold Council to tell you. Unfortunately, there's nothing I can do to change their decision. I've already tried."

Cody clenched his jaw, balling his fists. "You can't euthanize my wife. It's too soon to be sure she won't wake up and be fine, better than fine, back to her old self."

Andrea stared at Lisa's face. "She and I talked about you, Cody. I know how much she loves you and how adorable she imagined your children would be. She said you don't want kids, but after what I have to say, I hope you change your mind."

Cody looked from Andrea to Lisa. "I will do anything to save her."

Andrea faced him, taking Lisa's hand. "All right then, I'll tell you what they want you to do. It's horrible but necessary." She batted at tears with her free hand. "To justify the expenses for Lisa's long-term care, the Gold Council wants a return on their investment."

Cody narrowed his gaze at Andrea, sorting out exactly what she might mean. "I said I'd do anything, and I will. Lisa doesn't have the money to pay for extended care. She isn't paid even half of what a normal director receives, and then she gives most of her income to family, friends, and sometimes to strangers. It's cruel to think her naivete and generosity could lead to her death." That was true on many levels since she'd saved the life of her assassin only to have him make a second attempt to kill her.

Andrea took a cloth from her pocket and blew her nose. "Lisa gave me this. She said I should always be prepared." More tears fell. "Just let me say this because it's hard enough without thinking about what Lisa would want or what this is going to do to you. I'm incredibly sorry, Cody, but there's no changing the council's demand. They want a child."

Horrified confusion crashed around inside Cody's head, landing in his aching heart. "What do you mean by that?"

Andrea sobbed, wiping her face with the hanky Lisa had given her. "Have sex with her. If she's pregnant, they'll keep her alive long enough to bring the baby to term. It may buy her enough time to recover. However, if she never comes out of the coma, then they'll harvest her eggs and provide you with a surrogate to carry more children. You won't have to remarry unless you want to."

Stunned, he scoffed, disbelieving his ears. "That's insane."

Andrea knelt beside the bed, placing Lisa's palm on her cheek. "I know, and I wish it could be different, but it's what they require. It's also what Lisa would want."

Cody shook his head, pacing the room. "Lisa does not want me to rape her, trust me on that. She wants me to love her. There'll be no chance of that happening if I do this because she'll kill me when she wakes up."

Andrea chuckled despite her tears. "Lisa's aware of your intense feelings for her. There's nothing she wouldn't sacrifice for you. Since this will save you from some pretty harsh consequences, it would be wise for you to consider the council's offer."

Cody huffed, wishing he could lash out, but knowing Lisa's life hung in the balance caused him to hold his temper. "Can't you do it artificially? I don't think I can betray her like this."

Andrea met his gaze. "I asked the council for the resources required to do just that, but they refused."

Cody couldn't believe it. "Why?"

Andrea's head bowed as she stood. "They said it was an unnecessary expense when you could do the job with less risk to Lisa's health."

He stood there agape, unable to comprehend the callousness of his mother and her cronies on the council. How could this be happening? He couldn't do it. Maybe it was better for Lisa to die and for him to be court marshaled.

He shook his head. "I won't do it, Director Tran. The council can execute me if they like, but I'm not going to hurt Lisa this way. I can't." Unshed tears pooled in his eyes.

Andrea nodded. "I thought you'd feel that way, but you need to know that it won't hurt her. I mean, she's unconscious, so of course, it won't hurt. Besides, it isn't as painful as you think."

He frowned. "What are you talking about?"

Andrea set a tube of something on Lisa's bedside table and walked toward the door. "Sex. I'm telling you it's not as traumatic when you love each other. Use the lube. She wants you."

He turned his back on Andrea. "You should leave."

Andrea sighed. "You have until the thirty days are up."

The door opened and shut. Cody stalked over to the bedside table and threw the tube of lubricant at the wall, shattering the cap. He then dragged the recliner away from Lisa's bedside to the farthest point in the room.

He'd slept in the crippling recliner every night, holding Lisa's hand. He wouldn't do that again. Tonight, he'd sleep alone because even God could not escape his wrath.

Chapter Thirty-Three

Lisa didn't enjoy bodies of water. Call it a cultural fear, but she had never learned to swim. In her dreams, her toolkit fell into the ocean habitat. Each time it happened; she came closer to tumbling off the catwalk in the bio-dome.

She coughed in her dreams, gasping for air. The ocean habitat transformed into a water treatment facility and filled with smoke. Cody lay somewhere in that smoke, but she couldn't find him. She couldn't save him.

A splash of water heightened her terror. She heard him calling for help as the current pulled him toward the pumps. Desperate, she searched for the cutoff switch, but the layout of the room kept changing. Every time she thought she'd found it, her fingers hit a wall. Suddenly, the cries for help stopped, and the splashing ended.

Silence ensued.

The deepest kind of terror brought her to consciousness. Sucking air, she sat up in bed. In the dim light, she spotted Cody. He reclined asleep in a chair in the corner of a private hospital room she didn't remember being moved to.

She ripped off the oxygen tube. It was then that she realized a dozen more tubes and wires were attached to her. A great deal of equipment monitored her vital signs.

What had happened? A smile quirked her lips. That was Cody's favorite question.

Swallowing, she grimaced in pain. She steeled herself to call out to him with her damaged throat, but she couldn't think of what to say. The surge of love she felt for him didn't fit into words.

He believed she didn't understand him. Well, he was partly right. Even after living with him this long, she knew of nothing tangible that could explain her feelings for him. His file was no help because of the lies and omissions, and thus far, he hadn't chosen to fill in the gaps.

She lay in bed thinking about how little she comprehended his motivations. There were many things she hoped he'd share with her because she suspected he was hiding some hefty secrets. Even so, she wished for intimacy with him on every level.

Warmth flushed her skin. She couldn't help her attraction. She'd never tried to hide her need to be with him. An elusive something drew her in and held her captive.

She believed in eternity. So, it made sense to feel connected with someone she'd just met. She had friends she felt like she'd known from the first introduction, Andrea, for example. They'd been best friends from day one.

Andrea would be transferring to NINE soon, and Lisa couldn't wait. She needed someone to talk to. Andrea had married a few months ago and would have helpful advice.

Cody stirred. "Lisa?" He leaped out of the chair and rushed to her side. "You're awake." His voice cracked.

She smiled. "What happened?" Her laugh came out more like a croak.

He grasped her hand. "You died."

"Not possible." She glanced around the room as if there might be some evidence. "I feel fine." She squeezed his hand.

Unmoving, he stared at her in the light shining from the rectangular window in the hospital door.

"What?" She felt worse than she had the first time she'd awakened in the hospital but had no idea why.

"Do you remember the accident?" He kept ahold of her hand.

"A pump seized in the water treatment plant. Normally it wouldn't be a problem, except the ventilation system failed along with it. I cut off power to the pump, and that's it. Oh, I stumbled over an intern and nearly drown before I found the cutoff switch. I awoke in the hospital, but not this time, the first time." She frowned. "Why are you looking at me like that?"

"It's been sixteen days since the pump failed." His jaw clenched.

She laughed, and her throat felt better this time. "I feel just fine." She tried to leave the bed.

He planted a hand on her sternum and gently pushed her down. Distracted by his touch, but unwilling to be persuaded, she pressed the call button with an exaggerated motion. Cody frowned and withdrew his hand from her chest.

"May I help you?" A female voice sounded over the speaker on the wall behind her.

"I'd like to go home. What do I need to do to make that happen?" Lisa maintained eye contact with Cody.

"I'll notify the doctor."

"Thank you." Lisa grinned in triumph.

Tension eased from Cody's shoulders. He walked to the other side of the room, shaking his head. When he didn't sit, Lisa's unease intensified.

"I'm glad you're all right." He bowed his head. "Sleeping in this chair one more night was liable to leave me hunchbacked."

Her breath caught in her throat, and her lower lip trembled. "You stayed with me for sixteen days?"

"Fifteen." His voice fell flat.

"What?" Was he trying to confuse her?

"You told them not to send me a notification, remember? It took forever to find out what had happened to you. I thought you were dead." His back remained facing her.

"Cody..." She sat in bed. "I didn't want to bother you at work. I wasn't even hurt. I thought it was nothing."

He faced her. "It wasn't nothing. You could have died from the smoke inhalation alone. Though, you probably meant to say I'm nothing to you. That's pretty clear because a husband deserves to know when his wife is in the hospital."

She stared at him agape and at a loss for words.

He pivoted away. "Oh, forget it."

"You are my husband and a huge pain in my backside." She started coughing. "I told you I'm in love with you. How can you still be insecure?" She struggled to lower the rail on the side of the bed, but it wouldn't cooperate. "Fine. I'll spell it out for you. I love you more than my own life, Cody Greene. Don't ask me why. I just do."

He glanced at her sideways.

She coughed for quite a while before she could speak again. "I'm sure you're going to tell me I'm bossy and accident-prone. I know you're trying to push me away, but I'm not going anywhere."

The door opened, and a doctor strode in.

"Andrea!" Lisa welcomed the surprise.

"Hello, it's good to see you." Director Tran rushed over and gave Lisa a tearful hug. "That's from your mom."

Lisa choked on her emotions. "Please, let my family know I'm fine."

"I will as soon as I give you a once over. Now, lay back, and we'll have you out of here by morning."

Lisa obeyed. "Thanks, Andie."

Chapter Thirty-Four

Hours later, Lisa and Cody walked home from the hospital. As much sleep as she'd had lately, Lisa would have thought she wouldn't be tired. However, her limbs dragged, and she stumbled. Cody caught her by the elbow.

"I guess I shouldn't have turned down the offer of a wheelchair." Lisa couldn't keep her eyes open.

"There's no shame in needing a medical device. I thought you liked technology." Cody ushered her into their apartment.

Lisa smiled at what she assumed was his attempt at humor. "I'm sorry I'm not much of a conversationalist at the moment. I think I'll go to bed."

"Sleep with me." Cody shuffled his foot and blushed. "I mean, sleep beside me. I want to make sure you're all right." He straightened. "I want to be there if you need anything."

"I'd like that." She altered her trajectory, heading to his room instead of hers.

She gathered two blankets from the cabinet, unfolded one, and laid it on the floor. The other would cover them. A dim light from the kitchen shone through the open bedroom door to illuminate Cody's brown eyes.

"I probably snore or something." He fidgeted with his hands.

She took those hands in hers. "You don't snore, and I don't bite." She yawned as she went to her bedroom to dress in pajamas, returning to lie adjacent to him on the blanket.

He covered them with the second blanket. "I don't know what I would have done if you had died." Rolling onto his side, he traced her face with his fingertips.

His touch comforted her, and her eyelids drifted closed. "Will you hold me, please? I had a nightmare about you drowning."

"Me? You told me you were the one who almost drowned." He sidled his warm body close, wrapping an arm around her.

"I'm afraid of the water." She nestled her head on his shoulder.

"Don't you know how to swim?" He smoothed the hair away from her face.

"No. I never learned." She liked the smell of his skin.

"I'll teach you." He pulled her closer.

She imagined being in the water with him. "That would be nice."

"I'm really glad you woke up." The tone of his voice strained as if he were in torment.

Unable to believe it had been that serious, she contemplated the idea. "I've never considered death, not for me personally. I guess it doesn't bother me because I know where I'm going. The only thing that worries me about dying is leaving you. I'm glad you stayed with me. It was comforting to wake up and see you there."

He took her hand with a strange tremor in his touch. "They ordered me to force myself on you if you didn't wake up before the thirty days are ended."

She lifted her head to meet his gaze. "Why would they do that? I want to be with you."

He looked away, swallowing twice as tears filled his eyes. "Director Tran told me that you might never come out of the coma. She informed me that the Gold Council planned to keep you on life-support until our child achieved viability. After that, they intended to harvest your eggs."

The shock made Lisa light-headed. "I didn't consent to that. You know I wouldn't. It's against our religion to give up control of our biological material."

"That's the part that bothers you?" His voice grated in a gravelly way.

She considered another part of what he'd said. "If I'm pregnant and something happens to me, then you have my permission to keep me alive until our child is born. You will be a good father."

He released her. "You want me to rape you?"

She shook her head. "No, not at all. I mean artificially. The doctors could perform a procedure or something."

"That's not what they were talking about." He stared at the ceiling.

She had a hard time believing they would order him to do something so horrible. "Why would they put you through that, especially at such a traumatic time?"

His chest heaved with each breath. "Pragmatism."

She couldn't comprehend the word in such a context. "I don't understand."

"Conservation of resources." He looked away.

"How can that save..." The blood drained from her face. "I hadn't considered them to be this mercenary, but sex would be the most natural way to produce a baby. I'm not opposed to participating with you in the act of procreation. However, I definitely want to be conscious when it finally happens."

He snorted and shook his head. "Oh, woman, you are relentless."

She hugged him. "I'm sorry for what you've been through."

He cupped her face with his hand and wrapped his other arm around her to hold her close. "Please, don't ever shut me out again. I'm your husband, and I need to know you're safe."

She caressed the muscular contours of his pajama-clad chest. "I never meant to worry you. I won't keep things from you anymore,

I promise. In the future, I'll make you listen to me when I have something to tell you."

He chuckled. "That's good to know."

Tears piqued in Lisa's eyes as the impact of his revelation sunk in. "Would you have gone through with their orders?"

His stubbled chin brushed her forehead. "No."

"Even if they punished you for disobedience?" She knew the consequences might be severe.

"I would never hurt you like that." He took her hand in his.

Relieved, she relaxed until she realized something. "You're never going to sleep with me, are you?"

He stroked the back of her hand with his thumb. "As your caregiver, I slept with you every night."

Her eyes flew wide. "You nursed me through this?"

He nodded. "Does that convince you that you're important to me?"

She frowned. "Are you telling me that you..." She pulled away and rested her hand on her hip to avoid touching him. "You had no right. Well, I guess you do, but now you've seen every millimeter of me, and I still don't know anything about you."

"Look at me, Lisa." He looked at her intently.

"Why? Are you going to show me something important?" She stayed very still, trying not to overreact.

He rested his head on the blanket. "It's best if we sleep. You need time to recover."

She gathered her courage. "I'm not asking for sex, though I'm sure it's safe to try by now. Anyway, I just want to know what you're hiding from me. I mean, you bathed me and changed my diapers like a baby. Can't I even look at you?"

He raised a hand to sweep the curtain of her hair away from her face. "I never touched you inappropriately. I rehabbed your limbs with physical therapy and kept you clean, that's all. Don't be mad at me for taking over the job. They sent in a male nurse to do it, and I told him to leave because I knew you wouldn't want a stranger handling you."

She ground her teeth, trying not to feel the anger surging inside her. "Why would you take the trouble when you say you don't love me?"

His face constricted in a pained expression. "I've never said I don't love you. I almost lost my mind when I thought you'd died."

She stared at him, stunned by the confession of genuine affection. He moved as if to kiss her cheek, but something in his gaze intensified. He adjusted course to softly press his lips to hers. His hands gripped her back, and she cautiously returned the kiss.

Though she wanted to lose herself in the sensations that warmed her entire body, she knew he would push her away. Eventually, he released her, but not before he slid a hand down to grip her backside in a firm squeeze. Then, he relaxed on the blanket with a sigh, folding his arms behind his head.

"Do you believe me now?" He smiled.

Who was he trying to convince, her or himself? "Yes, Cody, I know you like me. I just don't understand why every encounter between us has to be completely one-sided?"

His smile slipped into a gentle frown. "What do you mean?"

Lisa's anxiety mingled with her pride to form a wave of powerful emotion. "Our intimacy is always on your terms. If I make a single move to initiate anything, then you run away." She forced herself to appear calm. "It frightens me when you withdraw as if I've done something in error."

His body tensed. "You haven't done anything wrong. I'm the one who has a problem with intimacy."

She tried to read his closed expression. "I don't like feeling as if I'm forcing you to do things you don't want to do."

The tension in his body stabilized, and he met her gaze. "Trust me, Lisa, I want to do the same things you do."

He pulled her into his embrace, holding her tight. She ventured to rest her head on his shoulder. Was it right to want him so badly that she would accept him even if he wasn't in love with her?

With her head tucked beneath his chin, she laid her hand on his chest. "I wish you would confide in me."

He took her hand. "I told you everything while you were in the coma."

"That's great. You knew I wouldn't remember." She lifted her head to look him in the eyes. "You're not really a massage therapist, are you?" She had grilled Jinhee and found out that Cody was level seven in Space Division.

He flattened Lisa's hand on his chest, covering it with his warm one. "I am a physical therapist, but I have a few more qualifications. I shouldn't be telling you this, but I just have to, because you deserve to know."

Her heart clenched. "Are you a perk?"

He stiffened. "No, that's not what I was going to say."

She started breathing again. "Oh, good. I thought for a moment that they'd forced you to marry me."

He held her gaze. "It's more like you were manipulated into marrying me."

Confused, she stared. "I wasn't forced to be your wife. I chose you. What I'm asking is if you have, um, an alternative skillset that you're not proud of."

He frowned. "I lie far too easily, and I'm sorry I've lied to you."

She shook her head. "That's not what I'm talking about." Heat warmed her cheeks. "I'm asking if you are embarrassed to tell me that you've had assignments like this before? Well, that came out wrong. I don't think you are assigned to me, are you? No, of course, not. Anyway, I'm talking about the past. Oh, forget I asked. I apologize." She pulled away.

His eyebrows raised. "You think I'm a prostitute?"

She stopped halfway to her feet and gaped. "No. I just thought you might have special training as an undercover agent to, um, keep people distracted. A man like that would resent being handed over to a woman he wasn't attracted to."

He rested his head on the blankets and cleared his throat, staring at the ceiling. "I am attracted to you, Lisa. As for skills in bed, I obviously have none. My career may be secret, but it's a legitimate profession."

"Oh." She'd always thought of undercover operatives as being willing to do unscrupulous things to achieve their objectives.

He chuckled and reached for her hand, drawing her back down and squeezing playfully. "A prostitute, seriously?"

A sad realization settled in on her, compelling her to be completely honest. "Aren't we all moved about by the government's whims? The Gold Council has tried to entice me into their sphere of influence in many ways. I'm glad you're not one of their ploys."

Tension locked his body in corded muscle. "And what if I am? I never meant to betray anyone, but I haven't been honest with you about why I'm here."

Lisa dreaded meeting his gaze, but couldn't help herself. "Then you are undercover in this marriage. I won't ask you why. I know you won't tell me."

He sat facing her, and she followed suit. "I have been investigating you for an air theft in THREE. I discovered the crime while I sat in prison awaiting execution for timing out so the case was given to me. You were my prime suspect, and I used your offer of redemption to insinuate myself into your life. I married you under false pretenses. I had nothing to do with the drugs and hormones we were injected with. I never would have slept with you, I promise. You can hate me if you need to. You have every right."

His confession shocked her. "I didn't expect it to be this bad."

"I'm sorry." He moved away from her, but she caught his wrist.

She shook her head, considering everything he'd said tonight. "Don't run away from me."

He ducked his head but didn't try to escape. "I should have said something sooner."

She realized she wasn't breathing and took in a series of shallow breaths. "I haven't stolen anything since I took Amy's pink eraser from her desk during a cleanup time in second grade. I was so ashamed that I put it back the next day. I'm not a thief, Cody."

He nodded. "I think I figured that out pretty quickly. I just held onto the pretense to avoid admitting how I feel about you."

She blinked and released his wrist. "Why?"

He shook his head. "I've lied to you about everything. I've kept important things about myself from you."

She frowned. "Like what?"

He avoided her gaze. "You talked about having bi-sexual attraction. Well, I sometimes have those feelings too. In fact, most of the time I feel anything for another person, it's for a man."

The blood drained from Lisa's cheeks, cooling their warmth. "Would you rather be with someone else?"

His head snapped in her direction and he met her gaze. "You think I want to be homosexual?"

She raised her eyebrows. "No. I just don't want you to be with me because you're avoiding the issue."

His intense gaze eased and his chest heaved in a sigh. "I was avoiding it, but not in the way you think. You are the answer to a lifetime of prayers."

She relaxed a little. "Well, that's good to know. I feel the same way about you."

He nodded, looking down and to the right. "I just need to understand one more thing. How has the government tried to draw you in? Be specific."

She shook her head and closed her eyes. "I told you that I had never dated anyone. It's true, but not because unworthy men haven't asked me out. I've been propositioned. I've been proposed to. I've been pursued until I nearly lost my sanity. I couldn't marry because I was being manipulated. I knew it, and I had no way of trusting anyone. Lucky for you, I still trust God."

Cody's breath came in gulps. "You really did receive an answer, didn't you?"

She nodded and met his gaze. "Yes. You should know by now that I don't lie."

He rubbed his face with his hand. "Then tell me why THREE is still losing air."

She tilted her head. "I have no idea. What makes you think it is?"

He reevaluated his position. "My ears popped twice while I was there infiltrating a group of criminals making and selling pornographic films. I was able to assist the local police in identifying suspects in a string of sexual assaults and child abuse cases."

She read between the lines. He must have seen things he couldn't unsee. Yet, he'd done it with the best of intentions and brought horrible people to justice.

She focused on the relevant observation that had led him to her. "A loss in air pressure would make your ears pop, but that should never happen if there are reserves and the lungs are partly full."

He cocked his head. "Lungs?"

She nodded. "All of the bio-domes and central tubes have lungs that expand and contract as the air heats and cools throughout the day. If there is a sudden loss of air, the section is sealed off as quickly as possible, but to avoid a failure, the air is rushed in from the reserves. Once the reserves are depleted, then the lungs begin to flatten. Once that happens, then that section of the colony fails. The system gives people time to suit up and do their jobs. It gives the repair crew a little time to stop the breach. It wouldn't happen without claxons sounding, people evacuating, and crews rushing around." She yawned, hiding her fatigue behind her hand.

He looked skeptical. "So, there are safety protocols in place that would prevent the secret theft of air and water? Did you design them?"

She nodded and wished she could lie down. "I improved them, giving the colonists a fighting chance. If you know your history, then you will remember that THREE failed fifty-two years ago. Everyone died in that accident except for a precious few who suited up quickly enough. It was a tragedy. I hope nothing like that ever happens again."

He frowned. "Are you telling me that you did not bypass the safeties and drain the reserves and the lungs for profit?"

She raised her sleepy eyebrows in an effort to lift her eyelids. "I only transferred a small percentage of air and water from each colony to TEN, and that was eight months ago. It was part of my job, and I didn't receive extra pay for doing it. No one else should be able to do what I did. I made sure of it."

He scowled. "How?"

She inhaled slowly. "I deleted the protocol. It won't be needed for another twenty years, and by then it would be obsolete. Can we go to bed now, please?"

He shook his head. "No, not yet. I need to know all of the ways the government has tried to influence you."

She rubbed her face in exhaustion. "Well, it started with my teachers in elementary school, asking me to focus on special projects. I didn't realize the danger until my parents warned me to be mindful of how my inventions might be used. I only saw the good, but my mother is wise enough to see the ways the government twists everyone and everything to their purposes. I can reassure you that I no longer accept any assignment that could be used to hurt people."

The muscles in Cody's jaw bunched. "The government doesn't take no for an answer, Lisa."

Calm, she had to disagree. "They do from me."

He raised both eyebrows. "What kinds of things have they done to try to change your mind?"

Heat raised in her cheeks. "It's embarrassing."

He rested his hands on her shoulders. "What?"

She folded her hands in her lap. "It started with money when I was very young. My family lived frugally, yet we suffered from poverty. I was tempted to help but soon learned that the rewards carried a heavy price. I stopped speaking to anyone who came to me with a request or offered compensation for my time."

Cody faced her, bending his knees and crossing his ankles. "What did they try next?"

She shook her head. "They made me famous. I think you know how painful that turned out for me."

He avoided her gaze. "What came next?"

The confession bubbled out of her, "Some of the men I worked with began acting strange around me. They winked or smiled. A few of them tried to touch me. I avoided the aggressive ones by working late at night, but they always found me. That's when the panic attacks started. My father began coming to work with me, and after a while, the unwelcome intrusions stopped."

Cody sat in silence, shaking his head until Lisa couldn't stand it anymore. She touched his face, and he closed his eyes. Covering her hand with his, he held it there for a long time.

His eyes opened. "Has anyone besides the government ever asked you to do anything for them?"

She searched his expression. "No. The only assignments I've received since I graduated from school have come through official channels. None of the recent ones have caused me any concern. I think they have given up trying to manipulate me."

His jaw clenched beneath her palm, but he moved her hand to kiss it before releasing her. "I believe you. Now, I need to make amends. I haven't been fair. I thought you had committed an unthinkable crime and had endangered the lives of hundreds of people. I'm sorry for misjudging you. I must have been mistaken about the pressure change somehow."

She considered his experience. "If you weren't mistaken, then something would have to be very wrong. I'll look into it."

He unbuttoned his pajama shirt and folded it. "I'd feel better if you did. Regardless, I've been a fool, and I've put you through a great deal of grief because of it. I apologize."

She watched him as he pulled off his socks. "Um, Cody, what are you doing?"

He tucked the socks together and laid them on the pajama shirt. "You're afraid of my body. He stripped his undershirt and laid it next to the other clothes.

She took his hand. "You don't have to do this."

He met her gaze. "Yes, I do."

"Why?"

He smiled for a moment before the glimmer of happiness drowned in something like regret. "I kissed you every day while you were in the coma."

Joy warmed her heart. "Like a hero in an old-time play?"

Cody held her gaze with fragility in his eyes. "Like a man terrified of losing the woman he loves."

A ray of sunshine burst in her soul. "Now that's the declaration of love I've been waiting for."

He looked away, brows lowering and shoulders curling inward. "I do love you. I just can't be with you in the way you want, at least not yet. Neither one of us is ready."

Lisa's breath caught in her throat. Her confusion made her unable to speak. Cody stood and stripped the rest of his clothes.

She stared as he turned around, curiosity taking over her senses. He knelt and placed her hand on his limp, warm mystery. She investigated each part of what he'd kept from her.

She marveled at his intricacy. "There's no bone." Someone had called it a bone once, and the idea had frightened her ever since.

"What are you talking about?" His agitation rebuffed her.

She withdrew her hand. "It's soft and not poking out like before. The kids in school said it had a bone...or something like that, but it doesn't. Does it?"

He rolled his eyes. "No, there's no bone there. Do you feel better about me now?"

She nodded, having trouble speaking for some reason. "Yes. This misunderstanding was my fault. I don't always know when people are telling the truth, teasing, or outright lying. I'm really stupid sometimes, and I shouldn't have bothered you with something so dumb."

He sighed, looking at her. "I'm not sorry you shared your concerns with me. Oddly enough, I feel relieved. I just wish you had been more candid upfront. I had no idea what you were worried about."

Her gaze lowered. "I've never talked about this kind of thing with anyone. Well, maybe a little with Andrea, but she never understands me. Like right now, I'm wondering if it's hydraulic. She'd probably think I was crazy for asking something like that. Do you?"

He chuckled and laid down. "No, I like the way your mind works. I guess blood pressure is a hydraulic system. Anyway, we'll discuss that at another time. For now, as your caregiver, I think you should rest up a bit."

Glad that he trusted her enough not to have dressed again, she covered his lower half with the blanket. "May I still sleep beside you?"

"That's your decision, but I hope you will." He smiled. "If it's not too distracting."

His words eased her awkwardness. "I'll risk it."

He beckoned for her to lie down in a side embrace. "I'm happy to hear you say that."

She nestled against his warm skin, breathing in his citrus scent. "You smell good."

He kissed the top of her head. "So do you."

With her head on his shoulder, she ventured to caress his chest. The hair didn't bother her like she thought it would. Before long, the steady rhythm of his breathing lulled her to sleep.

Chapter Thirty-Five

Cody awoke to the sensation of touch along the flat of his stomach. The downward motion stirred him. Groggy, he realized that Lisa's head and shoulders lay on his chest, and the touch of her hand had awakened him as it came to rest on his hip.

"Good morning." He concealed his panic with a welcoming tone.

Lisa didn't respond in the slightest way. Her head moved up and down with each breath he took, heavy as if she slept. He breathed a sigh of relief and carefully shifted her to lie on the floor.

Angelic, she captured his heart. The intensity of his love surprised him every time it happened. He dropped a soft kiss on her slightly parted lips. Her eyelids crinkled for a split second, but she didn't awaken.

This time, she wasn't in a coma, just resting. He smiled, wanting more than he should at a moment like this. If last night had proven anything, it was that she wasn't ready for a sexual relationship. He'd have to warm her up gradually, and that meant talking through all of her awkward misconceptions.

"Lisa..." He heard the smile in his voice when he said her name. "Wake up, Ribbon Dancer."

She continued to breathe deeply, giving no sign that she'd heard him. Charmed, yet disappointed, he lay down beside her to wait for her to come around. The blanket was tented with his morning blood pressure spike.

Cody raised his arms to support his head with his hands, satisfied that Lisa would enjoy his "hydraulics." Chuckling at her use of that word in context to blood flow, he imagined her response to experiencing a physical awakening of her own. He desperately wanted to please her because their first time together would set the tone for the rest of their marriage. If she enjoyed making love, then she would welcome him often.

A tinge of nervousness made his stomach churn. Springing himself on her wasn't going to produce the desired effect. He removed the blanket and sat facing away from her.

The clothes he had removed last night lay in a neat pile. He carried them to the bathroom, started the washing machine, and showered. Lisa liked everything clean and fresh.

He dried with the towel and added it to the washer. Brushing his teeth, he shook his head at the idiot in the mirror who was going to walk into his bedroom stark naked. He let out a breath and did it.

Lisa had rolled onto her side, but her eyes stayed closed as he walked past her. What was it going to take? He opened the cupboard and piled the clean clothes he needed into a stack, not wanting to put them on.

Did he dare cook in the nude? It could be dangerous, but like Lisa had said last night, some things were worth the risk. He abandoned the clothes and strode to the kitchen.

Changing his mind, he hurried back to dress for the day in khaki pants and a brown T-shirt. Why was it so hard not to rush into a physical relationship? He quirked an eyebrow, probably because every time he thought about her, his "hydraulics" went into high-pressure mode.

Before now, his idea of romance hadn't included much thought about the finishing touches. Instead, he had focused on the dating and gift-giving aspects of relationship-building. He wanted to enjoy being in love to the fullest without skipping any steps. Besides, Lisa deserved to be appreciated for every refinement and personality trait she had worked her entire life to obtain.

He returned to the kitchen, considering the way her trim, little body thrilled him. More than that, though, her uniquely intelligent mind delighted him with its quirky innocence. It shouldn't be too challenging to think of some fun ways to show her how much he admired her. Knowing some of her hang-ups helped him understand her, at least he hoped so.

He prepared the rice and started the rice cooker. Thus far, he'd managed to irritate Lisa more than anyone he'd ever met. Luckily, her Asian temper didn't include a resentful nature. Quick to forgive and forget, she moved on easily enough to make life smooth for them in the long term.

He washed, peeled, and chopped the vegetables. Establishing everyday routines might help them live together without clashing. He stir-fried the ingredients, set the table, and plated the meal.

The tea steamed in the kettle, and Cody shut it off. Leaving it on the stovetop, he strode to the bedroom. Lisa lay curled in the blankets with her face mostly covered. Her long hair stuck out at odd angles. Grinning, he knelt at her side and prodded the covers until he earned a groaning response.

"Come to dinner while it's hot. I think you'll like it. Your mom says you love shrimp." He unwrapped her like a gift.

She peeked at him through her lashes. "Is it morning?"

He chuckled. "No, it's early evening. I made shrimp-fried rice. Are you ready for your first solid food in weeks?"

He started to reconsider the digestibility of the food he'd prepared. Why hadn't he made something easier on the stomach? He'd hate for her to become sick.

Lisa's eyes opened fully. "You talked me into it." She took his hand as he helped her up, glancing at him sideways. "Did I dream this morning or did it actually happen?"

He smiled and kissed her on the head. "It was real. Come eat and we'll talk more about it."

She took his hand and stood on tip-toes to kiss his cheek. "Give me a minute to dress for the day. I don't feel right coming to dinner in pajamas."

He resisted the temptation to grab ahold of her and kiss her soundly. "Don't be too long or it'll be cold."

She rushed into her room, taking clothes to the bathroom. The shower turned on, and he shook his head. So much for not taking a long time. At least, he could keep the food warm in the oven.

Donning an apron, he washed the knife, cutting board, and frying pan. A knock came at the door. He dried his hands on a towel and opened the door.

Mr. Praetorius shoved his way into the room, knocking Cody's shoulder with the door. However, Cody's Space Division training kicked in, and he landed a solid left hook to the man's stone-like jaw. Shifting position, Cody barred the assassin's path to the bathroom.

They struck and blocked until Mr. Praetorius landed a kick to the liver that took Cody down. From the floor, Cody groaned in pain. The man tried to step over him, and Cody jerked his foot out from under him. The murdering rapist toppled with a thud that knocked the air from his lungs. Gaining the advantage, Cody pounded the larger man with both fists until Mr. Praetorius savagely backhanded him. Neck torquing, Cody nearly lost consciousness.

Mr. Praetorius pinned him face down on the linoleum. "I didn't come here to take out my frustrations on you, slave. I came to make Director Shim pay for killing my husband."

Cody gulped air, struggling to mount a defense against the stronger opponent. "She didn't kill anyone. If you're talking about the rover accident, well, Lisa and I had nothing to do with the cause of that."

Mr. Praetorius shifted his weight, crushing Cody's neck. "She paid for the promotion that put her on the highway that night with air and water stolen from every colony on the planet. They're all about to fail because of her greed."

Cody couldn't breathe. "No, that's impossible."

Mr. Praetorius flipped Cody over onto his back and sat on his chest. "Read the petition for yourself. All of the directors from ONE on up to EIGHT have signed it except your filthy wife. They're demanding the government stop executing Shim's Resource Transfer Protocol." He pulled a wad of papers from his back pocket. "She's the Gold Council's most valuable puppet and a whore for their praise. Don't stop me from crushing her soul because she deserves it after what she's done to me...and to you too if Shade was as important to you as you were to her. Shim is responsible for her death as well."

Cody resisted. "Who's Shade?"

Praetorius strained to keep Cody down. "She's the stupid blonde who used her tragic story to convince my husband to help her save you from a fate worse than death. He was always a sucker for women with a kid."

Cody had no time to ask more questions because two burly bodyguards rushed in through the open door. Papers flew as fists impacted in a whirl of motion. Mr. Praetorius escaped.

"After him," Cody commanded the bodyguards.

The two men ran after Mr. Praetorius. Unfortunately, their hesitation had probably cost them the capture. Cody climbed to his feet and stumbled after them.

He stopped at the sight of a different pair of bodyguards who lay dead in the hallway. Chilled, Cody returned to the apartment and secured the door. Protecting Lisa was the priority right now. It didn't matter what she was accused of because he needed to keep her safe. Except that it did matter. On a deeply personal level, this changed everything between them.

Shaking from the shock of Mr. Praetorius' words, Cody stared at the papers on the floor. His stomach flipped with unease. Positive proof that Lisa had lied to him would kill him right now, but he needed to know the truth.

Was she following the Gold Council's orders and siphoning off air and water from not just THREE but all of the colonies? Why? And where was it being sent? He rubbed his face.

The shower shut off. He stared at the bathroom door until his limbs took over for his stunned brain. Snatching up the papers, he stumbled to his room and locked the door.

Chapter Thirty-Six

The smell of strawberries awakened Lisa.

"Happy birthday." Cody walked into her bedroom, wearing pajamas.

She rubbed her puffy eyes and sat on the blankets. "Is it Saturday already?"

He sat cross-legged on the soft linoleum of the bedroom floor and placed a small, pink box in front of him. "All day long."

She met his gaze. "I'm sorry about disappointing you yesterday. I shouldn't have taken a shower. It was ungrateful of me to make you wait for dinner." Her lip quivered. "Anyway, I really appreciate you remembering my birthday."

He pushed the box in her direction. "I can't take the credit. Your mom mentioned it while you were in the hospital. I ordered this a week ago. It's a yellow cupcake with pink frosting and a strawberry on top. I hope you're not allergic. I didn't think to ask."

She smiled. "Thank you. I have no food allergies." She opened the box. "It smells heavenly. Share it with me, and it will taste even better."

His eyebrows shot up. "I was just being nice." He leaned back. "I didn't mean anything by it."

She groaned. "I'm the one who didn't mean anything. I was simply trying to include you in the Korean tradition of social eating. We believe good company makes food more delicious." She adjusted the blanket on her lap. "I wasn't pushing you to do anything other than have a bite of cake. Will you share it with me? This kind of thing should not be eaten alone."

"I can't." He frowned.

"Oh, I understand completely." She snatched the box away, shut the lid, and carried it to the kitchen.

Tossing it in the refrigeration unit, she slammed the door. Everything he did ended up making her angry, even when it started well. Perhaps, it was because things began great and went incredibly wrong somewhere along the way.

Yesterday had been amazing until she'd ruined it. How on Mars had she been so stupid? Cody's invitation to eat and talk had felt like a promise that the evening would end with making love. That's why she'd wanted to look her best, taking time to shower and shave.

Cody walked up behind her. "Lisa." He put both of his hands on her shoulders and coaxed her around to face him. "I'll eat it if you want me to, but we'll both regret it."

Her anger dissolved into a painful lump in her throat. "I don't understand." Holding back an emotional response, she searched his expression.

His cheeks flushed. "I'm lactose intolerant."

"You are?" She blinked. It wasn't in his profile. "I didn't know. Next time, buy something we can share." She gave him a hug that felt so good she forgot to let go.

He patted her back without returning the embrace. His rejection cut her deep, and she fled to the bathroom. He didn't follow.

She cried her heart out in the shower, wishing he would love her the way she needed. Unfortunately, she couldn't linger in solitude. She was being honored with another award ceremony. Both she and Cody were required to attend.

She dressed in a robe, wrapped her hair in a towel, and did her makeup. The event called for a dress uniform. The only consolation was that there would be a brunch afterward.

A knock sounded on the bathroom door.

"I need in there." Cody turned the doorknob and rushed inside.

"Come on in. Families usually share the facilities." She met his gaze hoping that he'd warmed to her again.

He pushed her out. "We'll talk about that later." He shut the door.

Unpleasant noises came from inside the bathroom.

"Everybody does that." She felt like an idiot.

Retreating to her room, she slipped into her new dress uniform. It was too tight and hugged her curves in irritating ways. Her old one had been tailored to be comfortable.

Everything bothered her these days. Of course, she'd never been married before. Apparently, it was the most annoying situation a human could endure.

Furthermore, she was married to the most incomprehensible man in existence. She guessed at a possible solution to her problem. But that frustrated her even more because sex was never going to happen at this rate, not even for her birthday.

She strode to the living area and punched the autodial button number one on the wall-vid. In no time, an image of her mother popped on the screen.

"Happy birthday, sweetheart. You look lovely." Her mother's struggle to subdue her relief was heart-wrenching.

"Thanks, Mom." Lisa put her hand on the side of the screen. "It's good to see you. Is anyone else there? Probably not, right? Why are you home?"

"Everyone's here somewhere except Sahra. She's already in TEN. We haven't heard from her. She doesn't know you recovered. Can you contact her?" Mother looked desperate.

"I'll try. I've already made inquiries on behalf of a church member. Unfortunately, I couldn't follow up while in the hospital." Lisa chewed her lip. "I've tried contacting TEN in the past, but the messages wouldn't go through. Whatever they're doing has a higher security clearance than I do. The only clue is that they requisitioned one of my inventions a couple of months back."

"The one with the diamond laser?" mother asked.

"No, they installed my lasers on the outpost towers ages ago. This invention improves the environmental controls and maximizes efficiency throughout the colony using infrared sensors."

Mother sighed. "That's great, Neesa. Can you send Sahra a letter?"

Lisa's heart warmed at her mother's Korean pronunciation of her name. "I might be able to if I ask one of the techs who are transferring over for a favor. It would be breaking the rules, but I'll try."

Mother gasped and turned her head. Lisa spun around. Cody, sort of, had a towel on. He ducked into his room and shut the door.

"Sorry," Lisa shouted after him.

Mother giggled. "I'll leave you to your day. I hope it holds everything you desire." Bethany winked and switched off the vid connection.

Lisa bit her lower lip. "That's unlikely."

Chapter Thirty-Seven

Lisa and Cody left the apartment for the award ceremony together. She sat beside him until called forward to receive her commendation. The number of people in the crowd exceeded her expectations, making her nervous because she didn't like large groups.

Soon, however, the ceremony concluded, and the brunch began. Cody strode straight for the food. Unfortunately, Lisa couldn't join him because a swarm of well-wishers and sycophants surrounded her.

"You saved the entire colony, Director Shim. How can we thank you?" Police Division Director Godfrey said.

"It really wasn't anything to worry about. The populace was never in danger. It was only smoke." She couldn't understand why anyone would make a big deal of her actions.

"You almost died." Godfrey's wife grabbed Lisa's hand in both of hers.

"And you saved that intern's life." A random woman wearing Health Division red swooped in to join the conversation.

"Now ladies and gentleman, give Director Shim a moment to catch her breath. I'm sure she'd like to enjoy the refreshments." Andrea guided Lisa away to a quiet corner behind the buffet table.

"Thank you, Andie." Lisa didn't like attention from strangers.

Andrea ladled a cup of punch for both of them. "I heard it was more serious than you seem to realize. Someone sabotaged the ventilation system. A technician confronted the man, and he strangled her. Didn't you know the pump seized because a body was in it?"

"No. I had no idea." Lisa's hand trembled too much to accept the punch. "I was told no one was hurt. Why haven't they questioned me?"

Lisa tried to think. Had she seen anything suspicious? Nothing came to mind.

Andrea sighed. "I overheard a conversation on the day I arrived in NINE. You were still in the coma. Apparently, they added a tracker to the receiver we collaborated on before they implanted it behind your ear. That's how they knew you were nowhere near the areas in question when the acts of sabotage took place. They're pretty sure the killer planned the whole thing to draw you to the water treatment plant and take your life. Haven't you noticed the security detail following you since you left the hospital?" Andrea pointed her elbow at two burly men with serious expressions standing nearby.

Anger steadied Lisa's hands. The malfunctioning device wasn't her fault because the government had altered it without consulting her. They had no right to do that.

Furious, she sipped the punch. The device drew a dangerous amount of power from her body. If Doctor Harper hadn't lowered the settings, then it would have killed her eventually.

"I don't mean to frighten you," Andrea said, "But someone made a second attempt in the hospital. I'm not sure what happened because I wasn't here. Anyway, you quit breathing. If the nurse hadn't returned to the room, then you could have died. You almost did die." Andrea put her hand on Lisa's arm. "You were dead."

Lisa dismissed the grim thought with a shake of her head. "Some friend you are, being so cheerful on my birthday."

Cody stood nearby, piling a small plate with delicacies.

"Don't eat that. It has cheese in it." Lisa stopped him before he took a bite.

He gave her a nod and returned the sausage on a toothpick to the platter from whence he'd selected it.

"You're taking this in stride." Andrea raised her eyebrows.

"Andie, what else can I do? I have no idea why anyone would want me dead." She met Andrea's gaze. "Do you?"

Andrea shook her head, and her dark curls bounced in the high ponytail at the back of her head. "Not a clue. But be careful." She kissed Lisa's cheek. "I couldn't stand it if I lost you."

Lisa squeezed Andrea's hand. "Stay clear of me, Andie. Whatever is happening is not something you want to be involved in. Thanks for warning me. I promise to be much more careful from now on. Though, I'm not sure how that will help."

This time, Andrea squeezed Lisa's hand. "At least you'll die with a chest full of medals."

Lisa rolled her eyes. "Only you would say something like that. This commendation is ridiculous. I tripped over that stupid intern and nearly drowned. If my sleeve hadn't caught on a tether hook, then I'd have ended up in a pump right along with the dead technician." Lisa surveyed the buffet table and selected the sausage Cody had put back. She didn't feel like eating it at the moment, but he shouldn't have returned it to the table after touching it. "How is the intern anyway?"

"Fine, I guess." Andrea dipped a piece of bread into the fondue. "I never heard about him at the hospital. I didn't know you'd saved anyone until today."

Lisa froze. "Do you suppose he was the saboteur? He was in the hospital room with me. He seemed like a brave man. Hey, how did he know about the fire alarm?"

Andrea's eyebrows rose. "No idea." She spoke around a mouthful of cheesy bread.

Lisa shook her head, laughing. "It's a good thing we're not in Police Division. We'd be booted out for incompetence for sure."

Chapter Thirty-Eight

Cody listened to Lisa's conversation with Health Director Andrea Tran. The two certainly acted like old friends. He pretended to be absorbed in the selection of food on the buffet table.

His research into Director Tran had revealed some troubling details. Firstly, her promotion from SEVEN to NINE had been largely due to her work with Lisa on multiple projects. Furthermore, Andrea had liaised with the government since they were in high school, sheltering Lisa from what the inventions were used to achieve.

Commander Simon Mambwe approached from a side entrance. Cody eyed the two goons who'd been on guard duty ever since the accident. They looked like they could handle things for a minute. That freed Cody to walk casually over to his commanding officer.

"Sir?" Cody ate a slice of starfruit from the plate in his hand.

"I should have you court-martialed for letting the assassin into your apartment." The color heightened in Commander Mambwe's dark complexion.

"Yes, sir." Cody had made a serious mistake. "I apologize."

The commander clamped a hand on the back of his neck. "That's not nearly enough to satisfy me. Fortunately for you, your mother has intervened on your behalf. However, the next time you do something that stupid, it could cost you your life." Simon scowled. "It could cost me mine too. If Director Shim dies, they'll shove you and me in the reclamation unit with her corpse."

The blood drained from Cody's face. "Understood, sir."

Commander Mambwe straightened his posture. "I had the papers you gave me analyzed, but the petition can't be authenticated. None of the directors will admit they signed it."

Cody scowled. "Are you saying that even with everything I've been reporting to you, there's no corroborating proof of Lisa's guilt?"

Simon shrugged. "Your wife wrote the protocol, but that doesn't mean she ran it."

Cody ground his teeth. "I think we know who's doing that. I just wish we knew why."

Simon squeezed Cody's neck a bit too hard. "Stop looking into it. Lisa's personality evaluations are definitively benign. She's not malicious. I'm here to order you to stand down. The investigation of her wrongdoing has been terminated."

Cody's blood chilled. "And the guilty go free."

Simon frowned. "Whoever ran that protocol is above our pay grade. Don't stick your nose where it doesn't belong. Stay on task?"

Cody nodded with great reluctance. "Yes, sir. What's my next assignment?"

Simon stared at him as if he were crazy. "There is no next assignment. Taking care of Director Shim is it for you. The Gold Council has decided that, and I quote, 'breeding her is worth forgiving whatever part she played in the resource theft. Childbearing will make her happy and keep her from causing trouble again,' end quote."

Cody clenched his fists. "I was promised a duty assignment on the next transport to Earth."

Simon's brows lowered. "There are no transports to Earth. No one from Mars has left the planet's surface in almost a hundred years. If we went to Earth, our elongated Martian spines would snap. It isn't possible. I'm sorry I lied to you, but it was under orders from your mother. Now, focus on what's happening here. Your job is easy. All you have to do is put part A into receptacle B."

Cody went numb as he absorbed the dream-crushing news about the Earth transport. "What are you saying, sir?"

The commander shifted his weight. "Don't play stupid. If you can't figure out how to do the job, then at least give her a chance to try. She's a genius, I'm sure she'll have everything worked out between you two in no time."

Cody clenched his jaw. "Your advice is that I should allow my wife to do it for me? Is that even possible?"

The commander clenched a fist. "Pretty much. Anyway, she's not fragile if that's what you're worried about."

Cody bristled. "What happens between Lisa and me is private."

Commander Mambwe shook his head. "No. It isn't. That's what I'm here as your friend to tell you."

Stunned, Cody looked him over. He wore casual clothes with no insignia. That meant he was here in an unofficial capacity.

Cody met the man's gaze, moved by the gesture. "Thank you, sir. It means a lot to know you care, even if you did lie to me."

The commander sighed. "I've known you for three years, and you've never let me down until now. It's hard to watch you hesitate when you have so much to gain."

Cody stiffened. "I don't know how to compromise my principles with a woman who aided someone in an act of treason that could soon cause thousands of colonists to lose their lives."

The commander's features pinched. "Don't worry about anyone dying. Safeguards are in place, and the situation is being remedied. The theft doesn't matter anymore. Just take your wife to bed as often as required to make her pregnant. That's what the Gold Council is asking of you."

Cody's mind filled with rage. "How do you know Lisa's not already—of course, she had one of her sensor-laden toilets installed in our apartment. Is the council monitoring our waste?"

The commander's face split in a grin. "I've seen the report for the past couple of days. You and your wife are both in perfect health. Furthermore, I came to tell you she's ovulating. That should make it easier on you. I know I can never resist my wife when she's in estrous."

Cody's ears burned with embarrassment at Simon's unasked for information. "Fine. I hope you're right, but I'll have to ask Lisa to fit me into her schedule."

Simon winked. "That shouldn't be a problem. Director Tran hasn't been cleared Lisa for duty yet. She has nowhere to go but home with you. She'll probably be on you as soon as you return to your apartment. All you have to do is let her have her way. It's a five-minute job if you warm her up properly."

Cody's jaw dropped, terrified at the prospect. "Lisa's still recovering from the coma. There's no way she has the stamina to initiate this, let alone follow through to completion."

The commander's brows raised. "Want to bet?"

Cody's mood darkened. "No."

The commander leveled his gaze on Cody. "Too late, you already have. I'm just here to make sure we don't lose our lives on this roll of the dice."

Cody glanced at Lisa who was laughing with Director Tran. "You think Lisa's body can take it right now?"

Simon sighed. "Director Tran doesn't foresee a problem. If you act today, then you may be successful on the first try. If you keep waiting, then you'll hit the thirty-day deadline. They won't execute your wife for noncompliance, but they will lock you in an outpost dungeon until you submit to their demands. This is a problem only you can solve. Lisa has never wanted anyone except you. I'm trying to protect you."

Cody's hands went cold. "Lisa asked for me to do this?"

Simon nodded, and his face warmed with a smile. "Your wife is in love with you. I guess she is a genius after all. Tell me this, since both of you have extremely high intelligence quotients, how many geniuses does it take to screw in a lightbulb?" He clapped Cody on the shoulder and left the reception room.

Cody understood the old Earth joke, but he didn't find any humor in it. Screwing Lisa was not something he wanted to do. She was one of the Administrative Division's pawns whether she realized it or not.

He had hoped she'd remained untainted. Unfortunately, that wasn't possible for anyone. Even he could be compelled to bow to their wishes, and that deadened him inside.

Lisa strode in his direction. "Are you ready to go home?"

His gaze snapped to meet hers. "If you say so."

She nodded. "I'm ready for bed."

He understood an order when he heard one. "I won't fight you on it."

She yawned and took his arm. "Thank you. I appreciate your understanding."

As the two of them walked home, his heart turned to stone. The assassin had been right. Cody was a slave.

Chapter Thirty-Nine

Lisa entered the apartment, and Cody shut the door behind them. She walked to the bathroom, stripped her uniform, and prepared it for laundering by removing the adornments. Cody followed suit, taking off everything.

She stared at him, taking in the bruises on his body. "Who hurt you?"

His expression became grim. "It's part of the job."

His vague answer triggered her anxiety. "Which job?"

He squared his shoulders. "You asked me to take you to bed."

Her heart pounded at the implied activity to be performed there. "Um, maybe you can tell me why you're angry with me first." Fatigue forgotten, she faced him.

He scoffed. "As if you don't know what you've done to me."

She glanced downward, but that wasn't the answer. "What?"

He took her by the wrist and led her to her bedroom. As soon as he released her, she faced the cupboard and opened it to look for pajamas. He placed his hands on her hips and pulled her toward him.

He unfastened her bra. "Our time is up the day after tomorrow."

His breath on her neck gave her the shivers. The sensation was partly good and partly frightening. Was she ready for this?

She faced him, allowing the bra to fall off. "You want to make love to me?"

He scowled. "That's how children are created."

Her heart soared at first but then crashed to the pit of her stomach at the cold look in his eyes. "Are you ready for a baby?"

He breathed deeply. "Do you think waiting two more days will make a difference?"

She raised her eyebrows. "Is that all we have left?" Because of the coma, she hadn't fully computed the math yet.

He nodded. "I've been really stupid about this whole thing, but not anymore. You should do what needs to be done." He dropped his hands to his sides.

She faced away from him, confronted by the cabinets with nowhere to go. Placing her head on the wood, she prayed for help. Cody wanted to make love. Her heart rate accelerated.

Her entire body pulsed with heat. "You've never asked to, um, well, anyway, you have my permission to touch me the way I did you."

Cody slid her panties down. "What do you want me to do?"

She faced him, marveling at the way his muscles rippled with tension. Unable to catch her breath, she stared into his eyes. His gaze lowered to her chest.

"Please." She swallowed moisture down her dry throat as her ragged breathing made her lightheaded. "Take it slow."

He gave a curt shake of the head. "It must be over with fast."

She searched his expression for an answer. "Will it hurt less if we do it quickly?"

He frowned. "I hope so."

She didn't want to do it this way, so she lifted his chin to meet his gaze. "I don't understand why we're rushing this. I mean, we have time left to wait and—"

Cody's eyebrows lifted. "Are you saying no?"

"No. I mean, I'm not saying no." Her heart said differently. "It has to happen. Please, proceed."

He took her hand and led her to the floor without putting down a blanket. She saw the practical aspect of that because the clean-up would be easier. Trembling, she tried not to think about what would soon take place.

On all fours, Cody placed one knee between her legs and then the other. He lowered his hips, and she squeezed her eyes closed, bracing for a pain that didn't come. He rubbed against her to no avail.

Cody growled, and her eyes flew open. "You're going to have to do something to make this work." His arms continued to hold his torso aloof.

Embarrassed that she didn't excite him, she touched his face. "Will you hug me, and see if that helps you to want me?"

He clenched his jaw. "No."

Hurt, Lisa quashed the anger that threatened to rise. "What has changed between us? Have I done something wrong again? I didn't mean to, and I'm sorry for whatever it was. Please, forgive me before we do this."

He ground his teeth. "You are forgiven. Why else would I be with you now?"

She searched his expression and tone of voice. Something wasn't right. "Are you sure? You can talk to me. I will listen."

He swallowed. "I don't want to talk."

His body lowered until he lay along the length of her. The sensation of his skin on hers scalded her senses. Crushed, but pleased at his decision to engage with her on an emotional level, she wrapped her arms around him and caressed his back. He relaxed in her embrace and let her kiss his shoulder, neck, and ear until she felt his hydraulics kick in.

Breathing heavily, she adjusted her hips to welcome him. "I love you."

Cody winced and said something, but she couldn't hear him because the receiver behind her ear voiced a summons from Director Xyler's office. Cody had finally decided to make love to her, and she wanted to experience this more than anything in her life. Involuntarily, her arms dropped from around her husband's chest and fell on the linoleum.

Cody pushed away from her and fled from the bedroom. Vertigo gripped her as the lengthy message from Director Xyler continued over the receiver, causing her stomach to heave. She fought against nausea until her head lolled to the side in blinding agony as the message droned on. He wanted her to report immediately.

Dazed, Lisa lay stunned on the floor. She had disappointed Cody. What had he said to her?

Her shoulders shook with silent sobs. It wasn't supposed to be like this. Her invention had ruined everything.

The sound of water running came from the bathroom. Cody must not have understood her distress because he surely would have stayed to comfort her. He always had in the past when the implant had incapacitated her.

A throbbing between her legs made her wish he had at least kissed her before he'd accepted her virtue. What had caused him to withhold his affections like this? He hadn't even touched her, at least not with his hands.

As her headache faded, she remembered Director Xyler's orders to report to his office. Faint, she replied to him on her wrist-vid: indisposed, standby. He responded by greenlighting the message.

Lisa rolled onto her side, willing her breathing rate to stabilize. Her bra and panties were only a meter and a half away. She crawled over to put them on.

A trail of blood droplets marred the floor behind her. Her gaze shifted to the crimson stain that had collected on the linoleum where she had lain. She didn't want Cody to see it.

Staggering to the kitchen, she bent to grab a cloth from under the sink. She armed herself with a bottle of disinfectant spray and took care of the mess. Returning the cleaning supplies to the kitchen she stooped to hide them away until she could launder the cloth.

More blood had dripped down her legs to the floor.

Her hands shook uncontrollably. Weeping, she collapsed to her hands and knees. What was wrong with her? She needed to report to work.

The faucet at the bathroom sink shut off, and panic struck her like a fist to the stomach. Lisa clenched her muscles to flee, causing more blood to drip on the floor. Mortified, she used the cloth and cleaner to make her way toward her bedroom, but she wasn't fast enough.

The bathroom door opened, and Cody stepped into the kitchen area. "Lisa, there's blood on me."

He held a pinch of skin with two fingers as he looked down at his body. She stared at his groin. He glanced at her, then his gaze followed the trail of blood droplets on the floor.

His knees buckled, sending him to the floor. "What have I done?"

Shaking too hard to do anything else, Lisa collapsed onto her backside, wincing at the pain in her most intimate place. "I don't know. A message came through on my implant when you did it. So, you need to tell me what happened because I missed the whole thing."

His face paled. "Whole thing? There was no whole thing. I couldn't go through with it. Nothing happened."

Stunned, she dropped her gaze to the bloody cloth in her hand. "Then why am I bleeding?"

He shook his head. "I must have caused it, but I didn't mean to. I'm sorry, Lisa. This wasn't my intention."

Her confusion caused more tears to stream from her eyes. "You were the one who insisted on doing this today. I just wanted to go to bed."

He blinked. "You didn't order me to impregnate you?"

Heat seared her cheeks. "No."

He scowled. "My commanding officer said you did."

She stared at Cody in shock. "I never asked anyone to order you to make love to me."

The muscles in Cody's jaw clenched. "Then how does the Gold Council know you want me, and no one else on this planet, to give you children?"

Lisa had no idea how the council always knew her innermost thoughts. "Cody, I don't talk to anyone about my deepest concerns, not even Andrea."

He clenched his fists. "Then how do they know?"

Stunned, she searched her heart for the answer. "I pray."

He tensed. "Out loud?"

She nodded. "I take my thoughts and feelings to the Lord. I've prayed for our marriage to work. I've asked God to bless us with children. I tell my Heavenly Father everything."

Cody's hands fell lifeless at his sides. "Don't you know they have you under constant surveillance?"

She met his gaze, searching for a confirmation of his words. "No. Why would they listen to my prayers." She glanced around the kitchen and into the bedroom. "How can they be watching us? I would have noticed a camera or a microphone."

Cody looked away. "They use the infrared scanners that you invented to see us. They don't need microphones to listen in because they have listening devices in the apartment next door that record everything we say. They obtained a warrant after the assassination attempt."

She forced herself to breathe. "You are still working for them, even after we talked, and you said you weren't investigating me anymore?"

His shoulders slumped. "Yes. Your protocol is still in effect. It's not just THREE that is in danger but all of the colonies. But then, you know that, don't you?" He adjusted his seated position to raise his knees and hug them.

She scoffed. "No. I didn't know that. I destroyed my protocol. I would never commit treason." Indignant, she climbed to her feet on shaky legs. "I've been nothing but loyal to the colonies. Everything I do is to protect the people who depend on me. You know this. Why would you doubt me? How could you be so cruel?"

He ducked his forehead to his knees, hiding his face from her. "I don't know. I'm sorry for hurting you. I didn't mean for it to go this far. I thought you had betrayed me."

She stood, staring at the top of his head. "You told me you were in love with me."

He nodded without looking at her. "Yes, I love you with all my heart and soul. I can't help myself. It doesn't even matter what you've done. I still want to be your husband."

The stubborn anger that had held her bound loosened its claw-like grip. "I don't know what you expect me to say."

His shoulders shook with sobs, and he buried his face in his knees. She watched him cry, naked and vulnerable, just as she had been. Forgiveness wasn't an easy thing under any circumstance, but she started the process inside her heart because she wanted to let go of the pain he'd caused.

She knelt in front of him and touched his hand. "Cody, I'm going to be all right. I hope you will be too."

He spread his fingers to accept hers between them. "I'm so sorry, Lisa."

She waited for him to look at her. "My name is pronounced Neesa in Korean."

His brows pinched. "What do you mean?"

She covered his other hand with her free one, and he accepted her fingers between his. "Because of the sound change. In Korean, my surname comes first, and that changes my given name's pronunciation."

His eyes became sad. "You mean, I haven't even been saying your name the right way?"

His contrition warmed her heart. "No, not really. I told you that a name was important. Well, this is why I kept mine. I don't care about that anymore, though. I want to be Mrs. Greene."

His eyes flooded with tears, and he took her hands in his. "You do?"

She met his gaze. "I really do."

He chuckled and used her hands to wipe his tears. "I don't deserve you."

She smiled. "I think you do."

He stared into her eyes. "I took your virginity. That's unforgivable. I thought I'd stopped in time, and that you weren't hurt. I told you I couldn't do it. I couldn't go through with my orders, Neesa. I'm sorry. I should have talked to you about why I was angry. I should have stayed with you."

She drew his hands away from his knees, and he let her. "Stay with me now."

He met her gaze. "I hurt you."

She assessed her pains. The throb between her legs had faded to a dull ache. Aside from the initial shock, it hadn't been as painful as she'd expected. He had strained the membrane that kept him at bay until it ruptured, but he hadn't realized that he'd broken through.

She shook her head. "You're thinking spatially."

He swallowed. "Are you saying I should think with my heart?"

She nodded. "I am."

He smiled for an instant, then took her into a warm embrace, but quickly let her go. "Sorry about that."

The hug had been very intimate. "I don't mind, Cody. I want to be with you."

He met her gaze. "You do?"

Her heart clenched. "Don't you?"

He shook his head. "You're hurt. You need time to heal."

Her heart surged. "I need a reason to heal."

His demeanor opened and he knelt before her, concealing nothing. "I'm all yours, Mrs. Greene."

She smiled at his invitation but came in for a kiss on the lips instead. "I'll start here, and we can work our way in that direction after a while. I intend to take this slowly."

He pulled her against him and kissed her deeply, caressing her back with his hands. She ran her fingers through his hair, kissing him with a steady love that inspired her to shift her attention. She captured his earlobe between her lips, and he shivered.

His skin broke out in goosebumps. "May I take you to the bedroom?"

She met his gaze. "Yes."

He kissed her neck and shoulders. "Thank you, Neesa."

She giggled at the caress of his lips on her skin. Gathering her in his arms, he carried her to the bedroom. She caught the edge of the door on the way past and swung it shut behind them.

Chapter Forty

Lisa's wrist-vid chimed, awaking her. She lay tucked in next to Cody with his arm behind her and her head pillowed on his shoulder. She'd never been so content.

However, the reminder summons from Director Xyler dispelled her bliss and worked knots in her stomach. She'd forgotten to report to his office and spent the midday making love to her husband instead. It was a dereliction of duty, but she couldn't help the smile that tugged at the corners of her mouth.

She caressed Cody's chest beneath the blanket. Oh, how she loved this man. She kissed his skin until he stirred from sleep because she couldn't leave him without an explanation.

His eyes opened in a moment of apparent alarm, then their brown depths warmed with a smile. "Good morning."

She raised to lay a kiss on his lips. "I'm sorry to disappoint you, but it isn't morning anymore, and I must go."

He wrapped his arms around her and held her against him. "Is there any way to change your mind?"

Naked and tempted, she debated how much trouble she'd be in if she stayed with him an hour or two longer. He caressed her brow with his thumb. She closed her eyes for a moment, enjoying his proximity.

Unfortunately, she had no choice. "I wish I didn't have to go, but I must report to Director Xyler's office, and then I have to submit to a compliance exam. I should be home for dinner."

Cody released his hold, though he did not remove his hands. "What is a compliance exam?"

She stood, and his gaze caressed her body. "I'm not sure what it entails, but regulations require me to see a doctor within twelve hours of, um, coupling." Heat blazed across her cheeks.

Cody stood in front of her. "Am I permitted to go with you?"

Since she'd averted her gaze, it now rested on his midsection. "I don't see why not."

He lifted her chin until her gaze met his. "Am I distracting you?"

She blinked. "Um, yes. Will you shower with me?" She smiled impishly. "I wish the mandate said to report within an hour of being together, but since it doesn't, I have no excuse to delay going in by being with you again."

Cody gave her a sideways smile as he took her hand, leading her to the bathroom. "Showers can sometimes take longer than expected."

She sighed. "No. This one can't. I'm already late as it is."

She turned on the water in the tiled room and stood outside the spray until it warmed. Wetting her hair, she shampooed it, rinsed, and reached for the conditioner. Cody stood before the squat toilet holding a pinch of skin and aiming to no avail. His hydraulics were partially pressured up, and she wondered if that was the problem.

"Impressive. Most impressive." The line from an old movie came to her mind, partly due to Cody's grim expression.

He chuckled but stayed focused until he achieved success. "The force is strong with this one."

She laughed and allowed him to urinate in peace. After conditioning her hair, she washed her body with a washcloth and soap. Cody stepped into the water with her, and she yielded the space to him after rinsing.

She lingered as she dried with a towel, watching him scrub his body clean. "You are a joy to me, Mr. Greene."

He glanced her way and a grin formed on his face. "That's a relief because you're never going to be rid of me after what we shared today."

His words made her happier than she'd ever been, and she knew what she needed to do. "I love you, and I'll see you in a while."

He reached out his hand, and she took it. "I love you too, Neesa."

She squeezed his hand, then wrapped the towel around her head. He continued to scrub his legs and feet. She removed her contact lenses, placing them in the container in the medicine cabinet above the sink. She had no idea what the exam entailed, but it might be a procedure of some kind and require her to come in clean as she had for surgery.

In her room, she put on her glasses and dressed in her blue uniform, dictating orders to her wrist-vid as she did so. "Order in three, two, one: celebration shopping list. Engage delivery: same day. Order in three, two, one: matching wedding rings as previously specified. Engage delivery: same day. File with record keeping: Lisa Shim requests her name to be changed to Lisa Greene. Requisition: uniform name patches for one dress uniform and two tech division uniforms with the name Greene on them, spelled G-R-E-E-N-E. Engage delivery: as soon as the name change is confirmed."

She hurried to Cody's room to swipe a name patch from his dress uniform and place it where her name normally resided on her blue uniform. Inexplicably giddy, she waited for Cody to finish in the bathroom. A message scrolled across her wrist-vid from record-keeping, granting her request for the name change.

Cody walked into the bedroom ruffling his hair dry with the towel. He stopped, eyed the name patch and her grin, then met her gaze. His eyes misted.

He swallowed, causing his Adam's Apple to bob. "You don't have to do this."

She nodded, undeterred. "I'm giving you a gift that you value, something that costs me little if you call me Neesa at home. I'm doing this because I want to unify our marriage through sharing your name and giving it to our children."

He closed the distance between them and crushed her in a huge hug. "Thank you."

She giggled with her cheek pressed in the center of his fuzzy chest. "You're welcome."

He rubbed her back, and she caressed him until his hydraulics kicked in. "Um, Neesa, you'd better go."

She hugged him once more, glanced down at his display of affection, and then walked to the apartment door to grab her toolkit. "I'm tempted to quit my job, but I just spent a small fortune on some orders that will be delivered sometime today. Will you coordinate with the services and be here for them to drop things off?"

Cody nodded, facing her with a semi-pained expression. "Hurry home."

She chuckled. "Don't forget to meet me at the doctor's office. I'll message you when I have an appointment lined up."

He strode toward her and captured her mouth in a deep kiss for a long time before letting her go. "I wish you didn't have to leave."

She did too. "It can't be avoided."

He took a breath and sighed. "Well, let me check to be sure your guards are ready to keep you safe. May I borrow your datapad for a minute?"

She opened her toolkit and handed the datapad to him. "Are you concerned? Surely, they've caught the assassin by now."

Cody finished with the datapad and met her gaze. "He's a hardened killer, Neesa. Be careful out there."

She caressed the smooth contours of his freshly shaved face. "Don't worry. Two bodyguards should be enough to deter him from trying anything."

Cody took her hand and kissed the palm. "Do what they say and come home as soon as you can."

She wanted to be with him more than anything. "I have duties to perform that will keep our family safe from penalties or punishments.

I'm sorry if you disapprove of my leaving, but I have to go." She avoided his gaze out of guilt.

Cody lifted her chin until she looked into his eyes. "I don't disapprove of you or want to keep you from your job. It's not that. I'm just being selfish. Anyway, I knew who you were when I married you, and I'm happy you're a capable leader. Never think for an instant that I don't want you to fulfill your duties or follow your dreams because your happiness means everything to me."

She pulled him into an embrace. "Thank you for believing in me. I want the same for you." With those words, she left him standing in their living room in all his physical glory.

Chapter Forty-One

Lisa walked a little more gingerly than her usual stride on her way to the elevator. Two hulking bodyguards watched over her. Whatever Director Xyler wanted must be critically important because he'd never summoned her with the implant before.

Would he be unhappy that she'd made him wait? She didn't care. The man had nearly ruined her first time with Cody, and she would have had a hard time forgiving him if he'd succeeded.

Lisa traversed the colony to the open doorway of Director Xyler's office. The broad man sat behind an enormous desk, idly running a rake through a desktop Zen Garden.

He squinted. "I'm not sure what to do with you, Director Shim. I'm leaving for TEN, yet here we are in this predicament."

"My apologies, Director Xyler." What did he mean?

"I'm not sure why you're apologizing. You are the best of the best, after me that is." He flashed her a greasy grin.

Why was he being cryptic? "Thank you, sir." Protocol dictated that she waited to be invited inside.

"You've earned the right to join the elite. I'm proud of you for your compliance this afternoon." He leaned back, meeting her gaze. "You are the future of Mars."

Anger surged in Lisa's chest. "What compliance are you referring to, Director?"

He chuckled. "I was a newlywed once. I know what indisposed for three hours translates to mean. Don't worry. I'm not upset in the slightest that you made me wait." He stood. "I'm vacating the office effective immediately."

He walked past her and headed down the hallway. Lisa stood locked in fury that the man had used the implant for something trivial. Xyler's leaving wasn't a secret to anyone, and there had been no reason to send the messages over her receiver.

Her outrage mingled with despair inside her chest. Cody had told her she'd made a mistake with the implant. He'd warned her that conformity led to victimization. She should report Director Xyler for his callous action, but her personal responsibility paralyzed her.

Staring at the clean desktop, she eventually shifted her gaze to take in the leather sofa, bare wall space, and the empty bookcase shelves. This was her office now. Xyler said she'd earned it with compliance, and the thought sickened her. Had she paid for this with her virginity?

A chill swept over her. She had cost Cody his virtue as well. He hadn't slept with her voluntarily, at least not in the beginning. The government had coerced him. That's why he'd behaved resentfully toward her.

Cody would have hated her if they hadn't talked through their differences. She might have hated him too if he'd done things the way he started today. Everything had turned out well, but it was an absolute miracle.

She stepped into the office. A distasteful smell in the air made her crinkle her nose. Did Xyler have halitosis? She left the door open.

Without taking a seat, she activated the equipment on the desktop. From here, she could monitor everything in NINE. If the air and water reserves were being depleted, she now had the authority to find out.

Access denied.

The message on the screen stopped her cold. She verified her status as acting technology director and attacked the inquiry from various angles. All of her efforts came up fruitless.

She snatched up her toolkit and headed for the juncture where the conduit inside the Glass Highway connected with the colony. Not many people realized what lay behind the door to storage locker one-eleven. Her bodyguards flanked her.

Their stern expressions darkened as she keyed in the access code. The keypad flashed red and sounded an angry beep. She tried to bypass the locking mechanism, but her hairpin trick didn't work.

"Director, you can't be here." A Space Division officer in full shock gear approached her from the hallway on the right.

She frowned, disliking the way his helmet distorted his voice. "I should have clearance to enter the conduit. I'm responsible for maintenance."

The short officer shook his head. "No, Director, this area is off-limits by order of the Gold Council."

Lisa lowered her brows even further. "Since when?"

The officer's helmet cocked to the side. "It's been a while. The policy was already in place when I transferred in seven months ago."

Lisa nodded, deep in thought. "Can you tell me if the valves are open?"

The officer shook his head. "I have no idea. No one has been allowed access to this door. My men and I are simply here to make sure it stays sealed."

Lisa inspected the doorknob, tracing a finger over the top of it. Dust coated it. That meant the officer was telling the truth and that no one had maintained the conduit for longer than seven months.

A sinking feeling settled in her chest. "Thank you, Officer. I will be on my way."

He nodded. "Glad I could answer your questions, Director. Have a nice day."

Lisa headed straight to the nearest lung. She descended in the elevator to sub-level four, walked a hallway, and flipped a light switch beside a window in the exterior wall of the central tube. Inside the chamber, a gigantic flat balloon lay on the floor.

Panic struck her like a slap to the face. The colony had no extra air. The reserve tanks must be empty. All they had was what was in the colony and it could be draining away at this very moment.

Lisa pulled her tablet from her toolkit and started a course of action that might buy the citizens of NINE some time. She ordered an evacuation of sub-level six and below. She initiated the draining of the aquatics facility located below the elite residencies on sub-level nine, routing that water into the filtration system.

While she waited in front of the window, she ordered replacement parts for atmospheric collector number five. Mr. Dean reported back when the items she needed were ready. One by one the evacuation teams sealed off each of the floors she'd specified.

When the water in the aquatic's facility had been pumped into the water treatment facility and routed to the ocean habitat, she initiated the vacuum sequence for the sealed-off floors. Pressure built in Lisa's ears, and she worked her jaw to pop them. Slowly, the lungs began to inflate.

She wiped the sweat from her brow. Flipping off the light switch, she raced for the elevator. The two men with her exchanged nervous glances. One of them pulled at his earlobe with a pained look on his face.

As soon as the elevator doors opened, she jogged to collect the parts from Mr. Dean. She had no intention of letting this colony fail. Whatever the reason for the air and water losses, she had to compensate by fixing the fifth collector. If she failed, then most of the populace would die in the emergency shelters awaiting a rescue that wouldn't come in time to save them.

Chapter Forty-Two

Cody gathered the blanket, cleaning cloth, and pink panties into a pile on the bathroom floor. He'd started rice cooking and chopped vegetables for a nice meal. Lisa had gone to meet Director Xyler.

While he waited for her to contact him about the doctor visit, he squatted to scrub her blood from the beige linoleum floor with a fresh cleaning cloth and a bottle of sanitizer. She had bled far more than he'd realized. The blood drained from his face to think of the pain he'd caused her. He'd almost done something unpardonable and it frightened him to know what he was capable of.

Walking to the bathroom he rinsed the blood from the cloth in his hand. Then he set to work scrubbing the blanket he and Lisa had made love on. The time they'd spent together had been beautiful. He had made her happy.

The bloodstain on her panties stubbornly refused to come out. He sweated with exertion to erase his horrible mistake he'd made. He hadn't been able to replace her virtue, but he had loved her properly after he'd accidentally taken it.

Lisa owned him completely now. No matter what she'd done wrong in the past or what she ever did in the future, he would always be hers. The memory of her sweetness melted him inside, and he closed his eyes as water ran over the panties in his hands.

He didn't deserve her forgiveness, but she'd given it freely. He finished with the panties and started the laundry. Standing in the middle of the bathroom, he turned on the water for a second shower.

He toweled dry and glanced at his wrist-vid. Lisa would be expecting him to meet her soon, but there was no news of when. He wrapped the towel around his waist and tucked it in on his way to the kitchen.

Seaweed soup as an appetizer with Korean fire meat as the main course would comfort Lisa when she arrived home tonight. He sliced the meat and prepared the marinade, prepping everything else to be finished after her compliance exam. How late would she work tonight?

He washed his hands and walked to his room, finally dressing to go out. Some part of him had hoped Lisa would come home and find him naked. She liked looking at him, and he loved the way she always asked before she touched him.

He dressed in the outfit she had selected for him when they'd shopped in EIGHT. Well, the clothes were replacements, but he smiled now at how annoyed he'd been when she'd bought them for him. He lifted his wrist-vid to queue up the picture of the two of them in the dressing room.

"Oh, how I love you, Neesa." He finished buttoning the shirt, humbled by the blessing of her love.

He knelt on the floor in his room and offered silent thanks to the Lord for making things right between him and Lisa. The miracle of forgiveness brought tears to his eyes. His wife had not held a grudge, she had accepted him with all his flaws from the beginning. Her faith had made their relationship whole.

A knock sounded at the door.

"Hello." His mother strode into the apartment with Commander Mambwe. "Son, are you decent?"

Cody's emotions surged with outrage. "I'm sure you knew the answer to that question before you entered."

Simon Mambwe cleared his throat. "No need for a poor attitude. You were informed of the warrant."

Cody climbed to his feet. "Did you enjoy the show?"

Simon avoided his gaze. "Of course, not."

Addison raised an eyebrow. "Nice recovery effort, Son. I was sure Lisa would bring you up on charges before you changed tactics with her."

Cody simmered in his anger. "Is that why you triggered her implant at exactly that moment?"

The look on her face confirmed his suspicion. Simon simply looked confused. Cody closed his eyes and clenched his fist to keep from voicing his profound disappointment.

"I was only trying to protect you from the consequences of your actions." Addison sounded contrite. "No one's first time should be a betrayal."

Cody's heart quailed. His mother was correct. He had almost done the unforgivable.

He faced them. "I made it right with Lisa. Now, she's expecting me at the doctor's office. I can't stay and chat about my private life with the two of you."

Addison shook her head. "She hasn't scheduled the exam yet. Regardless, we have other matters to discuss."

Cody frowned. "Lisa wants me there."

Addison squared her stance. "Yes, she does, but she's busy with work."

Cody looked away. "Is there an emergency?"

Addison's shoulders relaxed. "She's handling it. I'm just glad that it was good between you."

Cody snorted. "No thanks to your interference."

Addison let out a breath. "I admit, everything I did to force you to be intimate was a mistake, but I don't regret arranging things so that the marriage took place."

Simon nodded. "Lisa's promotion to NINE was the reason she requested the match. That was your mother's doing."

Cody rubbed his face with both hands. "Then Lisa didn't do anything to earn such a lavish reward?"

Addison scoffed. "Not even close. She isn't very cooperative. Anyway, her personality evaluations indicated that she would do anything for her family. It's easy to manipulate people when that's the case. It's why I keep you a secret."

Cody scowled. "I never asked you to protect me."

Addison dismissed Simon with a wave of the hand. "A moment alone with my son, if you please, Commander."

Simon's expression darkened. "I'll be right outside."

When he had gone, Addison met Cody's gaze. "Your resentful nature forced my hand. I couldn't let you die in that outpost dungeon a month ago any more than I could allow Lisa to blame you for what you did to her today. I had to give her someone else to blame. So, I rerouted Xyler's message to her implant. I knew it would incapacitate and distract her as well as give her someone else to be angry at for the loveless sexual encounter you were forcing on her. Rape is an ugly thing, Son."

Cody stilled, absorbing the truth of what had nearly happened between him and Lisa. "She consented."

Addison stared at him. "To be loved, not to be torn apart without affection."

Cody ducked his head and walked to the kitchen sink. "I love her."

"And I'm glad you finally showed it, Son." Addison's tone held tenderness. "However, you can never allow your rage to drive away your compassion again. Lisa trusts you, and you almost lost that today."

His eyes filled with tears. "Why all of this pressure to have a child?" He faced her. "You want grandchildren, that's understandable, but why force me to make Lisa pregnant so soon? What's the rush?"

Addison raised her eyebrows. "You think I'm the one in a hurry? No, Son, I would not wish children on anyone. They will bring you nothing but pain."

He squinted in skepticism. "No joy whatsoever?"

She stared at her right hand. "The more joy in life, the more agony in death."

Cody's anger slipped away. "What are you saying?"

Addison's dazed eyes met his gaze. "I'm saying, that someday, you will have to make choices that will haunt you for the rest of your life. I'm only glad that today was not one of those days."

Cody clenched his jaw. "You're not telling me something. Were you forced to do something to dad and the girls?"

Addison blinked. "I was allowed to save only one of you. You see, there weren't enough treatments for everyone. I chose your father. The Gold Council didn't like that. They wanted you. The Matchmaker chose you for his breeding program. I was left to watch the others die slowly. Well, I couldn't bear to see them suffer. Eventually, I took a pillow and held it over their faces to end their suffering. They didn't even have the strength to struggle."

Cody couldn't breathe. "You killed them? How could you?"

Addison blinked and two tears fell. "I loved your father more than my own life. I gave him my treatment, but it didn't work. He didn't respond to the medicine." She sobbed. "He was everything to me."

Cody watched her cry until he couldn't stand the distance between them and took his mother in an embrace. "I always thought you and dad had problems."

Addison wrapped her arms around him and held him fiercely. "Can you forgive me?"

Cody wanted to, but he needed time to process his feelings. "It was an impossible choice. I'm sure you did what you could for all of us. I have often wished I died with them."

Addison pressed her face into his chest. "Me too."

Cody rubbed her back. "I'm sorry I didn't understand you back then. I had no idea why you became distant. Anyway, you really need to explain that comment about a breeding program. Who is the Matchmaker? I thought it was just an algorithm in a computer."

Addison drew a shaky breath. "My father is the Matchmaker, and I've kept you safe from him as long as I could. Unfortunately, there's nothing I can do anymore." She plunged a syringe into Cody's buttock and depressed the plunger.

He flinched at the jab, then wobbled on his feet, and lost consciousness.

Chapter Forty-Three

Lisa determined via a comprehensive heat sensor scan that the colony's exterior walls had not been breached. That relieved her stress a little. Now all she needed was a miracle.

She lugged a specialized toolkit and an environmental suitcase that she'd acquired at the parts bay from Mr. Dean. One of her bodyguards carried a backpack full of replacement parts and a second environmental suit. Her destination was bio-dome five, the ocean habitat.

When the elevator doors opened on level three, she stepped from the box onto the balcony overlooking the water. She inhaled the salty air as the rush of the waves renewed her strength and centered her soul. The tension eased from her overtaxed body to see that the level was not much reduced from normal.

She had a lot to do and little time to achieve it. Yet, she looked through the transparent latticework of the structure at the first blush of sunset on the arid Martian horizon. The harsh beauty of Mars reminded her of her peril.

The brawny Mr. Trenton stood on her right side and glanced at his wrist-vid. It was enough to break her concentration. Lisa strode onto the catwalk.

High above the water, she traversed the length of the ocean bio-dome. The atmospheric collector lay at the far end. The task of fixing the stubborn thing had fallen to her because everyone else had failed.

Why that was, she couldn't guess. It shouldn't have been this difficult if only the technicians sent to do the job had known how. Retraining everyone in this entire colony would take time.

She huffed and puffed with the exertion of carrying the heavy toolkit and suit. It didn't help that this much water triggered her anxiety. She couldn't swim, and looking below made her chest tighten. Shortness of breath didn't bode well for the walk outside.

"Director Shim, I will be accompanying you outside the airlock. Grimes will remain inside to stand watch on the hatch." Trenton's deep voice rumbled.

Lisa shied away from the man. "As you like. I have a series of diagnostics to run before we go outside. There's a two percent chance I can start the collector from here."

He nodded, and both men took up defensive positions around her. She accessed the diagnostic equipment and ran her analysis. She'd done the math in her head with information from her technicians' reports. The imminent danger of an environmental collapse made the repair imperative.

That's why she was here instead of at home with her sweet husband. Her smile attracted a sideways glance from Trenton. She focused on her work with her fingers flying over the touch screen diagnostic panel. The results flashed in red.

She sighed. "Suit up, Mr. Trenton. We're going outside."

Chapter Forty-Four

Lisa worked on the atmospheric collector as fast as she could. Outside bio-dome five, the sunset blazed, but the temperature dropped. Her numb fingers could barely hold the socket wrench as she torqued a bolt tight.

Lisa slammed the collector's access panel shut. No sound reached her ears, but she felt the vibrations in the metal. Cranking the handle, she sealed the system.

"All done, Director?" Trenton held his pulse rifle aimed at the sky.

Lisa frowned as she gathered the broken parts she'd dropped on the ground. "I hope so. I'll be able to tell for sure when we're back inside."

"Hey, look at that, Director." Trenton pointed a gloved hand toward the nearest rock formation.

Lisa crouched to secure the flap on the backpack of parts. "I've never seen a whirlwind that big before."

Trenton hefted the heavy backpack onto one shoulder. "It could have been initiated by an off-road vehicle. We'd better head inside. I can't defend you against an armed vehicular assault."

Lisa grabbed her toolkit. "What do you know about the assassin that I don't know? Why is he hunting me?"

Trenton shrugged. "I'm not at liberty to say."

Lisa only knew what a shrug meant because Cody had explained it. In this case, Lisa was still puzzled. Trenton wasn't shirking responsibility, nor was he unsure, he simply seemed to be dismissing the question.

She quirked an eyebrow. "All of this secrecy and keeping things from me is ridiculous. I outrank you by, well, since you don't wear insignia, I have no idea, but I'd guess it's by a lot. I want to be let in on this so run it up the chain of command."

Trenton nodded inside his helmet. "Will do, Director."

Lisa punched in a code to open the airlock. "Thank you, Trenton. I need to know what the threat is."

Trenton kept his eyes on the area around them. "I understand why you want to know, but would it change the way you perform your duties?"

Lisa thought about that. "No, it wouldn't change anything for me along those lines."

Trenton entered the interim pressure chamber with her and sealed the hatch behind them. They waited for the pressure to equalize with the inside of the bio-dome. A green light flashed, and they removed their helmets and gauntlets.

Grimes opened the hatch from his side. "Well, Director, how did it go?"

Lisa wasn't sure yet. "There's a good chance the collector will work now. Let me run a diagnostic."

Trenton frowned. "How long will that take?"

Lisa ran the diagnostic. "Are you in a hurry?"

He nodded. "We need to be going, Director."

"Yes, you do." An elderly voice said from the catwalk.

Lisa glanced over her shoulder. "Mr. Albright, what brings you out here?"

He stepped onto the metal decking of the platform. "I've come to take you to safety."

When the diagnostic was completed, it showed all green lights. She ran the initiation sequence for the collector. Everything hummed smoothly as it came online. There were no malfunctions, and an influx of air whooshed from the small grate beside the control panel.

"Well, that ought to help ensure everyone's safety." She let out a breath she hadn't realized she was holding. "We have air." She walked over to a transparent panel and peered into a reservoir. "I saw a drop. Oh, there's another one. We have water." Grinning, she faced the men. "What?"

Mr. Albright shuffled closer. "It won't be enough. You must come with me. Your husband is already loaded into the rover."

Lisa frowned, checking Trenton and Grimes' expressions. "What are you talking about?"

Mr. Albright's expression became angry. "There's no time to argue. Come of your own free will or be dragged. Every second we delay increases our risk."

Lisa backed away, bumping into the control panel. "What risk?"

Trenton and Grimes grabbed her by the arms. She tensed and tried to stare Trenton down. The brawny men lifted her off her feet.

"Put me down." She kicked the men holding her to no avail.

Mr. Albright scowled. "This is for your own good. I thought you were smarter enough to know that."

She gritted her teeth, fighting with all her might. "Where are you taking me?"

The old man slapped her face with surprising force. "This colony is failing because this collector has been down for over a year. Do you want to die with the fools being left behind?"

Lisa fought even harder. "Yes, I will die trying to save the colony. There's still hope."

He stepped back. "Noble, but pointless." He waved to the bodyguards. "Pin her to the floor. I brought a paralytic."

Trenton and Grimes obeyed, slamming her to the deck with excessive force.

"Careful with her. She's already had enough trauma for one day." Mr. Albright rummaged in a medical kit, producing a syringe.

He stabbed the needle into her neck and depressed it. "I'm only giving her a half-dose. I wouldn't want her to stop breathing."

Lisa's body suddenly stopped responding to her commands. She couldn't speak. In fact, she couldn't even move her eyes.

Mr. Albright withdrew the needle, stowed it, and put drops in her unblinking eyes. "Remove the environmental suit. She needs a compliance exam before we take her to the docking hatches."

Trenton and Grimes forced the suit down over her lifeless body, leaving her naked. Grimes leered and reached for her breast. Trenton shoved his hand away.

"Spread her legs." Mr. Albright pulled a device from the medical kit.

Trenton and Grimes each pulled at a knee until she lay completely exposed. Mr. Albright knelt between her legs and thrust the device inside her body. The pain nearly caused her to pass out.

"I've never operated a speculum before, but I think this is how it works." Albright used the speculum to widen her passage.

She screamed in agony, but nothing came out of her throat. The old man stripped the paper packaging off of a long cotton swab. He thrust it in and stroked the strident swab around before withdrawing it and sealing it in a vial.

The sound of rapid footfalls on the catwalk grating preceded a tall man in full Space Division shock gear. Lisa's heart lurched. Was it Cody who had come to rescue her?

The man stabbed Trenton in the side with a serrated knife. Grimes fired a shot from his pulse rifle at point-blank to the chest of the attacker to no avail. The man wearing shock gear stabbed Grimes through the heart.

Grimes dropped beside Lisa. Wide-eyed, Mr. Albright staggered away in an attempt to escape. The attacker tripped the old man. Trenton lurched to smash the attacker in the back of the helmet with the butt of his rifle but took a knife to the neck in the process.

Trenton stared at the attacker before toppling to the deck. The space in which all of this took place was so confined that Lisa had been stepped on twice. She hoped nothing was broken, but the pain made her eyes stream with tears.

The attacker looked down at her, turned his booted foot to shove the speculum in deeper, and watched her reaction. She couldn't scream in agony. She couldn't even blink.

He crouched, removed the speculum, and stared from behind the tinted visor of his helmet at her bleeding body. She knew she was bleeding because of the sensation of hot liquid scalding her skin as it flowed from her wounds. He stood and threw the speculum at her.

It hit her in the ribs, causing pain and more bleeding. She didn't even flinch, but this time her eyelids twitched. Inside, she was crying.

He removed his helmet. Mr. Praetorius stared at her torn body. He slipped off his gloves.

He met her gaze. "I came here to kill you. You may not remember, but I choked the life out of you once already. I had plans to rip you to pieces, but I see someone has already done that for me."

Her vision narrowed. She wasn't breathing right. Would the paralytic wear off before she suffocated? Maybe that didn't matter since Mr. Praetorius planned to kill her.

He scoffed. "A virgin. I'd heard rumors, but I never believed a director could be virtuous. I guess you're every bit as noble as they say." He scowled down at her, meeting her gaze. "That's too bad."

Mr. Albright's shuffling step reverberated on the catwalk grating. He hadn't made it very far. Mr. Praetorius picked up the speculum and grabbed a handful of swabs from the medical kit with a sneer on his lips.

He strode after Mr. Albright. She couldn't see the confrontation, but she heard the old man threaten, bargain, then plead before he started screaming. Lisa had never heard anyone in that much pain before.

Chunks of something flew in an arc to land in the water below. Then a larger splash took place. Mr. Albright screamed and flailed in the water.

Mr. Praetorius stalked back to stand over Lisa. She met his gaze in defiance. He had no right to kill her, especially when she was probably the only one who could save this colony from catastrophe.

He stripped off his bloody silver shock suit. "Torturing you is all I've thought about since I found out Alik had died while intercepting your rover. I was sure you were to blame."

Open sores oozed on his genitalia. He reached into the medical kit, retrieved a tube of ointment, and spread it on himself.

A look of relief overpowered his features. He closed his eyes and tilted his head back. His heavy breathing steadied.

Lisa's helplessness overwhelmed her with anguish. How was she going to stop this man from killing her? There was nothing she could do.

Praetorius knelt between her legs, took her hand, and smeared ointment on her fingers. He then dragged her hand down to apply the ointment to her wounds. Her pain eased, and he dropped her hand.

"The virgin director is no more." He stared at her breasts. "Until today, you were chaste. That corroborates the Matchmaker's confessions. You are a slave, not a killer. I was wrong."

He stood and strode over to the storage lockers, grabbing an environmental suit. "You'll come out of the paralytic in half an hour. Unfortunately, that randy old goat will alert security in about eight minutes. I knew I should have cut out his liver. It was too much to ask that he'd drown."

Lisa blinked because that's all she could do.

Praetorius shimmied into the environmental suit. "If I want answers from you, then I have to take you with me." He clenched his jaw. "At least this way, the Matchmaker will be denied his prize."

Praetorius grabbed her suit, stuffed her in it, and sealed her up for the walk outside. He sealed his helmet and tossed her over his shoulder. Lisa's fingers twitched, but she couldn't stop the assassin from hauling her through the airlock against her will.

What she planned to do, as soon as she could talk, was convince him to help her close the valves siphoning away air and water from the colonies. After that, she would find a way to rescue Cody from TEN. She knew her enemy now, and she would fight the Matchmaker and the Gold Council until her dying breath.

Don't miss out!

Visit the website below and you can sign up to receive emails whenever S.V. Farnsworth publishes a new book. There's no charge and no obligation.

https://books2read.com/r/B-A-LKBI-VTBNB

BOOKS 2 READ

Connecting independent readers to independent writers.

Did you love *Hard Start: Mars Intrigue*? Then you should read *A Rare Connection: Inspirational Romantic Suspense*[1] by S.V. Farnsworth!

Flirty, French, heiress Nicole Moreau takes her hard-working, American best friend, Andrew Leavitt, for granted, until he puts his education at UCLA on hold to serve as a missionary in South Korea for the Church of Jesus Christ of Latter-day Saints.

She can't understand his devoition, can't seem to be happy without him, and can't stop herself from interupting his mission. Intending to propose, she botches the question and leaves heartbroken.

Andrew is deeply in love with her but doesn't react fast enough to prevent a tragedy.

---

1. https://books2read.com/u/bpElxz

2. https://books2read.com/u/bpElxz

Caught in the crosshairs of the private war between her French Intelligence agent mother and a deadly North Korean unit of kidnappers, Nicole becomes collateral damage.

Can her well-meaning grandmother give her a second chance to chose truth as well as love so she can heal from a #MeToo secret with the power to destoy her? Or will her mother's enemies exact the final revenge?

Read more at https://svfarnsworthauthor.com.

Also by S.V. Farnsworth

Fusion in a Fission World
Hard Start: Mars Intrigue

Modutan Empire
Woman of the Stone
Monarch in the Flames

Standalone
A Rare Connection: Inspirational Romantic Suspense

Watch for more at https://svfarnsworthauthor.com.

About the Author

S.V. Farnsworth speaks four languages and has lived in South Korea. **Issues with grit give her novels the traction to move you.**

Farnsworth is writing *Hard Start: Mars Intrigue* to be released October 10th, 2021. It's a sci-fi romantic suspense novel set on Mars 400 years in the future.

A Rare Connection: Inspirational Romantic Suspense is for anyone who needs a clean stay-cation in exotic locations.

Woman of the Stone and *Monarch in the Flames* are epic fantasy adventures with an appeal to readers who connect with #MeToo concerns and admire strong female characters.

S.V. Farnsworth graduated with a B.S. from SUU in 2002. She teaches ESL at Crowder College in southwest Missouri.

She is the 2020 and 2021 secretary of the Ozarks Writers League. She served as 2018 and 2019 president of the Joplin Writers' Guild, coordinated their conferences, and edited the guild's 2019 Anthology, *Seasons of the Four States*.

Subscribe to her newsletter for exclusive content and updates on her books at **svfarnsworthauthor.com**.

Read more at https://svfarnsworthauthor.com.

www.ingramcontent.com/pod-product-compliance
Lightning Source LLC
Chambersburg PA
CBHW021312190726
48288CB00003B/819